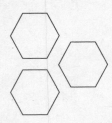

STUNG

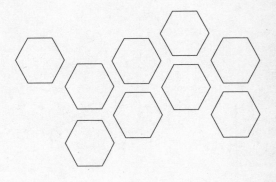

STUNG

BETHANY WIGGINS

SCHOLASTIC INC.

ISBN 978-0-545-61476-4

Copyright © 2013 by Bethany Wiggins.
All rights reserved. Published by Scholastic Inc.,
557 Broadway, New York, NY 10012,
by arrangement with Walker Publishing Company, Inc.
SCHOLASTIC and associated logos are trademarks and/or registered trademarks of Scholastic Inc.

12 11 10 9 8 7 6   15 16 17 18/0

Printed in the U.S.A.   40

First Scholastic printing, September 2013

Book design by Regina Roff

For Suzette Saxton and Lance Corporal Erin Owings, because love is the power of a true warrior, and those who are deemed weak, by its divine nature are made strong

STUNG

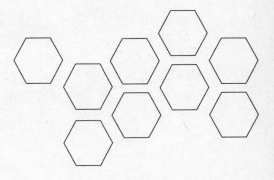

CHAPTER 1

I don't remember going to sleep. All I remember is waking up here—a place as familiar as my own face.

At least, it should be.

But there's a problem. The once-green carpet is gray. The classical-music posters lining the walls are bleached, their brittle corners curling where the tacks are missing. My first-place ribbons are pale blue instead of royal. My sundresses are drained of color. And my bed. I sit on the edge of a bare, sun-bleached mattress, a mattress covered with dirt and twigs and mouse droppings.

I turn my head and the room swims, faded posters wavering and swirling against grimy walls. My head fills with fuzz, and I try to remember when my room got so filthy, since I vacuum and dust it once a week. And why is the mattress bare, when I change the sheets every Saturday? And where did my pillows go?

My stomach growls, and I push on the concave space beneath my ribs, against the shirt sweat-plastered to my skin, and try to remember the last time I ate.

Easing off the bed, I stand on rubbery legs. The carpet crunches beneath my feet, and I look down. I am wearing shoes. I have been *sleeping* in shoes—old-lady white nurse shoes. Shoes that I have never seen before. That I have no memory of pulling onto my feet and tying. And I am standing in a sea of broken glass. It glitters against the filthy, faded carpet, and I can't remember what broke.

A breeze stirs the stifling air, cooling my sweaty face, and the gauzy curtains that hide my bedroom window lift like tattered ghosts. Jagged remnants of glass cling to the window frame, and a certainty creeps into my brain, seeps into my bones. Something is wrong—*really* wrong. I need to find my mom. On legs barely able to hold my weight, I stumble across the room and to the doorway.

Sunlight streams through the bedroom windows on the west side of the house, lighting the dust in the hallway. I peer into my brother's room and gasp. His dinosaur models are broken to bits and strewn across the faded carpet, along with the Star Wars action figures he's collected since he was four years old. I leave his doorway and walk to the next door, to my older sister's room. College textbooks are on the floor, their pages torn and scattered over the filthy carpet. The bed is gone and the mirror above the bureau is shattered.

Dazed, I walk through sunlight and dust, down the hall, trailing my fingers along the paint-peeling wall to Mom's room.

Her room is just like the other rooms. Faded. Filthy. Broken windows. Bare mattress. And a word I don't want to think about but force myself to admit.

Abandoned.

No one lives here. No one has lived here for a long while. But I remember Dad tucking me in a few nights ago—into a clean bed with crisp sheets and a pink comforter. In a room with a brand-new London Symphony Orchestra poster tacked to the wall. I remember Mom checking to see that I dusted the top of my dresser. I remember Lissa leaving before sunrise for school. And Jonah's Star Wars music blaring through the house.

But somehow I am alone now, in a house where my family hasn't been in a really long time.

I run to the bathroom and slam the door behind me, hoping that a splash of icy water will clear my head and wake me to a different reality. A normal reality. I turn on the water and back away from the sink. It has dead bugs and a rotting mouse in it, and nothing comes out of the rust-speckled faucet. Not a single drop of water. I brace my hands on the counter and try to remember when the water stopped working. "Think, think, think," I whisper, straining for the answers. Sweat trickles down my temple and I come up blank.

In the cracked, dust-coated mirror, I see a reflection, and the thought of being abandoned slips away. I am not alone, after all. She is tall, with long, stringy hair, and gangly, like she's just had a growth spurt. She looks like my older sister, Lissa. She is Lissa. And maybe she knows what's going on.

"Lis?" I ask, my voice scratchy-dry. I turn around, but I'm alone. Turning back to the mirror I carefully wipe away the dust with my hand. So does the reflection. *My* muddy eyes stare back from a hollow face, but it's not my face. I take a step away from the mirror and stare at the reflection, mesmerized and confused. I slide my hands over the contours of my lanky body. So does the reflection. The reflection is mine.

I stare at myself, at my small breasts. And curved hips. The last time I looked at myself in the mirror . . . I didn't have them. I touch my cheek, and my heart starts hammering again. Something mars the back of my hand. Black, spiderish, wrong. I take a closer look. It's a tattoo, an oval with ten legs. A *mark*. "Conceal the mark," I whisper. The words leave my mouth without me even meaning to speak them, as if someone else put them on my tongue. Yet I know in my gut that I must obey them.

I pull open the bathroom drawer and sigh with relief. Some of Lis's makeup is in it. I take a tube of flesh-colored stuff and open it. Concealer. What Lis used to use to cover zits. I remember her putting it on in the mornings before she went to nursing classes at the University of Colorado, when I was twelve and wishing I were as old as my big sister. I remember everything from back then. My sister. My parents. My twin brother, Jonah. But I can't remember why I have a tattoo on my hand, or why I have to hide it. I can't remember when my body stopped look-ing thirteen and started looking like . . . a *woman's*.

Outside the bathroom door, the stairs groan—a sound I remember well. It means someone is coming upstairs. For a moment, I'm giddy with hope. Hope that my mom has come home. But then dread makes my heart speed up, because what if it isn't my mom? I take a wide step around the spot where the floor squeaks and tiptoe to the door. Opening it a crack, I peer through.

A man is creeping up the stairs. He's wearing a tattered pair of cutoff shorts but no shirt, and his hair is long and stringy around his face. Muscles bulge in his arms, flex on his bare chest, and swell in his long legs, and thick veins pulse under his tight, suntanned skin.

Like an animal tracking prey, he leans down and puts his nose to the carpet. The muscles in his shoulders ripple and tense, his lips pull back from his teeth, and a guttural sound rumbles in his throat. In one swift movement, he leaps to his feet and sprints down the hall toward my bedroom, his bare feet thudding on the carpet.

I have to get away, out of the house, before he finds me. I should run. Now. This very second!

Instead I freeze, press my back to the bathroom wall and hold my breath, listening. The house grows quiet, and slowly, I reach for the doorknob. My fingers touch the cool metal and ease it open a hair wider. I peer out with one eye. The floor in the hall groans, and my knees threaten to buckle. I am now trapped in the bathroom.

I grip the doorknob, slam the bathroom door, and lock it, then yank the vanity drawer open so hard it breaks away from the cabinet. I need a weapon. My hand comes down on a metal nail file, and, gripping it in my damp palm, I toss the drawer to the floor.

The bathroom door shudders and I stare at it, wondering how long before the man breaks it down. Something crashes into the door a second time. I jump as the wood splinters, and scramble backward, never taking my eyes from the door. Something hits the door a third time, shaking the entire house, and I turn to the window—my only hope of escape. Because there's no way a nail file is going to stop the man who is beating down the door.

The window groans and fights me, the catch slipping in my sweaty grasp. As the window grates upward, the bathroom door implodes, a spray of splinters shooting against my back.

I grip the narrow window frame, just like I did as a kid, and swing my feet through. My hips follow, and then my shoulders.

A hand thrusts through the open window, attached to a scraped, straining forearm. On the back of the hand is the twin of the symbol that marks me—an oval with five lines on each side.

As I jump out the window, fingers slip over my neck, gouge into my cheek, and clamp down on my long, tangled hair. Fire lines my scalp as the skin pulls taut against my skull. I hang with my feet just above the balcony and flail, dangling by my hair. Somehow, the man's grip slips on my hair and my shoes touch the balcony. And then, with an unexpected release on my scalp, I'm free.

I glance over my shoulder. The window frames a face with smooth skin and hollow cheeks—a boy on the brink of manhood. He peels his lips back from his teeth and growls, and I stare into his brown eyes. For a moment it is like looking into a mirror, and I almost say his name. Until I realize his eyes are wild and feral, like an animal's. When he grips the outside of the window and swings his feet through, I scramble up onto the ledge of the balcony. And jump.

My spine contracts and my hips pop as I land on the trampoline my mother bought when I was eleven years old. The blue safety pads are long gone. I'm surprised the weathered black mat doesn't split beneath my feet as I bounce and come down a second time, stabbing the black mat with the nail file and dragging it as far and hard as I can. I jump over the exposed springs as my brother sails through the air behind me. The mat tears noisily beneath him and he falls through it, like jumping into a shallow pond. And when he hits the ground, I hear a snap and a grunt.

I run to the fence that separates my house from the elementary school and dig my feet into the chain-link diamonds. Just like when I was a kid, racing the tardy bell, I clamber up and over the fence in a heartbeat.

As I sprint across the empty schoolyard, past the silent, rusted playground, I dare a look over my shoulder. My brother is hobbling toward the fence, his ankle hanging at an odd angle to his leg. His eyes meet mine and he holds a hand up to me, a plea to come back. A sob tears at my chest, but I look away and keep running.

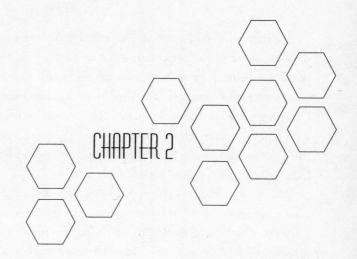

CHAPTER 2

A scorching sun beats down from the turquoise sky, gleaming off the distant buildings of downtown Denver. Yet no leaves grow on the skeletal trees, no flowers bloom in pots on front porches, no grass grows in dead front yards. Even the Rocky Mountains looming on the western horizon look brown and brittle. The only green in this world comes from brown-tinted pine trees—those that aren't as dead as everything else. I am in a world of winter being burned beneath a summer sun.

I stumble through a silent neighborhood. The houses' windows are shattered. Rusted cars sit atop flat tires in driveways. My shadow stretches long over the cracked, litter-strewn pavement. I skirt around a faded, tipped garbage can and walk faster, because deep down I can sense that this is a bad place to be when the sun sets.

My feet slow as I walk toward a telephone pole. The wires lie spaghetti-twisted on the ground below it, and tacked to the front is a piece of paper at odds with this trashed, forgotten neighborhood. The paper is daffodil yellow—not sun bleached or water warped or wind frayed. I take a closer look.

REWARD
1–4 marks = 1 oz honey
5–7 marks = 2 oz honey
8–9 marks = 3 oz honey
10 marks = 8 oz honey

To claim reward, marked one must be alive.
Payments made Sundays @ Southgate or Northgate.
No payment for dead body.
Sincerely, Governor Jacoby Soneschen

I walk past the daffodil-yellow paper and round a corner in the deserted street, and a dog barks—the first sound that I haven't made myself since leaving my house. More dogs join in, and my heart speeds up, a weak, dehydrated fluttering against my ribs. Four houses ahead, a window reflects evening sunlight . . . and the window is whole. Several dogs stand in the front yard below that window, teeth bared, saliva strings dangling from their barking mouths, yanking against the chains that keep them from charging me. My steps slow and I glance at my right hand. The flesh-colored makeup still hides the tattoo. When I look back up, four men stand in the yard with the dogs, and each man holds a gun pointed at me.

M16 assault rifle. The name flitters into my confused brain. And I can remember the day my dad taught me to shoot.

The guys at the Buckley Air Force Base always saluted Dad, even though he wheeled himself up to the platform in a wheelchair—his final badge of military duty, one he could never leave home without.

"This your kid?" one guy asked, looking at me where I cowered behind the wheelchair. I stared up at his camouflage clothes, his broad shoulders, and tried to imagine my dad dressed like that and standing tall.

"Yeah. She's eleven," Dad said. "Figured it was time to teach her to shoot."

The guy nodded approval but looked skeptical. "Never too young to start 'em out. Just warn her about the recoil. We wouldn't want her leaving with a black eye."

The rest of the time at the shooting range was a blur of guns, noise-muffling ear covers, and recoils that flung me backward, but I remember the look in my dad's eyes at the end of the lesson. And the other men's eyes. Surprise.

"With the finger control you're learning in piano, you'll be a sharp-shooter in no time," Dad said, his hazel eyes glowing with pride.

One by one, the M16s are lowered as the men study me. I take a tentative step forward, and all four guns point at me before I can flinch. I don't move.

"Ellen, come here!" one of the men calls, staring at me through the scope on his gun. He seems to be the oldest of the four. His hair is white, at least.

The front door opens, and a thin, hard woman steps onto a

front porch edged with shrub skeletons. The white-haired man nods toward me. The woman puts her hands on her bony hips and squints. I have seen her before. She is the mother of one of my schoolmates. I used to play at this house, and this woman was always baking. She used to be as soft and round as her cookies.

She presses a hand to her heart. "Dear Lord Almighty, that's Fiona Tarsis. If she doesn't have the mark of the beast, let her pass."

Three of the four guns lower.

"Hold up your hand," the white-haired man calls. I lift both my hands over my head, palms facing them—a sign of surrender. "No. Your right hand," he says, voice hard and mistrusting. "Show me the back of your right hand."

Of course. He wants to see my tattoo. I turn my right hand, palm facing me, tattoo facing him.

Ellen sighs, the sound carrying down the quiet street. "She's clean."

The fourth gun is lowered, but none of the men relax.

"Get on past here, Fiona," the white-haired man calls. I nod and start jogging. As I pass the house, the dogs go ballistic, jerking against the chains anchoring them in place. I stare into the front yard and study the men. But I was wrong about something. Only three are men. The fourth, the one who kept the M16 trained on me the longest, is Jacqui, my old schoolmate.

But there's something really wrong with her. She's on the verge of being an adult. And her thick brown hair is cut like a boy's—short as a soldier's.

"Get on by," the white-haired man warns. I stare straight

ahead and jog as fast as my weary legs will carry me, which is not very fast.

Just as I pass the edge of their property, a shadow appears beside me. I gasp and cover my head with my arms.

"Fo—Fiona!" It's Jacqui—the older, womanly version of her in spite of her boy hair. Her hands are in my hair, twisting it, shoving it down the back of my shirt. "Cut your hair off," she says, eyes scared. She presses something into my hand and retreats to her front yard. I look at what she's given me and frown. A half-eaten snack pack of crackers. The sight of them makes my parched throat clamp shut, so I stuff them into my pocket.

Movement catches my eye. In the last rays of the setting sun, a child perches on the roof of Jacqui's house, a gun in his small hands, his eyes darting all about. Behind a fence in Jacqui's backyard, I can see the tops of cornstalks. *Green* cornstalks. In the midst of the corn stands Ellen, trailing a fine-bristled brush over the feathery wisps that shoot out at the top of the corn, moving from plant to plant in a methodical, deliberate manner. Painting the corn.

I look back up at the boy. He can't be more than eight years old, but the way he holds the gun, he might as well have held it in the womb. He glares at me and aims in my direction. I turn and continue down the littered, deserted road.

When I get far enough from Jacqui's house that I can no longer see the boy, I stop. With the sun gone, the air fuses with twilight and darkness creeps in, unsettling my nerves, giving me the impression that something hides in the shadows. Something teases my ears. I pause and survey the decrepit houses haunting the street. I peer into the black, glassless windows and feel as if someone is watching me. I pray I'm imagining it.

Shelter. I need to find shelter. I step over trash, over bleached human bones, over tree branches and tumbleweeds and empty plastic bottles strewn across the road. With every step the approaching night grows darker, making it harder to see, harder to tell the difference between trash and road. Harder to tell the difference between real and imagined.

A dog barks behind me, and the desire to find shelter makes me frantic.

I run, dodging trash, and jump over a mangled car door. When I land, my knees buckle beneath my weight. I squat on my heels and rest my hands on my knees. Panting, I lick my peeling lips, but my tongue holds no moisture. I need water almost as much as I need air. More than I need shelter.

Another dog joins the first, a distant barking that echoes down the road, driving me to action. I stand unsteadily and face the silent houses. There has to be water in one of them. Maybe left in a toilet tank. Or forgotten in a teakettle. Or caught in the coils of a garden hose. Ignoring the instincts that warn me to stay out of the houses, I walk toward the closest one, staring at the gaping windows.

I step up onto the sidewalk and pause. My skin tightens as if something is watching me, like the darkness will devour me if I take another step.

More dogs start barking. A gun explodes, echoing like thunder. I turn and look down the dark road toward Jacqui's house, and the gun explodes again. Raised voices fill the night, mixed

with the frantic barking. Someone screams—a deep, male scream—and a gun goes off again. And then there is nothing but the ringing in my ears.

Something grabs my arm and I am yanked backward, tripping over trash and the curb and my own feet. I scream, but my throat is too dry to muster up anything more than a croak.

"Shut up!" someone snaps, the person dragging me to the middle of the street, to the black ring of an old tire. The person, a short wisp of a human—a child—releases my arm and shoves the tire away. Beneath it sits a barely visible manhole. Metal echoes hollowly as the lid is slid aside, and then the shadow launches itself into the hole in the road and disappears. I peer down into the blackness and cringe at the dead-animal-and-raw-sewage smell wafting up.

A pale hand darts out of the opening and grabs my ankle.

"Hurry up and jump, or you'll be worse than dead!" the child hisses, digging ragged nails into my skin. And then I hear a new sound. Footsteps. Lots. Pounding against pavement faster than my frantic heart pounds against my chest. Getting closer.

"Fine! Stay up there. Freaking idiot!"

The manhole starts scraping back into place as the footsteps thump closer. I peer down the dark road toward the sound of the footsteps and see a hoard of shadows approaching—big, broad-shouldered shapes silhouetted by starlight.

I swallow, step, and plummet into darkness.

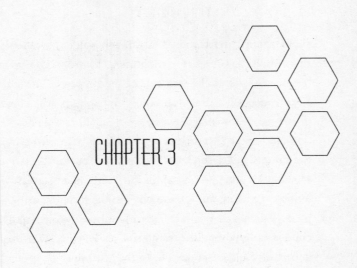

CHAPTER 3

I soar through darkness but only for a heartbeat. My feet impact the ground and sink, the squishy floor absorbing the jolt from my fall. It is like standing at the edge of the ocean and letting the incoming tide wash the sand over my feet until I can't pull them out without wiggling them loose. I move my feet and the ground squelches.

Above me, stars shine in a sphere, a halfmoon, a crescent, and then there's darkness as the manhole locks back into place, the child panting with the effort of it. My feet squelch again, and the child leaps to the ground and grabs me, nails digging into my shoulder and pulling me down.

Lips are on my ear, and I can't tell which smells worse—the child or the air. "Shut up or I'll kill you," it whispers. A small hand comes over my mouth, and something cold and rough slides against my throat. I swallow a spitless swallow, and my throat bobs against sharp roughness. I hardly dare breathe.

Above, the hollow smack of feet echoes. The child and I stay frozen in a tense embrace, my mouth still covered by a grimy hand, the sharpness warming against my neck.

The footsteps pass, but the child doesn't move a muscle. Yet the child's heart thunders against my back. We stand frozen together for a long time—until the child's heart slows—and then, without a sound, I'm released. I stumble forward, arms flailing in pitch-blackness. A hand grabs my elbow before I fall, and the child starts guiding me through the darkness, over the squelching floor. The child's feet don't squelch. Just mine.

I hold my hands forward like I'm sleepwalking, but the child obviously knows where to go. In spite of the blackness, we walk at a steady pace. The child counts under its breath, and when it gets to a certain number, it pauses and we turn . . . left or right, always different. Every once in a while starlight, slatted by the bars of a storm drain, filters down to where we creep. And every time we pass beneath a storm drain, the child clasps a grimy hand against my chapped lips.

We walk a long time, silent, until the child asks, "Why are you so clean?" The whisper, out of place in the dark tunnels, startles me.

"What?" I say.

"You're *clean*. Your clothes, your skin. And you smell like . . ." It sniffs. "Plants and iodine. Are you from the right side of the wall?"

"What wall?" I whisper.

"Shut up!" The hand is over my mouth again. We turn a corner, and blue starlight glows down from a storm drain. I walk on my toes, and the squelching becomes a muted wet squish. We pass the glow and walk for a few minutes in silence before the child speaks again.

"Are you from inside the wall?"

"What wall?" I ask a second time, my voice a whisper. Even if I wanted to speak louder, I don't know if I could. "I'm thirsty," I say, panting.

We stop walking and the child releases my arm.

"Look here, *girl*," the child growls. "I just saved your life. You're the one who should be giving *me* water. You owe me. And you're gonna pay me back, or I'm gonna leave you here. In the dark. Right now. To shrivel up and die like everything else." The child's voice is high. Feminine.

"Pay you back?" My hand goes to my throat, tracing the dip of my collarbone, searching for a necklace. But there's nothing there. I lower my empty hand. "How can I pay you back?" I ask. "I don't have any money or jewelry."

"*Money? Jewelry?* I can't eat those, or trade them. Do you have any food or honey?"

Honey. I remember honey. Gold. Sweet. Melted with butter on wheat toast at breakfast. Drizzled in tea. Made by bees. Bees are on the endangered species list. And now I can hear my sister's voice like she's standing beside me.

"Since the bees are endangered, we have to plant these special flowers to help feed them." Lis dug a shallow hole in the dirt and dropped a seed inside

for Jonah and me to see. "Bees love lavender—the color, the smell," she explained. "And so do I. Here, you guys plant some."

She put three small pale-purple seeds into my hand and three into Jonah's.

Using my fingers, I dug a shallow hole in the damp soil.

"What will happen if the bees go extinct?" Jonah asked, burying his first seed.

"First of all, there would be no more honey. It would become the world's most rare, most precious food—even more precious than gold," Lis said. "But that's just the beginning. Bees pollinate a huge percentage of the world's crops. If bees die out, things like apples and peaches and vegetbles will die. Lots of plants will die without the bees' pollinating them. And if the plants start dying, then the things that eat plants will start to die, like cows and chickens, which means no more meat for us to eat. If we have no fruits or vegetables to eat, and no meat, our world will experience a major famine. People will start starving to death worldwide."

I looked at the tiny seeds in my hand and wondered how something so small could make a difference if the bees were already going extinct.

"Don't look so scared," Lis said, patting the top of my head. "My biology teacher says that the government has their top scientists and biologists working on a solution."

"Hello! Can you pay me back now or what?"

I shake the memory from my head. "No. I don't have anything to give to you."

"Whatever. You can pay me back with a favor. And when you complete it, *then* I'll give you all the water you can drink," it says.

"No. I need water now."

The child sighs and mutters under its breath. The sound of water swishes, and my dry throat clamps tight with desire. A narrow container is pushed against my hands. I grab it, open the lid, and chug it down, but before my thirst is slaked the water is gone, leaving sand in my teeth and the taste of copper on my tongue.

The empty bottle is yanked from my hand. "I just saved your life twice now, idiot. You owe me double." Fingers find my elbow and, clutching it a little too hard, guide me forward again.

My feet squelch against the floor, and my mouth is deliciously damp. I sigh, content. "I'll repay you double," I say, willing to do anything for more water. Not a smart thing to do when you haven't been told the price.

When we finally stop walking, fatigue drags at my body. A *scritch* disturbs the silence, and a match sparks to life. I squint against the tiny flame and look around. I stand at the end of a tunnel surrounded on three sides by concrete. Above, pipes slowly drip water into waiting, dented pots. And above them, darkness.

The child lights a candle and grabs my right hand, big, hungry eyes examining the back of it. "So much for paying me back double," it grumbles, shoving my hand away.

The child, slight and bony, wears baggy clothes a grimy shade of gray, the same color as its sickly skin. Its dark hair is short everywhere but in the front, where long greasy bangs cover most of its face, except for a pointy nose sticking out. I lean toward the child, trying to peer beneath the thick hank of hair. It sounds like a girl, is small like a girl, but there's something masculine in the way she—he?—stands.

"Are you a boy or a girl?" I ask.

The child whips the bangs out of its face and grins at me with stained teeth. "Does it matter?"

I stare at the child's dark, shifty eyes. "I guess not."

The child gnaws on its thumbnail and studies me for a moment, eyes calculating. "I'm a girl. But when things get ugly, looking like a boy is more protection than a hidden knife." The way she says it, she sounds way more grown-up than she looks. "Rest. You'll need it. You're paying me back tomorrow. Double."

A pile of blankets are heaped in a corner where the cement walls meet. I walk toward them, but the girl steps in front of me and puts her hand against my shoulder. "Sorry, Flower. That's where *I* sleep."

"My name's not Flower. It's . . . Fo."

"Arrin. Nice to meet you." Arrin takes a blanket from the pile and chucks it at my feet. "And just so you know, Fo, if you try and ditch me while I sleep, the others will kiiiiiill you," she says.

I peer over my shoulder, toward the dark tunnel. "Others?"

"Yeah. The *others*. You know, the people who've banded together and hide down here in order to survive. They kill wanderers before they ask questions. So don't wander off if you ever want to see the sun again." Arrin collapses onto the pile of blankets and blows out the candle. My eyes open wide and I swing my hand in front of them. I see nothing.

Reaching down, I spread the blanket on the cement floor

and ease onto it. And gag. The blanket smells like vomit, moldy cheese, and urine. My stomach turns, and I scramble to my feet. Wadding up the blanket, I toss it away. Cold, hard cement over the smell of that? Any day.

I lie on my side with my arm under my head, but I don't sleep. Not yet. Not with my body screaming for the water dripping into a pot not three feet away. When Arrin's breathing grows deep and methodical, I roll onto my hands and knees and stick my face into the pan. Water drips onto the back of my head as I drink, but that doesn't slow me down. I drink until my belly wants to pop. And then, finally satisfied, I lie on my back.

Arrin mumbles in her sleep, something about bacon, her voice a deep grumble. I try to block her out by focusing on the rhythm of dripping water—a liquid metronome. My fingers move to the beat, tapping out the notes to the second movement of Beethoven's Seventh against my thigh, and as I play the silent music, I cry myself to sleep.

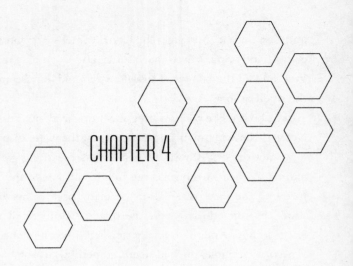

CHAPTER 4

"First thing we have to do is cut your hair."

I still hear the rhythm of water dripping onto water. Beethoven's Seventh still haunts my groggy brain, keeping time with the dripping.

"And then we'll make you dirty. Really *filthy*. You stand out, and not in a good way. Sad fact about cleanliness—it makes you a minority if you're on the wrong side of the wall. Who are you, anyway?"

I open my tear-crusted eyes, and the music in my head jolts to a stop. A glowing candle flashes against Arrin's close face. She sits cross-legged beside my head, holding a rusty dagger in one hand, tugging my hair out of the neck of my shirt with the other. I push against the cement floor and sit. "What are you doing?" I croak, staring at the knife.

"Waking you up, idiot. The early bird always gets the worm. And I have a mighty big worm that needs getting."

"What time is it?" I wonder aloud, looking at my empty left wrist. I always wear a watch. Correction—*wore*.

"There is no time down here," Arrin says, rubbing a strand of my hair between her thumb and finger. "So, what are you doing on the wrong side of the wall?"

I think about the meaning behind her words. At least I try to. But I don't know what she's talking about. "You mean, what was I doing out in the street? Last night?"

"Duh." She rolls her eyes.

My brother's face wavers in my mind. A younger face, smiling, gentle. Not how he was yesterday—if that was yesterday. But there's no way I'm going to tell Arrin that I was running from my own brother. "I was running from . . . something."

"Yeah, I got that. You caught the attention of the raiders. What'd you do to make them come after you?"

"Them?" I think of the shadows running down the street toward me just after sunset and shrug. "Nothing."

"Whatever. I totally saved your butt. They *never* let anyone get away, especially girls. And now you've got to repay me. *Double*. As soon as possible, because I can't have you depending on me for anything. Including water." She glares at the pot I drank from the night before. "And if you want to succeed in that payment, you gotta look like a boy, and you gotta be dirty." She lifts the dagger, and candlelight flickers against the rusty blade. I lean away and press a hand to my neck.

"I'm not going to kill you, idiot. You're worth too much alive. The knife's for your hair," she says.

I grab my hair and wind it around my hand. It hangs down to my hips—longer than I remember it ever being in my life. And thicker.

Arrin rolls her eyes. "Yeah. So it's glossy and smooth and the color of wheat. You'd be in a shampoo commercial if we still had television. Thing is, no one but the lice can appreciate it down here. Just hold still." She holds the knife toward me, and I flinch. "Look, Fo. You'll be thanking me for getting rid of it. Trust me."

I hug my knees to my chest. The knife saws against my hair, tearing it from my scalp more than cutting it. But then I feel a release, and my sheared hair falls around my shoes in a shiny, honey-gold pile. Arrin takes a chunk of the hair still attached to my scalp and hacks it even shorter, until she's moved around the entire back of my head. Until I imagine I look just like her— short, uneven hair on the back and sides of my head, chin-length hair in front that covers most of my face. Totally ugly. My mother would be mortified. The thought makes my heart ache. Where *is* my mother?

Arrin grins, a flash of teeth as dingy as her skin. "Perfect," she says, eyeing my hair. Her breath smells like the tunnels. "Are you rested? Because the sun is going to set in a couple of hours. And that's when you are going to pay me back. *Double*."

"Right." My stomach growls, and I remember the half-eaten pack of crackers from Jacqui. I take them from my pocket and slide one into my hand. It is a peanut-butter-filled sandwich cracker dusted with little grains of salt. My mouth waters.

A black weight hits my chest, and I fly backward. The candle wavers and goes out just as my head crunches against cement. Heavy darkness sits atop me, pinning my arms to the ground, clawing the crackers from my hand.

"Air did oo get dese?" Arrin asks, mouth full. She swallows noisily. "I haven't tasted peanut butter in two *years*." She climbs off me. I hear the crackers crunching in her teeth. "These crackers, they can help pay off your debt to me."

Hunger stabs my hollow stomach. "Not if I die of starvation first. I need food," I retort, climbing to my knees and rubbing the goose egg on the back of my head.

She laughs, and I can smell peanut butter on her rancid breath. A match scrapes and a flame flickers. She relights the candle, and shadows dance against her greedy, chewing face.

"Here. Gnaw on this." She tosses something at me. Relieved at the thought of eating, I snatch it out of the air and frown. A leather belt, half eaten and covered with teeth marks, dangles from my hand. I toss it back and stare at her like she's crazy. Arrin lets the belt fall to the ground and shrugs. "Suit yourself. But there ain't nothing else to eat down here." She looks at the last cracker, golden and clean in her discolored hand, then breaks off a tiny piece, barely a morsel. She holds it out to me. "Here." She says it like she's just sacrificed something priceless. I guess a crumb *is* priceless to someone who is starving—someone like me. I take it and swallow without chewing. My stomach growls for more.

Arrin holds the last cracker with the tips of her fingers and nibbles toward its center, like a mouse, beady eyes focused on me as if she's afraid I might fight her for it. I stare and she glares, but I don't take my eyes from her. It isn't the cracker that holds my attention. Something darkens the back of her right hand. An oval with three lines drawn through it like insect legs—two on the left, one on the right. I glance at my own hand. The edge of my mark is showing through the makeup and dirt. My palms turn icy-damp, and I wipe them on my shirt.

"I need some privacy," I blurt, touching the tube of makeup in my pocket.

"Pee over there." She nods toward the darkness, and I wander out of the ring of candlelight. "But, Fo. The others. Don't go far."

I stumble through the darkness and come to the end of the cement. My feet sink into goo and squelch with each step. When I am sure Arrin cannot see me, I slip the makeup from my pocket and dab it on the back of my hand, smoothing it over the tattoo. Over the ten-legged spider. When I'm done I squat and relieve myself, and as I am retying the drawstring waist on my knee-length shorts, a squelch echoes behind me, followed by a gasped curse.

I flip around and face the black tunnel. Someone could be standing six inches from me, engulfed in darkness, and I wouldn't be able to see him.

I turn to the flickering candle and hurry toward it, easing my feet onto the slick floor with each step, trying not to squelch. And then I am on cement, inside the glow of candlelight. Arrin lounges on her nest of nasty blankets, hands behind her head, staring at the pipes on the ceiling.

"Arrin," I whisper.

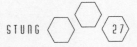

She looks at me with heavy eyes. "Those crackers," she says with a sigh. She grins and licks her teeth.

"I think someone is in the tunnel," I whisper, glancing over my shoulder.

Her eyes snap wide, and she springs to her feet, dagger in hand.

"We know you're there. I'll kill you if I see you," Arrin snarls, her words ringing with violent truth. She slices the air for impact, and I take a step away from her. There is no reply. Crouching beside the candle, she blows it out. We plunge into darkness so thick I can hardly breathe it into my lungs.

"Why did you blow out the candle?" I ask.

"So they can't see us. If they can't see us, it makes it a hell of a lot harder to kill us."

I gasp.

"Stop breathing so loud," Arrin whispers. "They won't need the light to kill you if you keep making noise like that. And I'm *not* going to save you again."

I open my mouth and take slow, silent breaths, straining to hear the warning sound of approach.

A long time passes—my legs begin to itch from standing still for so long. I sink down to the ground and sit on the grimy cement. Icy hands are on me, touching my face, wiping my arms. I pull away and whimper, expecting a knife in the back.

"Hold still, idiot," Arrin breathes. I force myself to freeze beneath her hands. She keeps touching me, wiping grit onto every inch of my exposed skin. When no skin is left untouched, she whispers, "Take off your clothes."

"What?"

"Hurry up! Just take them off. We need to trade." Fabric rustles. A warm mass is dropped into my lap. Her clothes.

I pull my shirt over my head, and after taking the concealer out of the pocket, slip off my shorts, holding them in what I assume is her direction. She snatches them away.

"But first," she whispers, "you need to wrap this around your . . . you know whats." She drops something else in my lap, a long, thin strap of fabric.

"Wrap this around my what?" I ask, baffled.

"How dense are you? Do I seriously have to spell it out?" When I don't answer, she blurts, "Around your *knockers,* Fo. No one's going to believe you're a boy if they get a look at those. Even if they are small. Sheesh." She mutters under her breath as I struggle to bind my breasts, tying the fabric into a knot below my left armpit.

When I'm done, I fiddle with her clothes until I find the shirt. As I pull the stiff, greasy-feeling fabric over my head, I gag. The stench is unreal—sweat, urine, dirt, sewage. I pull on the pants, barely manage to squeeze them over my hips, and, sucking in my stomach, force them to button.

"You are so fat," Arrin whispers, her voice filled with wonder. "It's a good thing these shorts have a drawstring."

I press on my bony hips. "I'm not fat."

"Don't you know a compliment when you hear one? You're lucky. Even with the drawstring, your shorts will barely stay up on my bony butt." Arrin inhales deeply. "And you smell like flowers, I think. I can't quite remember."

Flowers. I remember how they smell. Beds of lavender and forget-me-nots lined my driveway. Lis put lavender in matchless socks and stuck them in her drawers. She always smelled like lavender.

"It's almost time to go," Arrin whispers.

"Where?"

"Up. You're going to pay me back. Double. Tonight. *Remember?*"

My heart starts drumming. Something in her voice makes me wonder what I have gotten myself into. "*How* am I paying you back, Arrin?"

She chuckles, and goose bumps shiver down my arms. "You'll see." The air shifts, and then she pulls me to my feet. "Now, someone is stalking my tunnel. You've got to walk behind me and hold on to my shirt. And don't let go! Even if we have to run. *Especially* if we have to run."

I nod and blindly run my hands over her bony body until I find the back of her shirt. And then we start walking through the black tunnels, and all I can think of is the person who was watching us, who might be about to pounce. Her shirt grows damp from my hand, and my feet squelch no matter how I tiptoe.

CHAPTER 5

"Why's the ground so squishy?" I whisper.

"You're walking on dried-up human sewage. Only it's not completely dry," she says, her voice barely audible.

I shudder.

"Haven't you ever been down here, Fo?"

"No," I say without thinking. And surely I'd remember a place like this. Wouldn't I?

"Lucky you. It used to be worse—a canal of slime that reached up to my knees. I had to hide in it once, buried up to my nose." She says it like she's bragging.

I cringe and wonder if the clothes I'm wearing are the clothes she wore in the sewage.

"Don't you wanna know why?" she asks.

"Why?"

"The militia was hunting me. Almost caught me, too. One of them waded right past me and didn't see me because he didn't look down." She laughs under her breath.

"What happened?" I ask.

"They all got sick—the militia. They're a bunch of wimps, can't stand the smell down here, I guess. They started barfing up perfectly good food. A total waste. And then they left."

"What is the militia?" I ask. Arrin stops walking.

"Seriously?" she says.

"Yeah."

"You don't know what the *militia* is?"

I search my muddled brain, trying to put a picture with the word, but come up blank. "I don't think so."

"You know, the guys with the big *guns*? Who patrol the wall and catch Fecs for the lab? And shoot the raiders on sight?"

"Oh. Right. The guys with guns that guard the wall and catch . . . whatever . . ." I have no idea what any of that means, and my brain won't supply the answers.

The shirt tugs against my grasp, and we continue winding through the dark, my feet the only sound.

"Fo, where did you come from?" Arrin whispers after we've walked a while. "It's like you're straight out of a fairy tale, or another dimension."

Sleeping Beauty, I think, *just woken from a hundred-year sleep*. "I don't know where—" Arrin's shirt tears out of my clammy fingers.

A wet smack echoes through the tunnel and then I am knocked onto my back, the impact absorbed by the spongy, damp ground. The breath gushes out of me but stops prematurely as a pair of massive hands clamp around my neck. I try to gasp but can't. The hands squeeze harder, crushing my windpipe, and jagged fingernails dig into my flesh.

I claw at the huge hands, wiggle beneath them, try to force air into my body. But I can't. I ball my right hand into a fist and swing at the darkness above my face. My fist contacts rough, hairy skin, and the hands on my neck loosen a fraction. My blood starts to boil as fury fills me, seeping fire all the way to my toes. I pull my hand back again and ball my fingers so tightly my fist trembles. This time when I swing, my entire body bolts energy into the movement. My knuckles contact flesh and bone, the fingers on my neck loosen and fall away, and something crumples on the ground beside me. I roll to my side and gasp for air, pressing my cheek against the slimy ground.

Noise fills the tunnel—grunting, struggling, and breathing loud enough to wake the dead. Arrin whimpers and lets out a cry. I climb to my feet, turn toward her voice, and nearly trip over something. A body. My hands flutter over it; feel the gentle inhale and exhale of a living person; feel broad, square shoulders with lines gouged into the bare skin and a face covered in coarse hair. My attacker.

I yank my hands away and stand, shuddering.

The sounds of struggle still haunt the black tunnel. I follow the gasping and grunting and growling and stumble into flailing bodies.

"Arrin?" I ask.

"Help me!" she gasps. I freeze. Help? I can't see anything. If

I start kicking, I might kick Arrin. If I punch, I might hit the wrong person.

"Jump on him, Fo!" Arrin calls.

I take a deep breath and halfheartedly throw myself toward the sound of the human skirmish. I land atop a roiling, lurching pile of arms and legs. And then I can tell which is Arrin and which is the other. He's big and muscular with arms like fur-covered clubs. She's a pile of skin and bones. I grab a handful of greasy, coarse hair and yank his head backward. Arrin grunts. Without warning, the man jerks twice and goes limp.

"Get him off me!" Arrin cries. I push the man over, and my hands come away wet. "Hurry. They travel in packs." Arrin grabs my hand, and we start staggering through the dark. Before my heart has had time to calm, we stop.

"Bloody hell," Arrin whispers, her hand tightening in frustration on mine.

"What's wrong?" I ask.

"We're lost." She yanks me forward once more.

After a few minutes of staggering, I make out a hazy glow down a tunnel to my right and tug Arrin to a stop. "Light," I say.

Arrin curses and pulls me into a crouch. "Don't say a word," she warns. "Or make a sound! Walk on the outside edge of your feet, Fo. Because if they hear you, they'll murder you. And I'm not going to save your sorry, fat butt a third time."

"Even though I just saved you?" I ask, trying to understand her logic.

"Whatever! I had that under control. Now shut up," she hisses.

I struggle to balance on the outside of my feet and manage

something close to silence. But as we approach the light, confusion fills me. They don't look like murderers. Arrin stops.

A hollow-cheeked woman sits on the ground beside a candle. Four children huddle at her feet. One child, the tallest, a boy who can't be more than ten, holds a dingy plastic container in his hands. He fishes around in the container and pulls out something long and thin. It curls and coils in his fingers. I blink and stare at the child holding the earthworm, wondering what he's going to do with it.

He hands it to a wisp of a child—a girl, I think—wearing an oversize T-shirt that hangs down to her knobby knees. The girl shoves it into her mouth, chewing and sighing like she's eating chocolate.

My jaw drops, but I snap it shut. I can taste the sewer when I breathe through my mouth.

The boy gives each child a worm, then hands one to the woman. Once everyone else has had one, he takes one for himself, eating the wriggling creature in little bites, savoring it.

"Why are they eating worms?" I whisper.

"Obviously their father, wanting to live a life of leisure inside the wall, abandoned them," Arrin whispers, voice bitter.

"No way. A father wouldn't do that."

"Wanna bet?" She squeezes my hand, mashing the bones together. I gasp and try to yank my hand away, but she clings to it. "Shut up, Fo!"

In one collective movement, all four children whip around to face us. A knife appears in the boy's hand. Another appears in the wispy little girl's hand. They stare into the darkness, poised on the balls of their feet. The woman, eyes panicked, leans forward and blows out the candle, and the safety of darkness swallows them.

Arrin yanks me in the opposite direction of the worm eaters. We run until she jolts to a dead stop, and I slam into her back. She groans and drops my hand, but our palms don't come loose. I pull and our flesh peels apart.

"Why were our hands—"

"Shhh!" Arrin hisses, smacking me. "You are going to get me killed! Just shut up long enough to pay me back!"

There is a wet thud by my feet. "I crashed into a wall and hit my head." Arrin's voice comes from below. "And the guy in the tunnel cut me. I've got to rest. Sit, if you want."

I don't sit. Not when I know what coats the floor.

"Here's what you're going to do, Fo," Arrin says a few minutes later. "My nine-year-old brother was picked up yesterday morning. You're going to create a distraction so I can get him out. After that, you're on your own."

"Why was your brother picked up?" I ask.

"He's a Level Three," says Arrin, as if it's the most obvious reason in the world.

"A Level Three what?"

"Where are you from, Fo? How can you not know what a Level Three is?"

"I'm from . . ." Fuzz fills my brain. I can see my house, see my brother, remember how my sister smells, remember my dad teaching me how to shoot and my mom cooking pancakes on Sunday morning. I can even remember how to make music with my fingers. But I can't remember where I have been.

"That was a rhetorical question, moron. I get it. You don't remember. Help me up." I pull Arrin to her feet. "Next rain gutter we see, we're going topside."

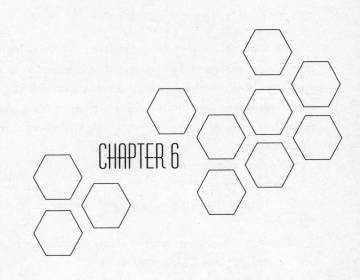

CHAPTER 6

The late-afternoon sky burns my vision. I press my palms against my watering eyes and fill my lungs with clean, bright air.

"The bad news is, we're still about half a mile from the wall," Arrin says, sliding the grate back over a rain gutter. "Good news is, I don't think there's a hive between us and there. All we'll have to watch out for is patrolling militia and raiders. But raiders usually don't come around the militia's camp, and they never come out before sunset."

I pull my hands from my face and squint. We stand on the side of a deserted street surrounded by crumbling factories, abandoned cars, and broken traffic lights. Garbage and tumbleweeds blow down the street, the only noise in this arid world of silence.

Arrin starts to run. I lope to her side and for the first time, truly see her.

She is tiny, the top of her greasy head barely as high as my chin. One of her eyes is bruised and nearly swollen shut, and her lip is split. Greasy-looking grime covers every inch of her skin and darkens her pores into a constellation of black dots. Yet, beneath the dirt and filth, she is a child. She glares at me with cold blue eyes.

"Why are you staring at me, Fo?"

"How old are you?" I ask.

She thrusts her square chin and pointy nose forward. "Thirteen."

"So am I," I say. I can remember my birthday cake, remember the pink candles. Thirteen of them.

Arrin raises one dark eyebrow and looks me up and down. "Liar. You're an adult."

"No. I remember turning thirteen," I say. My hand wanders up to my throat again, feeling my collarbone for a fine chain. But there is nothing hanging around my neck.

Arrin shakes her head. "What you are is messed up in the head. You have hips. And *knockers*. And you look like an *adult*." Arrin tilts her head to the side, her eyes suddenly alert. She grabs my arm and yanks me toward the nearest building. We dart through a missing door and Arrin dives into the shadows. I crouch beside her, perplexed.

"What's wrong?" I mouth.

She points toward the doorway, and I peer around the splintered frame. Six men are marching down the street toward us, the bases of long black rifles cupped in their hands, the other ends resting on their shoulders. They wear crisp brown jackets and crisp brown pants, and their hair is slightly long on top but short on the sides of their heads. Above their left ears, each one has horizontal stripes shaved into his scalp, and pinned over each of their hearts is a shiny silver star.

Aside from having different colors of hair, they look like paper dolls, all symmetry and rhythm, even down to their staccato march. Tchaikovsky's "March of the Wooden Soldiers" echoes in my head, and my fingers begin to move, playing imaginary notes. "Militia," I whisper.

Arrin tugs me away from the door and presses a finger to her lips. Her nails are ragged and caked with dirt and blood. The creases on her finger are dark-red stripes. I frown and look at her clothes—my old clothes. Blood is spattered on them, like crimson fireworks. She raises one eyebrow and points at me, and I look down. Blood coats my hands, clings to the pale hairs of my arms, and covers my clothing. I gag and my stomach heaves, but nothing comes up. I am too empty. Arrin clasps her hand over my mouth, and the smell of blood makes me dry heave again.

Outside the building, the militia march past, their footsteps a fading cadence. When the evening grows quiet, Arrin removes her hand from my mouth. Silent, she stands and darts out the door. I follow on her heels.

We cling to the shadows, hugging the bases of factories until the sun sets and the entire world is in darkness. And then something changes. My stomach growls, saliva fills my mouth, and I turn my face to the twilight sky and sniff. Images of roast turkey and grilled steak pop into my brain. Clutching my concave stomach, I whimper. I will do anything for food.

Too focused on food to realize she's stopped, I crash into Arrin. She gasps and hunches over.

"Arrin? What's wrong?" I put my hands on her shoulders and try to help her stand. She whimpers and pulls away, and my hand comes away wet. Even in the dusky light I can see my palm is coated with something dark. I squeeze my hand shut. When I open it, my fingers are sticky. "Blood," I whisper, not so hungry anymore.

"I'll be fine. I've had worse," Arrin says.

"You have?"

"Yeah," she says, peering up at me with a gleam in her blue eyes. She chuckles and stands tall. "Lots worse. Those guys in the tunnels, they come down and prey on the Fecs all the time. I've dreamed about killing them for years. You have no idea how good it felt when I stabbed that one!"

My stomach turns. "You stabbed him?"

"Yep. One swift slice to the carotid artery." She grins, and her face looks like it did when she was eating my crackers—filled with greedy satisfaction.

"The *what* artery?" I ask, slightly sick to my stomach, slightly terrified of this . . . *child*.

"Carotid? It's in the neck. My dad's a doctor, and he taught me how to kill. Where'd you think all the blood came from?" She looks pointedly at my blood-covered arms and hands, and I cringe. "Come on. We're almost there."

Arrin cradles her arm as we continue down the dark street. The smell of food grows stronger, along with other smells that tickle my senses. Wood smoke. Laundry detergent. Sweat and soap. And then the smells are accompanied by sound. Laughing. Singing. Talking. A dog barking.

Suddenly something different floats on the air, and my heart skips a beat. I press my hands to my ears, wondering if my imagination is going wild, wondering if the sound I hear is trapped in my head. But with pressure on my ears, the melody dies. When I uncover my ears, the music returns—Beethoven's Seventh—the same song I heard in the dripping water as I fell asleep the night before. Only this time, instead of remembering the tune as I played it on the piano, guitar strings sing the melody.

We round the corner of a building and halt, and my eyes grow wide. A wall, taller than all of the factories we just passed, juts up from the sidewalk on the other side of the street, so long it disappears into the night. At the base of the wall sits a village, or rather a camp, swarming with men in brown uniforms. Fires glow orange, making shadows dance on the wall, revealing triangular tents, releasing the scent of cooking meat, illuminating a lone man playing the guitar—playing the song I played a thousand times on the piano before . . . before everything changed. A spit of meat roasts above the guitar player's fire, and the music combined with the food . . . he's like the pied piper. And I'm a rat. Without thinking, I take a step forward.

"Idiot! You don't even know the plan yet!" Arrin grabs my hand and stops me. She pulls me toward her and puts her mouth to my ear, explaining how I'm going to pay her back. With each whispered word, my pulse beats a little faster and my palms begin to sweat. When she stops speaking, I stare at her like she's insane. And judging by the look in her eye, maybe she is.

"Are you serious?" I whisper, glancing at the camp again.

She nods. I look past the men in brown, past the tents and campfires, to two people slouching at the wall's base, their backs pressed against it. One is small, a pile of bones in a heap of grimy clothes, the other is slightly bigger, a little more filled out but still scrawny. Firelight glints off metal shackles encasing the lower halves of their arms. I look at the men in brown again and realize almost every single one of them holds a gun.

"What if they shoot me?" I ask.

"Then you won't owe me anymore. We'll be even," she says.

I try to take a step away, but she grabs my wrist in an iron-strong hand. "No. I'm not doing that," I say. "I'll find another way to pay you—" The tip of Arrin's knife finds the soft flesh under my chin and all I can think is *carotid artery*. I don't dare breathe.

"You can die right now, Fo, or you can help me and have a chance to live," she warns, her voice a low growl.

Slowly, I put my hand on her wrist, soft and gentle, like I'm trying to pet a dog that wants to bite me. She pushes the knife a little harder so the tip digs into my skin, and I know if I'm not careful, she'll kill me right here, right now. Releasing her wrist, my hands slowly go up in surrender. She moves the knife so it no longer touches my skin, but barely.

"So will you help me or not?" she asks.

"I'll do it," I whisper, my voice trembling. She nods and tucks the knife into a fold of her clothes. I turn and stare at the camp, take a deep breath, possibly my last, and take a step forward.

"Fo," Arrin says. I jolt to a startled stop and look at her. "If they catch you, say you're a boy. Since you don't have the

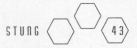

mark, they'll probably let you go. Might even let you inside the wall if you qualify."

I glance at the back of my right hand. The mark is still covered, but by blood and grime as much as makeup. I run my ice-cold hands through my butchered hair and sigh.

"Which one's your brother?" I ask, looking at the two hand-cuffed people with their backs against the wall.

"The little one. He's eleven."

"Wait. Eleven? I thought you said he was nine."

She gnaws the skin on the side of her thumb and then swallows. "You obviously need to clean the wax out of your ears," she retorts. "What are you waiting for?"

I clench my teeth and take a deep breath, brace myself to run and—

"Fo?"

I jump again and glare at Arrin. "What?"

"Thanks."

I nod, like I had a choice in the matter. Facing the camp, I dig my toes into the pavement. And I sprint.

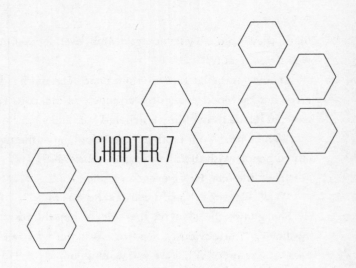

CHAPTER 7

The funny thing is, what I am doing right now is exactly what I wanted to do the minute I saw the camp. In spite of the fact that I'm starving, my legs are strong and swift, stronger than they've been since the moment I awoke in my bed.

Reaching the closest fire, I tear a spit of meat out of a stunned militia man's hands and keep running. At the second fire, I do the same . . . take the meat and run. Without slowing my pace, I press the hot meat to my mouth, burning my tongue and gums as my teeth tear into it, and swallow without chewing. And then I am passing the third fire. And people are yelling, swarming, aiming guns at me. A siren blares.

Before I reach the fourth fire, something catches my ankle and I crash to the ground in a heap of hot meat and dust. I don't care. I've created the distraction Arrin wanted, and now I can

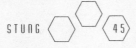

eat. With my eyes staring at the star-freckled sky, I gnaw half-cooked meat, letting the grease and blood coat my fingers, throat, cheeks. Until someone tears it from my hands.

I scramble to my feet and try to run, but a shock of pain freezes my muscles and shatters my world. My legs forget how to work, and I crumple to the ground as spasms rack my body. Someone yanks my hands behind my back and slings cool metal around my forearms. I blink through a haze of pain and find myself staring at the wall and a frenzy of men in brown. They're running around like headless chickens, yelling, swinging their guns. And then I see Arrin and her little brother, tiny even compared to her, leaping over the fire at the farthest edge of the camp. The smaller shadow stumbles and Arrin grabs his shoulders to steady him. They keep running, are almost to the street. Nearly touching freedom.

"Stop them!" a man bellows. "He's a Level Three on the verge of turning!"

Silence smothers the camp, like being dunked under water . . . one minute there's noise; the next, nothing. Every single militia man has his gun to his shoulder and is taking aim. The night explodes in gunfire. Arrin's brother just explodes.

My jaw drops and I'm too stunned to breathe—almost forget that my muscles are twitching with the aftermath of pain. The guns are lowered and sound returns to the camp. The militia pat each other on the backs, chuckling, sighing with relief. I press the balls of my hands against my eyes and try to forget the last image I have of Arrin's brother, silently cursing the meat in my stomach that is about to come up.

Hands grip my biceps and I'm yanked to my feet.

"What've we got?" a deep, gravelly voice asks. A gray-haired man steps in front of me and frowns.

"By the smell of it, we've got us another Fec, sir."

"What level?" the man with gray hair asks.

Someone behind me turns over my right hand. My legs tremble, and it has nothing to do with being Tasered a moment before.

"Huh. No level. He's clean." I can hear the wonder in his voice. My shoulders sag and my legs stabilize.

Gray Hair's eyebrows shoot up. "You sure? I thought all Fecs were marked. Why else would they hide down there?"

The man behind me fiddles with my hand again, rubbing the spot where the tattoo is.

"No. No mark. He's clean, sir."

I peer at Gray Hair through my thick bangs. He studies me with eyes as mistrusting as Arrin's, and his lips grow thin. "Bring him to central. I'm going to do a scan."

A militia man escorts me through a throng of men with wary eyes, to the center of their camp and into a spacious wooden structure—a log cabin—with a row of empty tables and a paper-strewn desk. Overhead, lights hum and buzz. *Electrical* lights.

"Uncuff him, Rory, so I can get a pure read," Gray Hair says. There are lines shaved into his hair above his left ear. Six of them. He has a star on his brown coat. Embroidered above the star is the name *Micklemoore*.

"Yes, sir." My hands are lifted, along with my cuffs, and then the cuffs snap free of my arms. I let my hands hang casually at my sides and try to appear like I am not searching for an escape. The other man, Rory, steps in front of me and aims a Taser at my chest. There are only three lines shaved into his blond hair.

Micklemoore walks to the desk and opens a drawer, removing a metal box the size of my palm. Rory turns from me, hand out held for the metal box. And I run.

Micklemoore yells. Rory turns and clutches my shirt, but I tear away from him. The outside darkness fills the log cabin's door, and I know it's my only hope.

I pass from light into dark and slam into something hard and warm. We topple to the ground, and the unpleasant smell of digesting garlic and onions tickles my nose. Rough hands grapple against my body and latch onto my hips, flinging me aside. The icy barrel of a gun finds my temple, and I squeeze my eyes shut. Instead of feeling my head explode, I hear a low, humorless chuckle.

"Len, you always seem to be in the right place at the right time," Micklemoore says, still chuckling. He crouches beside me, lifts my right hand, and holds out the metal box. The box lights up, a cool, soothing blue that makes my skin crawl. And when the light touches my hand, my tattoo shines through the layers of dirt and blood and makeup like a bike reflector. The box wails a warning siren.

Micklemoore drops the box and lurches away from me faster than anyone with gray hair should be able to move. And then I can't see anyone, because a hundred automatic weapons are pointed at every inch of my body, blocking my view.

Like Arrin's brother, I wait to explode.

CHAPTER 8

"Bowen!" The name echoes and I flinch, expecting gunfire. "Electromagnetic wrist cuffs and ankle cuffs! Now! We got us a Ten!" Micklemoore barks.

A moment later, a small section of guns part and a square-shouldered man fills the space. Darkness hides the features of his face, but his voice resonates deep and soft and soothing, just a tremor above a whisper. "I won't hurt you if you hold still," he says, kneeling beside me.

What he doesn't know is that I couldn't move even if I wanted to. My whole body has turned numb with fright, right down to my lips. He leans over me and an image of a high-mountain lake settles behind my eyes. Or, more accurately, the giant pine trees that encircle the lake and sway in the wind and smell . . . just like this man. I stare at him and breathe, and a temporary calm settles over me.

"That's it, kid. You got a name?" He lifts one of my arms and clamps something onto it, something that stretches from my wrist to just below my elbow and is cool against my skin. "I'm Bowen." He takes my other wrist and clamps the same thing onto my forearm. I open my eyes and lift my head to look at my arms. Bowen leaps away from me, points something in my direction, and the devices on my arms hum to life and of their own will meet, like two magnets attracting each other. I try to pull my arms apart but can't.

Bowen kneels beside me once more and lets out a deep breath of air. "Don't. Move." His voice has turned hard and cold. "I will kill you if you do." With damp, unsteady hands, he lifts my ankle and pushes the pants up around my knee, then attaches a cool metal casing around my calf and shin. He puts one on the other leg, and when it clamps into place, he scrambles away from me like I'm liable to explode at any moment. From a few feet away, he points something at me again. My legs slide together and fuse into one.

The crowd sighs and gasps, and then some men start laughing, like they just witnessed a lion tamer caging his fiercest beast.

"That was awesome, man," someone says, patting Bowen on the back. "First Ten we've ever caught! Must be beginner's luck." The hundred guns disappear, replaced by the starry sky, as men move away. But not Bowen.

"Kid, if you move I'll release a current of electricity through you that'll stop your heart before it can finish a beat. Got it?" he warns.

I don't dare answer. Don't dare to move my jaw—just shift my eyes to stare at Bowen's silhouette.

"Unless you need to talk. Or grunt, or whatever a Ten does," Bowen says, like he can read my mind. He leans a little closer to me, body still tense. "Can. You. Understand. What. I'm. Saying?" He overenunciates each word.

My stomach growls. "I'm hungry," I whisper.

Bowen jumps at the sound of my voice, and his pale eyes catch moonlight. "Whoa. You can *talk*?" He looks from side to side, then reaches into his pants pocket. "You bite me, I shock the crap out of you," he says. "Open your mouth."

I obey. Bowen places a large round disk on my tongue. It dissolves into foam, and I taste pork chops and gravy and green beans. I sigh and close my eyes, and the world wavers beneath me and disappears.

Voices tug at my sleep, whispers dancing with my hazy dreams.

"Come on, man. I'll keep him until Sunday and then take him to the lab. You can have the pay," someone says, his voice hushed.

"Why?" another voice asks.

"I don't know. 'Cause you're new at this job? And I don't want to see someone as young and healthy as you dead. How 'bout I give you eight ounces?"

"For a *Fec*? You want to *buy* him from me?" the other man

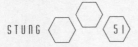

answers, his voice deep and distinct. I know this voice—Bowen. I try to open my eyes, but my body is as unresponsive as stone.

"Sure," the first voice says.

"Why?"

My dreams overpower the voices, dreams of a world lush with budding plants and birdsong, as if the dead summer has turned to spring.

CHAPTER 9

A smell wafts at me, burning my sinuses and making me gag—a smell like rotting meat, morning breath, and dog crap—pulling me out of a deep, troubled sleep. I turn my head to the side and gasp for fresh air.

I am lying on my back, on something hard, and my muscles feel as if I haven't moved them in a year. I try to stretch, but my forearms are stuck together, from my elbows to my wrists. My legs, too.

A breeze stirs the air, and the rancid smell surrounds me again. I gag and open my heavy eyes. A low army-green canvas roof stretches overhead, bright with sunlight. A threadbare sleeping bag is zipped around me, pulled snug at my neck. I try to move again, and when the sleeping bag shifts, a gust of air escapes it. My eyes water and I gag again, my hollow stomach clenching. The nasty smell that pulled me from sleep? It's *me. My* smell.

I cough and wheeze, stretching my head as far to the side as it will go. Someone throws the tent flap open, and a black man whose shoulders fill the entire tent opening sticks his head inside. Covering his mouth and nose with his hand, he glowers down at me.

"Tell Bowen it's awake," the man says, his voice muffled beneath his hand. "And it needs a hose down." He drops the tent flap back into place.

I clench my stomach muscles and do a shaky sit-up, and the sleeping bag falls around my waist. The tent flap opens again. I try to twist around and see who is there but can't.

Someone gasps. "Don't move a muscle, kid."

I recognize this smooth, deep voice—Bowen—and do what he says, turning my aching body to virtual stone. He coughs and then squats beside me, unzipping the sleeping bag. He hooks his hands under my armpits and drags me into sunlight. Four armed guards move from the four corners of my tent and point their guns at me.

"If I release your legs, you must not attack," Bowen says from behind me, emphasizing each word like I'm dense. "Nod once if you understand the meaning of my words." I nod once and Bowen sighs. "Shoot him if he does anything, boys."

Without warning, my ankle cuffs separate from each other. I twist my ankles and point my toes. Hands are in my armpits again, lifting. Someone groans behind me. "Better burn his sleeping bag, guys. I don't think anything will remove the smell,"

Bowen says. He coughs and gags. "Walk," he commands, shoving me forward. On legs stiff and awkward, I put one foot in front of the other. Bowen walks behind me, his voice directing me through the camp with the command "left" or "right."

The entire camp stares as I wind past tents and burning fires. Words follow me. *Security hazard. Level Ten. Mark of the beast. 8 ounces. Black market. Fight. Honey. The pits.*

"Stop," Bowen orders. I am at the log cabin from the night before. I freeze, my back to the camp, and stare at a knot in one of the round logs that make the cabin's walls. Out of the corner of my eye I see a garden hose being pulled from a hook on the cabin.

Water hits me from behind, and I gasp as a shiver makes its way from my scalp to my feet. I guess I'm taking a shower. In frigid water that sprays so hard against my shoulders I almost fall forward. But I can feel the layers of grit and sewage and blood and Arrin dripping off my skin and clothing, and welcome the cold water. A puddle forms beneath my feet—hazy gray swirled with deep brown.

Squinting, I slowly turn into the spray, ducking my head into it, letting it drench my thick bangs and squirt them out of my face. Next, I bring my shackled forearms to my face and, coughing and spluttering, scrub my skin.

By the time the water stops, my entire body is trembling with cold and covered with goose bumps, my clothes are soaked, and the tattoo on my hand is a dark, visible warning. I shake my head from side to side, flinging drops of water from my hair.

"The bathroom's on the other side of the cabin," Bowen says. I nod my understanding, relieved. My bladder is about to burst.

Blinking water from my eyes, I start walking. Like before, Bowen stays a couple of paces behind, remote always pointing at me.

When we get to the bathroom, my stomach starts to hurt as a new fear descends. There are no stalls, no toilets, just a trough.

Three men occupy the bathroom, talking, joking as they stand side by side peeing into the long, narrow trough. One looks over his shoulder, and his eyes meet mine. His pee stops, and he's out of there before he has his pants zipped. The other two look at each other, and then over their shoulders at me. They're gone before their pee hits the trough. Bowen, behind me, chuckles under his breath.

I stand shivering, dripping a puddle onto the bathroom floor, but don't make a move toward the wet, brown-stained trough.

"What's the matter, kid?" Bowen asks from the doorway. I peer over my shoulder and look at his annoyed face through my stringy, sopping bangs. Whipping my bangs aside, I take a closer look at his face. My heart lurches.

When I was eleven, I fell in love with my neighbor. He was gorgeous, sixteen, drove a motorcycle, lived across the street, and made out with his girlfriend on his porch swing in the summer.

I'd climb the tree in my front yard and watch him and his girlfriend through the leaves, fascinated, disgusted, jealous. Sometimes when they were making out, he'd look across the street without taking his mouth from hers, and our eyes would meet. He'd roll his eyes and then they'd slip shut and I was forgotten.

My mom called him an inconsiderate, hormonal teenager who should take his personal affairs where the whole neighborhood didn't have to see them. When she found out I'd sit in the tree and watch, she called his mom and complained.

He didn't stop making out on the porch swing—started making out more, in fact. And when he caught me spying, he'd yell, "Hey, kid, why don't you go find someone your own age to spy on?"

His hair was the color of milk chocolate, and his eyes were somewhere between blue and gray. And his name was . . .

". . . Duncan?" The word leaves my lips before I can stop it.

Bowen's eyes narrow, and his hand, the one that has been pointing the remote at me all morning, drops to his side. He blinks and the remote is aimed at me again. "What did you say?" he asks.

I bite my tongue and look at the floor. "Uh, I need, you know, like . . . walls?"

"You gotta be kidding me, kid. You want privacy?" he grumbles.

I'm a girl. I can't pee standing up, especially into a trough. And Arrin said pretending to be a boy is a safety precaution. "Need to take . . . a dump," I whisper, trying to sound like a guy. The lie floods my cheeks with warmth. Bowen presses himself against the wall beside the door and groans.

"Get out," he snaps, motioning outside.

"But I—"

"Just do it, Fec! Out!" His voice is cold and hard. A voice to fear.

Careful to give him a wide berth, I step through the door and into blazing sunshine. Something hard rams into the back of my thighs. With my arms cuffed, I can't find my balance. I topple forward, skidding to a stop on my forearms and knees. Bowen grumbles something under his breath, something laced with cuss words.

"Get up or I'll kick you again," he says through gritted teeth.

It takes me a minute, but I climb to my feet despite the fact that fear makes my muscles weak and tears have filled my eyes. I'm not crying because my elbows and knees are scraped. The tears are of self-pity. Tears that no one else is going to cry for me, a prisoner in this camp, with no family and no friends.

"I need an armed guard!" Bowen bellows, making me flinch away from him. The camp shushes. After a long silence, three men reluctantly grab their guns and circle me.

"What's the problem?" a big black man asks—the same man who opened my tent flap. Heart pounding, I stare down the barrel of his gun and wonder the same thing—what is the problem? That's when my arms swing free, no longer fused from elbow to wrist. The guards, though armed with rifles, take a giant step away from me.

"He's gotta do his business, Tommy," Bowen says, shoving me forward hard. My arms flail and I barely manage not to fall to the ground again. Tommy laughs and casually swings his gun into the side of my head, and I do lose my balance this time.

"Get up, kid." Bowen laughs, kicking me firmly in the butt. Quickly, I scramble to my feet.

With my hand pressed to my aching head, I bite my trembling lip, blink away fresh tears, and follow the sound of Bowen's voice as he guides me to another bathroom. One with stalls and doors and toilet paper. And even though I only need to pee, I sit on the toilet a long time, letting tears stream down my face.

When I've gotten control of myself, I wipe the moisture from my cheeks with my hands and, hair hanging in my face, come out. Bowen activates my arm cuffs. As I walk out the door, I brace myself for a gun to the side of the head or a kick in the butt. But they don't come this time.

I spend the day baking beneath the hot sun with my back to the wall, arms and legs fused together, head and knees throbbing, surrounded by four armed men.

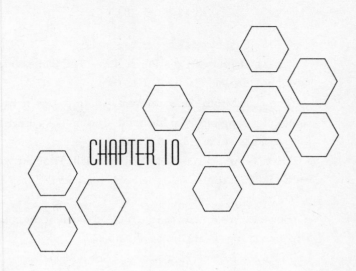

CHAPTER 10

When the sun is low in the sky and shadows stretch long, Bowen, eyes wary, comes for me. We walk through the camp—me in front—and stop at a cold, deserted fire ring constructed from a handful of small boulders.

"Sit," Bowen orders, motioning to a large, flat boulder a few feet from the ring.

I sit and try to stare without staring, peering at him through my tangled bangs while he stacks pieces of wood that look like broken table legs inside the ring of rocks.

Can this cruel man be the same person who lived across the street? I wonder. My butt still throbs from his kick. He sprays lighter fluid on the varnished wood and holds a match to it. Flames flare up, heating my face. I quickly lean away and Bowen jumps, aiming the remote at me, eyes wide with fear.

"No sudden moves," he warns.

"Sorry," I grumble, glaring at him. "The flames burned my face. I couldn't help it."

The guard from the bathroom—Tommy—walks over to us, something dangling from his hand. Bowen looks up and shades his eyes against the glare of sunset.

"Hey, Bowen. I caught this by the wall. Thought you might want to feed it to the Fec." He holds out a wet, skinned carcass and grins.

Bowen takes it and frowns, then looks up at the man again. The man shrugs beefy, broad shoulders.

"Thanks, Tommy. I'll cook it up. See how he likes it," Bowen says.

Tommy chuckles and studies me with dark, satisfied eyes. I look away and stare at the flames eating the wood. "You want me to hang around? Just in case?" Tommy asks.

I can feel Bowen's eyes on me. "I think I've got it under control," he says. "But I'll let you know if he starts scaring me more than he already is."

"You just say the word, and I got your back," Tommy says. He walks away.

Bowen slides a long metal rod through the carcass and balances it across the fire pit, turning the meat as the flames jump up to lick it, and I study him again. Aside from the dark scruff covering his lower face and framing his lips, he's hardly changed. If anything, time has made him more handsome than he was when I'd stare at him on his front porch—even with the scruff.

The smell of roasting meat makes my head spin and my stomach growl, and Bowen glares at me, mouth hard, as if he's mad that my stomach is making noise. I shrug.

The sun shines into his face and lights up his eyes, and I completely forget about the roasting meat. I was wrong about him. He is *not* Duncan—not the gray-eyed teenager I'd stare at across the street. Bowen's eyes are too green, like grass and mint and dandelion leaves. Yet, I know him.

I look away from his guarded eyes and study my brown-stained pants, worn so thin above my knees they are sheer, and try to remember who he is, why he's so familiar.

His hand is on the spit again, a hard, strong hand, brown from days in the sun. His long fingers turn it, making grease drip from the meat into the flames. I dare another look at him. This time he's waiting. Our eyes meet. His eyebrows lift, his face hardens, and the remote is pointing at me.

"You planning something?" he asks with a smirk.

Like I can *move* with my legs and arms locked together. If I even attempted to stand, I'd topple forward into the fire. Not to mention I'm in a camp filled with men who would shoot me if I so much as stepped wrong. I laugh at the absurdity of it.

Bowen leans forward, eyes intent, and I stop laughing.

"Open your mouth again," he says. I open my mouth and he peers inside. "Huh. Your teeth aren't rotten. How old are you?"

"Thirteen?"

"You're tall for a thirteen-year-old, Fec." He leans back, but his eyes don't leave me. They slowly cover every inch of my body, as if they can see the secret lying beneath my clothes. I hunch forward, praying he can't tell I have breasts. "Lift your hands. Show me your palms."

I bend my arms at the elbow, forearms still locked, and splay my fingers. His hand leaves the spit. Without lowering the remote, he trails a finger over my palm and frowns.

For a heartbeat his eyes meet mine, and then I am forgotten. Turning the meat takes all his attention. More grease drips from it, popping in the fire. For a long time we sit in silence, Bowen intent on the meat, me intent on looking at him without looking at him. Without him noticing, at least.

He looks up and catches me staring again, but I don't look away this time—not when I almost remember where I have seen eyes the color of summer. But then he says something and I forget that he looks familiar.

He says, "You're not a Fec."

I catch my lip in my teeth, heart pounding with fear. "What *is* a Fec?" I whisper.

His brows draw together. "Didn't you come here with one? The kid who tried to break that Level Three out last night?"

"The one you shot?"

"Yeah. He was a Fec. A feces dweller—*F-E-C*. You know, the people with the sign of the beast who didn't go to the lab, and didn't go instantly mad, so hide out in the sewers instead of turning themselves in?"

A wave of anger makes me bold, and I glare right into his eyes. "Why did you have to shoot her little brother? He was only eleven! She was trying to save him."

His jaw muscles pulse. "She? I only saw two boys. And

shooting him was the humane thing to do." His gaze flickers to my hand, to the tattoo, and his mouth puckers in distaste.

"What are you going to do with me?"

Instead of answering, he focuses on the roasting meat again. He lifts the spit away from the flames and sets it on a chipped plaster plate.

"What *am* I going to do with you?" He says it like he's asking himself, his eyes never leaving the meat as it drips tiny beads of moisture onto the plate. "I don't know. I could take you to the lab and get eight ounces of honey. And be well off for a year. Or I can sell you to the black market and get eighty ounces of honey. Eighty ounces of honey would buy me a life inside the wall. I could quit the militia."

"The black market?"

"Yeah. The black market runs the pit. Where they put people like you to fight to the death."

Fight to the death? Me? "You're joking, right?" I ask, my voice disbelieving.

He shakes his head but doesn't look at me. "The pit is the best form of entertainment the wall-dwellers have." His voice is full of bitter sarcasm. "They don't get to see all the violence on this side of the wall, so they make their own."

"Don't sell me to the black market," I whisper.

"I have until Sunday to decide." He gives the meat a little shake, letting grease splatter off it.

"Sunday?"

"The only day of the week they open the wall. So if you can manage to keep yourself alive for five days . . ."

He whips his head to the side, swinging his brown bangs from his forehead, and makes eye contact. Years melt from his face, and I see him how he used to be, fuller cheeks, no scruff on his chin, a gleam of mischief in his eyes. His eyes narrow, dark lashes framing bright green irises, and I realize my mistake. He's not Duncan, the guy I watched make out with his girlfriend on the porch swing. It's Duncan's younger brother, *Dreyden*. Dreyden Bowen.

We were the same grade in school. He was the boy who always teased me about playing the piano and threw snowballs at me when we walked home from school. But something's so wrong with how he looks now that I almost don't believe my own memory. Because . . . He's a . . .

Man.

Which means that I should be a—

Panic overwhelms my better judgment, and my entire body starts to tremble. "How old are you, Dr—" I snap my mouth shut, cringing at the near mistake of saying his first name.

He tilts his head to the side and studies me with his vibrant eyes, looking at me like I'm a freak, like my skin has turned green and is covered with scales.

"Why are you looking at me like that?" I ask, my heart hammering my ribs. Does he recognize me?

"You're so *normal*," he says, brow furrowed. "I keep waiting for you to start drooling and bite me, or tear my head from my shoulders with one sound twist, or yank my beating heart out of my chest and eat it. I mean . . . you're a Level Ten! I don't get it!" His gaze lowers. "What happened to your arms?"

I look at my bound arms. "You locked them up?"

"No. Right in the creases above your elbows," he says. I look at the creases. On both arms, the skin is clouded purple and green.

"I don't know," I answer, thinking I should remember how the bruises got there. Bruises form from blood pooling beneath the skin. Getting them must have hurt. I close my eyes and think. And am met by a gray wall of nothing.

"Your neck, too. You have bruises in the shape of hands circling your throat."

Those I remember. Vividly. "I was attacked in the tunnels." I open my eyes and swallow. My throat still hurts. "Someone tried to strangle me. Yesterday. I got away. Arrin was attacked too, but she killed the man."

"Arrin?" he asks, still studying me like I'm liable to explode at any moment.

"The girl who tried to save her brother. You killed her brother. He was only eleven."

"I didn't pull the trigger, kid," he grumbles, picking up the spit. He holds it out to me, an animal the size of my forearm, with a long scaly-looking tail that has been blackened by the fire.

I take it from him and, with my fused arms, attempt to eat. I shove my face against the food, suck the grease from it, and gnaw the flesh from the tiny bones like I am eating corn on the cob. Nothing has ever tasted so good, and I sigh.

Bowen watches me eat with a fascinated frown. When more than half of the meat is gone, he says, "I heard Fecs will eat rat. I just never believed it." Looking away, he shudders.

Rat. I know the very thought should make my stomach turn, should make me want to vomit. But starvation doesn't discriminate. And besides, it's better than wriggling earthworms or a leather belt. Way better.

"They eat worms, too," I mumble, my mouth full. "The problem is, I'm not a Fec." I might not remember a lot of things, but I know this.

CHAPTER 11

By the time the sun sets, my shoulders ache, my neck is cramping, and my head throbs in time with my pulse. I desperately need to move my arms.

"Hey, Bowen," I say, shrugging my shoulders and rolling my neck.

He looks at me and shivers, though the evening is hot. "You seem so normal," he says. "How old did you say you are again?"

My brain swirls, trying to remember when I aged, when I grew into a body that is definitely older than . . . "Thir . . . teen?"

"You've got a high voice for a thirteen-year-old boy."

I cringe. Mental note to self: try to sound like a boy. I clear my throat. "I have to . . . take a dump." Bowen's eyebrows rise and I look away. "The rat. It didn't agree with me," I say in a deep voice—a lie. My stomach is sluggishly thrilled with the meat inside it. But I've been holding it all day. Pee. Because, well, like I said, I can't pee standing up.

"Dude." Bowen sighs, shaking his head like he's got the worst life in the world. I brace myself for a sound kick, but he doesn't kick me this time. "Can I get an armed guard over here? The Level Ten's got to take another dump," he yells. The whole camp turns and stares at me, and a slow burn creeps up my neck, all the way to my hairline. I hang my head so my hair hides my entire face.

Five brown-uniformed, gun-wielding men come forward, and Bowen pushes the remote. My legs unfuse. I wobble, lose my balance, and fall on my face beside the warm fire ring, my cuffed hands pinned painfully beneath me. Men start laughing and guns dig into my back, jabbing at my ribs hard enough to make me gasp.

"Stupid Fec," Bowen mutters, and wraps his hand in my shirt. He pulls up. The fabric strains in his hand, and I rise off the ground, hovering just above the dirt as I try to maneuver my feet below my body. My shirt pulls against my armpits, and a loud rip grates against my senses. I fall back to the ground—face-plant, really—and dirt goes into my mouth, digs into my cheek, my naked stomach, and my bare shoulders.

Oh, crap.

The fabric binding my breasts is the only thing that hides the truth about me.

A hand grabs my elbow. "Someone get his other elbow," Bowen grumbles.

"You serious, man? You want one of us to *touch* it?" someone whines.

"Just hurry up," Bowen snaps.

A warm hand clutches my other elbow, and I'm heaved to my feet. I hang my head low and hunch my shoulders forward, too scared to spit the dirt out of my mouth. Too scared to even breathe—I'm practically naked, standing in a camp filled exclusively with armed men. And then I understand Arrin's insistence on my looking like a boy. I hunch forward even more and press my arms against my chest until my shoulders want to pop. I might be able to hide my breasts, but I can't hide the way my hollow stomach curves outward to meet my wide hips.

"You got a broken rib?" Bowen asks, jabbing my back hard with his finger as if he hopes I do. I can't form words—am still gasping for breath—so I shake my head.

My escort and I walk to the bathroom in silence, with only the evening darkness keeping my secret. I step into the dim bathroom, and the light automatically flickers on. The armed guard wait outside, but Bowen stands in the doorway and glares at me. I hunch even more, straining my shoulders forward, forcing my chest concave, mentally cursing my body for growing breasts and hips.

"Well?" he says, crossing his arms.

I peer at him through my hair, too scared to move.

"What'ya waiting for? Hurry up." Without uncrossing his arms, he pushes the remote and my arms unfuse.

I am at the stall in two steps, slamming the door behind me and sliding the lock into place. And then I look down. The binding is still securely in place over my breasts, but without my oversize T-shirt, it is obvious. I am a girl. Nearly a woman. I stare down at my body and marvel at the slide of waist leading to hips, the small bulge of breasts that makes my skin crease just above the bindings. Because the body I'm looking at? It is not the body I remember belonging to my head and brain.

Where have I been that my body has grown up so fast?

"Kid. You almost done?" Bowen hollers. Men snicker. I drop my pants and sit on the toilet. When I'm done, I pull the pants back up and squeeze the waistband over my hips, barely able to button it. And that's when the siren blares.

Without warning, electricity hums in my wrist cuffs, and my forearms fuse together. The stall door crashes open, slamming into my face and cutting my mouth, and Bowen is there, dragging me out of the stall by my arm. He curses under his breath, yanking me out of the bathroom, through the dark night, and we merge into groups of running men holding their guns on their shoulders.

The night turns to day as lights built into the wall flood the ground. And then I see the reason for the commotion.

A guy has entered the camp—young, black haired, shirtless, with straining muscles and bulging veins beneath skin the color of coffee. He's growling and throwing men around like they're paper dolls dressed in brown paper uniforms.

"No guns! Taser the beast! Taser to *stun!*" Bowen roars beside me, pulling me faster. Toward the uproar. Toward the *beast*. "Tasers! Now!" he shrieks.

Several men release their guns and grab palm-size black

devices from their belts, aiming toward the beast. With a zip of electricity I can feel in my cuffs, the Tasers go off, zapping the men surrounding the beast with a quick flash of blue as tiny metal prongs embed into their skin. They crumple to the ground, eyes rolled back in their heads, mouths slack, bodies convulsing. With them down, there is a clear path to the beast. My cuffs tingle with electricity again, and blue sparks light the air, but when they hit the beast, he growls, yanks the small metal Taser plates off his skin, and keeps attacking.

Surely Bowen can see how insane this person is, I tell myself. Yet Bowen still drags me toward it. And all I can think is, *Is he crazy?*

I dig my feet into the ground, dragging against his hold. He pulls harder. I dig my feet deeper. His eyes meet mine, full of fury, and he smacks me upside the head, knuckles slamming into my temple.

The world swims before my eyes, a blur of brown coats and guns, and my knees buckle. Bowen's arm snakes around my waist, and he drags me the last few steps toward the beast. In one swift move, he throws me down to the ground. And then he sits on me, his legs on either side of my hips.

His eyes flicker to my bound chest and he freezes, as if everything in the world but the two of us has disappeared. Time stops, my eyes grow wide, and his green eyes take in every detail of my body before meeting mine again. When our eyes lock, his brow furrows, his eyes narrow in confusion, and he blinks. But then the cuffs on my arms fall from my skin. Bowen picks them up and stands, taking a slow step away from me.

I roll onto my side, toward the beast, and whimper at what I see. A circle of militia, at least twenty thick, surround the beast and two other people. The militia have their Tasers and automatic weapons trained on the beast, following its every move. The beast's muscles twitch and spasm from the electrical residue of the Tasers, but it doesn't seem to care.

Bowen, his hands raised, speaks soothing words to the beast as he slowly walks toward it. But the beast isn't paying attention to him. It is looking at the third person trapped inside the armed circle of militia.

Me.

Its dark eyes, the irises overwhelmed with pupil, devour me. And there is nothing human about the way it stares. I am looking into the eyes of a wild animal. A very deadly, brawny wild animal. Bowen looks between the beast and me as if debating something. His jaw pulses, his body goes taut, and then, as if it pains him, he steps between the beast and me.

"You move, you die," he says to the beast, his voice no longer calm and soothing.

The beast growls and fakes a lunge forward, but Bowen doesn't budge. A deep, gravelly hum interrupts the silent night, growing slowly louder, like a jet tearing across the sky. And then the sound grates against the night, vibrating in my ears. It is coming from the beast's mouth. It leaps forward and swats Bowen aside, flinging him through the air. And then it is just the beast and me. It stares at me, lips pulled back from its stained teeth, drool coating its skin, eyes starved, as if it is about to devour a feast. Me.

But as Bowen flies through the air his voice rings out clarion clear:

"Taser to kill!"

Never taking its animal eyes from me, the beast leaps. Streams of blue lightning flash above my head, disappearing into the creature's dark skin. Its feral eyes stop staring as they roll back in its head, gleaming bloodshot white, and its body convulses as it soars through the air.

It lands on me, crushing me into the ground, and electrical current enters my body, boils my blood, and jolts my heart.

The beast spasms atop me and my eyes roll back into my head.

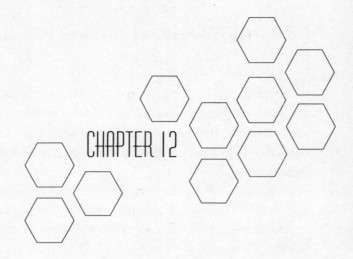

CHAPTER 12

My tongue sticks to the roof of my mouth like a fly on flypaper. I work it free and part my swollen lips. Pain pulses in my head in time with my heartbeat. I bring shaky fingers up to my temples and the pain intensifies, making me cringe.

I force my eyelids up over my parched eyeballs and see nothing but darkness. But to the left of me, the darkness is somehow darker, and shaped like shoulders and a head. I reach toward that darkness and feel fabric, and beneath the fabric, warm skin.

"Are you awake?" the shadow whispers.

I jerk my hand away, startled. "I hope not," I croak. Every single bit of my body aches. I groan.

"Definitely awake," he says, voice a deep, quiet rumble. Bowen.

"Crap. I was afraid of that. Why do I hurt so much?" Even talking hurts. I gingerly lick my swollen lip and taste blood.

"Let's see. You were attacked by a beast filled with electricity. Before that, I hit you upside the head because I had to get your cuffs off. Oh. And the bathroom door split your lip."

Bathroom door? And then I remember—he tore the shirt from my body. Revealed my secret. I gasp and run my hands over my chest and down to my hips. A shirt covers me, a shirt that smells like a high mountain lake. My eyes slip shut in relief. My secret is still safe.

"So, when were you going to tell me?" he asks.

My eyes pop open, and I gulp down a resurgence of fear. "Tell you what? I don't know what you're talking about."

He chuckles. "Whatever, Fotard."

That name on his lips sends my heart racing. It is the name he made up to torment me when we were in third grade. I push up onto my elbows to get a better look at him and realize that for the first time since I've been in the camp, my cuffs aren't fused together. Bowen scrambles backward and bumps up against the wall of a tent.

"Don't move or I'll activate your cuffs," he says, voice hard.

I lower myself back onto the sleeping bag and lay my arms flat against my sides. "I'm not moving." I look at his silhouette out of the corner of my eye. Slowly, he eases closer to me, juts a bit.

"Can I ask you something, Bowen?" He knows my secret. There's no use in pretending anymore.

"Yeah. I guess."

"Are you Dreyden? Or Duncan?" I already know the answer—I just need to hear him say it.

There's a long pause before he answers, "You spent enough

time staring at my brother. Can't you tell the difference?" There is resentment in his voice.

I see the two faces from my past, the two brothers, one with gray eyes, one with green, one my age, one several years older, and know without a doubt which one sits beside me. "But you're too old to be Dreyden," I whisper.

"Too *old*? We're the same age," he says.

I take a deep breath, grateful for the darkness that hides my face when I ask, or rather squeak, "How old am I?"

"What do you mean? You don't know?" Skepticism taints his voice, as if he thinks I'm lying.

I'm thirteen. One-three. I can remember blowing out thirteen candles on my last birthday cake. Remember my twin brother blowing out the candles on his cake at the same time. I wore a yellow sundress. And mascara on my pale lashes—my first time wearing mascara. My mom gave me my first bottle of perfume, and my dad gave me a gold treble-clef charm on a gold chain. My hand gropes my empty collarbone, feeling for the necklace even though I already know it isn't there.

"Seventeen." Bowen's voice interrupts my memories.

My breath comes too fast and my hands grip my too-big hip bones. There is no *way* I'm seventeen. He's got to be wrong, got to be lying to me. I push up on my elbows again to tell him so, and hear the hum of electricity. My arms are yanked out from under me and meld together, pinned awkwardly over my stomach. I fall back and land with a thud, and all the air jolts from my lungs. Pain shoots through my throbbing head, and my stomach roils with nausea. I whimper and squeeze my eyes shut.

"I told you not to move," Bowen says, his words laced with anger. He opens the tent flap and leaves.

After a moment of lying perfectly still and taking deep, even breaths, the nausea subsides and I can think despite the pounding of my head. *Seventeen*. That's how old my body looks. But I don't remember turning fourteen or fifteen. Or sixteen. And I definitely don't remember seventeen. I remember . . .

Lavender and forget-me-nots blowing in the wind.

Being forbidden to go outside.

Jonah staring out the music-room window while I practiced piano.

Wearing clothes to school that covered me from my neck to my fingertips to my toes, with a hat that draped bee sting–resistant netting over my head like a veil.

I remember a yard with grass that hadn't been mown in so long it died and was replaced by dandelions even though my dad was anal about paying someone to keep the lawn mowed and edged.

And Mom and Lis coming home from the grocery store wearing their netting veils, and all they'd purchased was bags and bags and bags full of canned fruit and dehydrated meat substitute.

I remember the sharp prick of a needle, hardly bigger than the tip of a pencil, and a deep voice that didn't belong to my father: *You have to relax your muscles, Fiona.*

And every month when Jonah and I went to the health clinic to get another shot, I cried, so Jonah held my hand.

"Bowen," someone outside my tent whispers, scattering my memories. "Can we talk?"

"Yeah. What?" Bowen says, his voice still tinged with anger.

"Mind sending the armed guard away first?"

"Take a break, men. I don't think the kid's going to try anything in the next ten minutes," Bowen says.

"Yessir." The hollow thump of boots echoes up through the ground.

"'Sup, Len?" Bowen asks.

"I want to know your answer regarding what we talked about last night," Len says, his voice hushed.

"Refresh my memory," Bowen snaps.

"I want the Fec. I'll buy him off you for eight ounces." There's something about Len's voice that makes me squirm. It has the same emotion I saw in the beast's eyes when it looked at me—hunger. *But is hunger an emotion?* I wonder, shivering.

A shoe scrapes in the dirt and there's a long silence. Bowen finally says, "So, why d'you want him so bad? You've never shown interest in *anyone* with the mark before."

"What's your problem, Drey?" The other guy sounds offended. "I'm offering to take a Level Ten off your hands *and* pay you! You should be the one paying me!"

"Yeah. I don't buy it. What's your real motive? Why the sudden interest in someone with the mark?"

"I'll give you sixteen ounces, man," Len whispers. "That's double what they'll pay for him at the lab. *Sixteen ounces!*"

"Sixteen ounces?" Bowen's voice is shocked. "Where'd you get sixteen ounces?"

"I've got my sources. So, what do you say?"

"Well, crap, Len. Sixteen ounces of honey? Let me think about it," Bowen says. "Hmmm. Thinking hard. Thinking, thinking. And the answer is . . . no. Get out of here."

"Twenty-four ounces of honey. That is my final offer. An offer you'd be a fool to refuse," Len says, his gravelly voice mad. "Take it or leave it."

"Twenty-four ounces? I could practically retire on that and live inside the wall. No more special forces," Bowen says, and I can hear the yearning in his voice, as loud and clear as the hunger in Len's.

"Please, no," I whisper, straining to hear his answer.

Bowen sighs. And then groans, as if facing a painful internal struggle.

"Like I said. An offer you can't refuse," Len says eagerly. His tone makes me feel . . . dirty. I burrow deeper into my sleeping bag, shut my eyes, and pray Bowen says no.

After a drawn-out silence, my pounding heart the only noise, Bowen says, "You wanna know the funny thing about making me an offer I can't refuse?"

"No. *Tell* me what's funny about it." Len is practically panting.

"I'm afraid I'm going to have to refuse it."

My eyes pop open, and a small smile pulls painfully on my split lip. Tears fill my eyes, the first *good* tears that I've cried since waking up in my abandoned house. *Thank you, Dreyden!*

"Now get out of here before my men come back and I have them escort you away," Bowen says, voice taut.

Len growls, an animal sound of frustration. "Let me know when you change your mind."

"Won't happen. Get. Out. Of. Here."

Footsteps pound over the ground, fading to silence. Bowen exhales and swears under his breath. A light flickers. The tent flap opens, and I squeeze my eyes shut against the glare of a flashlight.

Bowen squats beside my head and shines the light on my chin. I squint up at him. His eyes move over my face, searching for something. "Is it possible Len knows?" he whispers.

I frown. "Knows what?"

"That you're . . ." His eyes travel over my sleeping bag and grow wide, as if he can see my female body through the bulky material.

"That I'm a gir—"

Bowen claps a hand over my mouth, gently, though, so his callused palm doesn't hurt my split lip. He puts a finger to his lips and removes his hand.

"You dragged me around the camp half-naked last night," I whisper.

Bowen shakes his head, brow furrowed. "No. He knew before that. He had to have known the first night you came into the camp."

"Why does it matter? What's the big deal about my gender?"

Bowen smirks. "Where have you been the past few years? Seriously?"

I open my mouth, but no answer comes out. I sigh and finally say, "I don't remember."

Bowen rubs his eyes and leans as far from me as the tent allows, setting the flashlight in his lap. "You really don't remember? It's not some sort of *act*?"

"I remember turning thirteen. But I don't remember any birthdays after that," I say. "What's wrong with being a girl?"

He sighs and his breath stirs the air. "Well, for one thing, there are seven living men for every one living woman. Being a woman outside the wall is the worst thing you can be. Women are hunted even more than beasts."

"Why?"

"Because they bring the highest . . . the gangs pay . . . some men are . . ." Bowen presses on his eyes with the balls of his hands. "So now . . ." His hands drop to his sides and he looks at me. "On top of me protecting the entire camp from you, it looks like I'll be protecting you from them."

Footsteps stir outside the tent and fabric rustles. Bowen sits tall.

"Bowen? You in there, man?" a voice rumbles.

Bowen's eyes meet mine and he presses a finger to his lips. "Yeah, Tommy. Just keeping you guys safe from the Fec. You boys have a nice break?"

"Sure did. Thanks, man."

Bowen turns off the flashlight, and the tent goes dark. There is warm pressure on my lips, and my heart flutters before I realize what he's doing. I obediently open my mouth, and a wafer is

placed on my tongue. It tastes like hamburgers and French fries, and as it settles in my stomach, it brings a food-heavy tiredness to my entire body that makes me think of Thanksgiving Day.

As I drift off to sleep, I believe being cuffed is worth tasting food again, even if it is in wafer form.

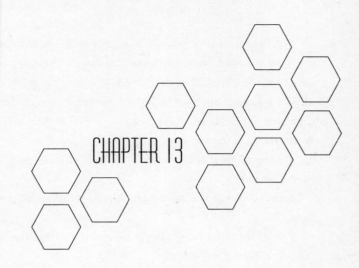

CHAPTER 13

Sunlight blazes against the tent's canvas walls, making it impossible to stay asleep. Not that I was sleeping well, with my legs and arms immobile. I open my eyes and try to stretch, but pause. Bowen is still in my tent, sitting with his back against the canvas, head slumped sideways on his knees, eyes closed, remote clutched in his hand. Air whistles between his soft lips every time he exhales. There's a faded scar on his left cheek, and a fresh scar on the side of his chin, a white slash where dark stubble doesn't grow. Looking at him, I get a funny feeling in my stomach—an ache, like I'm hungry, but not quite.

His dark lashes flutter against his cheeks, and I look away fast, studying the top of the tent like it holds the answers to my missing past. I count to twenty and he hasn't made a sound, so I look back and stare right into his narrowed eyes.

"You've *got* to keep your hair in your face," he whispers. "No one's going to believe you're a boy if they get a look at your eyes. Who am I kidding? They won't believe you're a boy if they actually look hard enough, even if your eyes *are* covered." His words make my cheeks burn, and he clears his throat. "I'm serious. Put your hair back in your face."

I glare at him. "I can't *reach* my hair," I snap, wiggling my bound fingers.

Bowen's eyebrows shoot up. "A bit snarky this morning, Fotard?"

I sigh, feeling a bone-deep, weary ache in my whole body. "Can you blame me, *Botard?*"

He runs his fingers over his scruffy chin and studies me. "No. I'd be pretty snarky if I smelled like you. And I bet you're dying to brush your teeth."

I run my tongue over my disgusting teeth and glower.

He lifts his hands. "Don't look so ornery. The smell of the tunnels isn't easy to wash away." His face softens and the sides of his mouth twitch. "It's not you that stinks. It's your pants. They are pretty . . . disgusting."

"I know. My clothes were clean. These pants were Arrin's. She told me we had to trade clothes so that I looked—and smelled— like a Fec. They're too small."

"Yeah. They looked really tight when I dressed you last night."

My eyes grow wide. "You *what* me last night?"

Bowen's smile deepens and he shrugs. "Someone had to dress you. I'm the only one who dares to stand within arm's reach, let alone touch you. So I put a shirt on you. No biggie. It's not like you were *naked*."

If my hands weren't cuffed, I would pull the sleeping bag up over my burning face. Instead I squeeze my eyes shut.

"Hey, kid," Bowen says. I look at him from under my lashes. His face is hard again, not even the memory of a smile dancing in his green eyes. "I'm going to release your legs, but don't try anything. Just because you *seem* harmless doesn't mean I'll hesitate to kill you if you make one wrong move."

I swallow and nod. The cuffs on my legs release, and I bend my knees with a groan of relief. Bowen points the remote at me.

"Don't move until I get out," he says, eyes like steel. I freeze.

Once he's crawled from the tent, I follow. Slowly, awkwardly—my wrists are still melded together, my body aches, and my legs feel like an awkward mixture of rubber and lead. I flinch against the blazing morning sun just as four pairs of booted feet surround me.

"At ease, men," Bowen says with a weary sigh. "In fact, why don't you take the morning off?"

"You don't want an armed guard?" a deep voice asks as I try to stand. A gun jabs against my shoulder, men snicker, and I fall forward. Warm hands grab my biceps and heave me to my feet before I have a chance to crash to the ground. Bowen. But unlike yesterday, when he practically wrenched my shoulder from its socket, there's gentleness in his touch. He holds on to me a little longer today, making sure I've found my balance before removing his hands.

"I'm not going unarmed," he says. "I'll have my rifle, my Taser, and the electromagnetic cuffs. I'll just go without the armed guard."

There is a collective gasp from the men pointing guns at me. "But he's a *Ten*," Tommy states, swinging the barrel of his rifle toward me.

Bowen's wrist intercepts the rifle a split second before it would have collided with the side of my face. "Yeah. Tell me something I don't know, Tommy."

"A *Ten*, man. You turn your back for one sec and you're dead! Remember what happened to Charlie last year? I don't want to lose my best friend that way!"

Bowen shoves Tommy's rifle away and lets his gaze travel slowly over me. "I've been watching him, and he doesn't have a single symptom. If I see the slightest change, anything at all, I'll call you over."

"But, Bowen—"

"If the kid was going to kill me, I'd already be dead," he growls, glaring into Tommy's eyes.

Tommy is bigger, older, and looks twice as mean as Bowen, with muscles that bulge and gleam beneath his skin. He glares and says, "Yes, sir. But if you die, I'll never forgive you. Come on, guys."

The guards walk stiffly away.

Bowen guides me to a tent—the only tent near mine, secluded from the rest of the camp. "Go in," he orders, remote pointing at me. I duck into the tent and he follows. "Sit in the corner." I do, right beside a guitar.

Without thinking, I swish my fingers over the strings. It's been recently tuned. And polished to a high shine. I look at Bowen, then at the callused tips of his fingers, and understanding sinks in.

He's digging through a black backpack when I say, "You're the one who was playing on the night I came to camp."

His hands pause, and he looks up at me and nods.

"You were playing my favorite song. Beethoven's Seventh."

"You played it at least a thousand times before everything changed. The tune is sort of ingrained into my head."

"When did you learn to play classical guitar?"

He shrugs. "I taught myself after everything changed. My whole life I'd always been surrounded by music—by your music, you practiced so often. I guess I . . . missed it."

A small smile flutters against my sore lips.

Bowen pulls a bundle from the bag and holds out a pair of faded jeans with ballpoint-pen ivy decorating the pockets. I look from the jeans to him. "They don't stink, and I don't think I can stand another minute in your presence unless you take off your pants," he says, scrunching up his nose at my—Arrin's—pants.

I take the jeans, press them to my nose, and inhale. They don't stink at all. Quite the opposite, in fact. They smell like Bowen.

"So, hurry up and put them on," he says, watching me. "I'm on pollen duty today."

My heart starts to pound and my cheeks burn. Again. As if I'm thirteen. "Put them on right now? Aren't you going to wait outside?"

"And leave you completely unrestrained *and* unobserved?

Sorry, Fotard." Mischief gleams in his eyes, and I have the feeling he's trying hard not to smile.

I roll my eyes, and his mouth flickers into a quick smile. Electricity hums and my cuffs unmeld, freeing my arms.

I tug Arrin's pants from my legs and, while Bowen stares, pull the jeans on over a pair of plain white granny underwear that goes up to my belly button. I don't remember ever owning granny underwear. As my fingers loop the button through the buttonhole, Bowen hands me a brown leather belt. I take it and stare at it.

"You got a problem with the belt?" he asks.

"When I was in the tunnels, I asked Arrin for something to eat. She gave me a leather belt," I say with a shudder.

"Fecs don't have much food. Lots of them starve to death before they have a chance to turn."

"Turn? Turn how?" I ask as I loop the belt through my new pants and cinch it into place. The moment it's latched, electricity hums and my forearms meld back together.

"I'll tell you while we pollinate," he says. He slings one strap of the black backpack over his shoulder. Next, he gets a rifle and slings it over the other shoulder, making an X across his chest with the straps. He eases out of the tent, and I follow.

We walk past the camp—everyone stares at me—and then go to the base of the wall. And I see the first living plant I have seen since I saw Jacqui's mom painting corn. Many plants, actually, in an assortment of mismatched pots—terracotta, plastic, clay, a few even grow in dirt piled in the interior of old car tires, or in paint cans.

I step up to a plant and trail my fingers over the pulpy green leaves. Tears sting my eyes and my throat constricts. "It's beautiful," I whisper. "What kind of plant is it?"

"A tomato," Bowen says, looking at me like I'm nuts. "Are you crying?"

I sniffle and shrug. "It reminds me of . . . the world I used to know." The world I belong to, where I am thirteen and Jonah is normal and plants grow. And I have never seen a pair of electromagnetic cuffs, not to mention been forced to wear them.

"Here." Bowen holds out a fine-bristled paintbrush, and I take it. "We need to pollinate them or they won't produce any fruit."

Like Jacqui's mom painting the corn.

"What you do is stick the paintbrush into the little yellow flowers, like this." Instead of watching his little demonstration, I stare at his profile, wondering if he misses the old world as much as I do, wondering if he misses his family. "And then move to another flower. Until we've done it to all of the flowers. Got it?" He looks up and I nod.

I stick the fine bristles of my paintbrush into the flower. Tiny, pale grains of dust cling to it—pollen. I move to the next flower and do the same, brushing the dust from the first flower into the second, while taking dust from the second to place in the third.

"You asked me what it means to turn," Bowen says, his voice warm and deep and grown-up. I pause and watch him move his paintbrush from flower to flower, his strong, callused hands gentle and precise. "Your tattoo. Do you remember getting it?"

I look at my hand and can remember the needle darting in and out of my skin faster than I could see. I remember the sound, a grinding buzz—like getting a tooth drilled. I remember crying. "A little," I say.

"Well, that tattoo was given to the kids who were lucky enough to get the bee flu vaccine," he says, looking at me. "Only problem was, they didn't know about the vaccine's long-term effect. So everyone who got it, even one dose, is infected. If they haven't turned into a beast, like the Fec you came here with, they will before long. But the Fec was a Level Three. You are a Ten."

I stare at the tattoo. "So what does Level Ten mean?"

"It means you were one of the special kids, one of the very first to get the vaccine. *Our nation's hope for the future.*" He says this last part with bitter sarcasm. "Probably because of your father's military connections and your musical talent, you qualified for the earliest possible dose. And because of that, you got ten months of the vaccine. The highest dose given." Bowen points to my tattoo. "Each of those marks," he says, motioning to the legs coming out of the circle, "represents a dose of vaccine. Ten months was the longest anyone took it. Because after ten months, every kid who'd been *lucky* enough to qualify for the shots started showing signs of insanity."

My brother's animal-crazed face flashes into my mind. "What do you mean, insanity?" I whisper.

He takes a small step away from me, hand on the remote, eyes wary. "You know the thing that attacked you last night?"

I nod. My body still hurts.

"That was a Level Eight. Totally insane."

Anger flares in my chest. My brother can't be insane.

"He didn't look *insane* to me. He looked like a wild animal," I snap.

"Yeah. Insane wild animals that massacred their own families and neighbors and friends. And then ate them if they couldn't find anything else to eat!" Bowen glares at me, and his jaw muscles pulse.

I think of my brother trying to catch me as I slid through the bathroom window. Did he catch the rest of my family? My stomach starts to hurt, and I can hardly hold the paintbrush in my trembling fingers. "Dreyden—"

"Don't call me that," he growls, glancing over his shoulder to make sure no one's around.

I look at my feet. "Sorry. Bowen. What happened to my family?" Did my brother eat them or kill them? That is what I'm really asking. I stare at the scuffed toes of his brown army boots. When he doesn't answer, I look at him.

He studies me for a long minute, searching my face with his wary, uncertain eyes—eyes that know more than a seventeen-year-old's should. "Lissa lives inside the wall. I saw her a couple of years ago. She looked good. Your mom . . ."

I hold my breath, my entire body tingling with hope. "Is she alive?"

He frowns and looks away. "I saw her once inside the wall. At least I think it was her. She was old, right? She had you and your brother when she was, what, forty?"

She couldn't get pregnant after she had Lis. After trying to have a baby for seven years, Jonah and I were her in vitro miracles. "She was thirty-nine."

"She'd be over the government-enforced age limit. Most likely she's—" His mouth snaps shut, and he begins furiously painting flowers.

"Can you take me to her? On Sunday?" My voice is desperate. I know that if I find her, she'll be able to fix everything. I ache for my mother.

He shakes his head, glaring at the paintbrush in his fingers. "No. She's gone by now. The Sunday after she turned fifty-five, they—can we not talk about this?" he snaps, scowling at me.

I shake my head. "I need to know. What happened to my mom?" I whisper, sick with dread. Already I can tell what he knows isn't good.

"Are you sure you want to know?" he asks.

I nod.

"Life inside the wall has *rules*." His mouth puckers, as if the word *rules* leaves a bad taste on his tongue. "No one with physical disabilities is allowed inside the wall. No one's allowed inside who suffers from any type of mental illness—even depression. If you are an unmarried male age fifteen or older, you are assigned to work in the militia unless you have an invaluable skill, like farming, engineering, or medical expertise. The inner-wall age limit is fifty-five. After that people are too old to be much worth, so they . . ." He sweeps his hand through his hair, moving it from his forehead. "After that they're either kicked out or . . ." Bowen mumbles something so fast I can't understand him.

"Kicked out or what?"

The color drains from his tan cheeks and he whispers,

"Offered medically assisted suicide. Put to sleep. Terminated. They say it's painless."

Heavy numbness settles over me. My mother is dead. That's why he didn't want to tell me. "And my father? Would they let him inside the wall even though he was disabled?"

Bowen tilts his head to the side and frowns. "Your father? I thought that . . ." He clears his throat. "No wheelchairs inside."

I turn to the plants and quietly pollinate, letting the reality settle in, letting silent tears wash over my face. My mom and dad are dead.

A long time passes, maybe hours. Bowen and I have pollinated nearly all the plants, and my tears have finally stopped falling. "What is the lab?" I ask, sticking my paintbrush into a flower.

"The lab is the place where they test different strains of antivenin in search of the cure. On, you know, the beasts. Sort of like animal testing."

My eyes grow round, and I look up from the tomato plant. "Wait a sec, I'm going to a lab to be their human guinea pig?"

"They test insane, beastly humans, Fo. Not regular people."

"But I am a regular person. I'm not a beast!" I say, panicked.

He studies the paintbrush in his hands as if it's the first time he's seen it. "You're a Ten. You could turn any second. Break my arms from my body. Shatter my skull with your bare hands."

"Tear your beating heart from your chest and eat it?" I say.

"Yeah. That, too. Charlie, my old friend, was torn in two by a beast."

I take a step toward him. He darts backward and holds the remote toward me, his eyes scared.

"I'm not like that, Bowen." My voice trembles.

"Well, you've got to cut me a little slack, here," he mutters, slowly lowering the remote. "Guardians don't live all that long."

"Guardians?"

"A guardian is the person in charge of taking the beasts to the lab. That's me. I'm the guardian at the south gate of the wall." He points to the lines shaved into the side of his head—four of them. "Four lines mean I rank higher than anyone in that camp except Micklemoore. And it's because I'm a guardian."

"Are you my guardian? Or the militia's?"

"The militia's. I'm guarding them from you," he says as if I'm stupid for asking. As if it's obvious. But the way I see it, *I* need protection from *them*.

"How long have you been the south gate guardian?"

His mouth thins. "I've been guardian since Sunday."

"Only three days?"

"Two and a half days. It's Tuesday."

"So, why did you become a guardian on Sunday?"

He tilts his head to the side and frowns. "They shut the gate at eight p.m. like usual. And then, first time in the two and a half years since I've been posted at the wall, they rang the bell and opened the gate *after* eight p.m. Had a piece of paper signed by the chief medical officer dated that day, stating Dreyden Bowen was to become the new south gate guardian. I wasn't aware the CMO even knew my name. But get this. They appointed a new north gate guardian at the same time. Richard Kimball. Remember him? He was in a grade above us and lived a block away."

A boy's face flickers in my memory: blond hair, pale-blue eyes, and freckled skin. He tried to kiss me when I was in first grade and he was in second. "I remember him. So, what happened to the old guardians?"

Bowen shrugs. "I can't say for the guy at the north gate, but ours was thrilled. Not only is he relieved of the worst job in the world, but he gets to live inside the wall. He was a guardian for only four days."

"And the guardian before him?"

"Got his beating heart torn out of his chest. He lasted eighteen days."

"Seriously?" I say.

He glowers at me. "Do you think I'd joke about something like this?"

I shake my head. "Then why don't you resign? Or do a different job?"

"Because I am stuck in this job until I die. Or qualify to live within the wall."

I start dusting pollen again. Bowen does the same, careful to always stay two steps behind me, always have me within view, and always have the remote in his free hand.

After we've dusted four more plants, I turn to him. "Why don't you just run away?"

He looks over his shoulder, at the dead expanse of the world and abandoned buildings. "I have a better chance of surviving as a guardian than out there. And besides, I want to live inside the wall one day, even if they do terminate their population at fifty-five. From where I'm standing right now, living to fifty-five sounds ancient."

Pollen forgotten, I ask, "Then what are you waiting for? Go live inside the wall!"

He laughs, a dry, humorless laugh. "First of all, the gate is locked. You can't open it from the outside—a safety precaution. And then there's the fact that I'm not allowed to live there. Not until I either make enough money to buy my way in; get an education that makes me potentially useful; or meet some nice girl, get married, and start helping the effort to repopulate the—"

A siren wails. Before I can blink, Bowen jumps in front of me, rifle on his shoulder and aimed toward camp.

CHAPTER 14

"Stay behind me," he orders. We run toward camp, a good half mile away, but when it comes into view, I stop, my feet frozen to the ground. If Bowen wants me to follow him a single step farther, he'll have to hit me upside the head again and carry me.

Bowen doesn't notice I've frozen in place, or he doesn't care. He throws himself into the middle of a swarm of brown-clad militia interrupted by patches of bare skin.

I crouch as low to the ground as I can get, an unassuming human rock, and stare.

Young, exceptionally healthy-looking men are tearing at the militia, flinging them, biting them, snapping their bones, splattering blood. They're like Jonah, these freakishly strong young men—beasts. A gun goes off, and one beast staggers, looks down at its muscular chest, at the gaping bullet wound in it, and then jumps toward the man who shot him. The man shoots again, and the beast jerks to a stop, falling lifeless to the ground.

There are four other beasts. Three are men, dressed in tattered rags, but the fourth is female, wearing torn pants and a thin tank top that hangs to her thighs and barely covers her small breasts and bulging muscles.

The female beast turns her face to the sky, and her eyes slip shut. Her nose wrinkles and her chest expands as she takes a deep breath. And then her eyes pop open and slowly travel to mine. Her lips pull away from her teeth, and above the din of the fighting I can hear the deep, guttural rumble that comes from her throat.

The three male beasts freeze, look at the female, and follow the line of her glare. And then all four are staring at me. As one, they face me, crouch, and balance on the balls of their feet. The militia surrounding them pause, their faces baffled.

The beasts lunge forward and sprint, flinging bodies out of the way to reach their target. *I* am their target. A target with fettered arms and nowhere to flee. But it doesn't matter. They move like the wind and whirl around me before I have time to stand. Finally, as if it is a sound I have been waiting my entire life to hear, guns go off, a sudden, deafening explosion of a hundred discharged bullets that topples three bodies to the ground beside me.

The fourth beast, the female, is already on top of me, crouched on my chest, flattening me to the ground, fingers forcing my chin up. She opens her mouth and lunges for my exposed neck. Electricity hums in my electromagnetic cuffs. My forearms grow hot and my body convulses, my jaw rattling with the force of it. The thing on top of me absorbs half of the current boiling through my flesh, leeching the heat away so it's almost bearable. Her back arches and the grip on my throat loosens. She is yanked from me and the electricity stops. I stare at the blue sky, my body numb.

The cuffs on my wrists separate and release, and my burning arms fall limp to my sides. Bowen is beside me, face freckled with crimson, straddling the female beast, my cuffs in his hands. The female writhes beneath him, and he slams a cuff into her face, making blood splatter from her nose. She growls and lunges at him, her bloody teeth barely missing his chin.

"I could use a little backup here!" he roars, smashing a cuff into her face again. Three more men throw themselves onto the beast, and Bowen secures the cuffs on her arms. They lock into place, and he jumps off the writhing creature. Crouching by my legs, he removes my ankle cuffs, but before he has a chance to put them onto the beast, she throws the three men from her and is back on her feet.

She launches herself at me, mouth open, cuffed and fused hands reaching toward me. I lift my gloriously free arms and, using her momentum, push the female over the top of me.

A lone gun goes off and the beast hits the ground, skidding to a stop in the dirt. She does not move, does not blink her eyes. A pool of red forms beneath her and soaks into the dusty earth.

I look up in time to see Bowen lower his rifle.

"*That*," he says, his voice trembling, "was a Level Ten."

CHAPTER 15

I am shut away in a tent, one of the few that wasn't ruined in the skirmish earlier that day. My forearms are covered with burn blisters, and the hair is singed completely off. But I am not restrained in any way for the first time since I entered the camp. And the armed guards are throwing a fit. Every time I so much as breathe too loudly, they panic.

But it feels so good to move that I stretch my legs, point my toes, and sigh. Late-afternoon sunlight blinds me as the tent flap is whipped aside and four guns are thrust inside, inches from my face. I don't blink.

"Did he touch the flap?" someone asks, and if I had to guess, I'd say his voice is hopeful. They've been given strict orders from Bowen: shoot if I so much as touch the tent flap—shoot *me*.

"No, the flap didn't move," Tommy says. "Bowen?" he shouts,

not taking his gun from my face. "You almost ready to put his cuffs back on? Because I can't guarantee the Fec'll live much longer if he isn't restrained! The men are jumpy from the attacks!"

"I'll take care of it," Bowen calls.

The guns are moved aside and Bowen leans in. He pauses as uncertainty and fear dance across his face, but then he drops the tent flap behind him and crawls toward me, crouching at my side. He takes a small bottle out of his jacket.

"About your arms, the burns," he says, his voice hardly more than a whisper. "I had to shock you. I didn't know what else to do to stop her—the beast—from . . ." Face grim, he looks down, studying the tent floor.

From tearing my throat out with her teeth, I think. "I'm alive," I answer, voice as quiet as his. "My arms hardly hurt." My arms throb with every single beat of my heart and radiate fire that goes all the way to my stomach and makes me feel like I have the flu. Bowen holds the bottle out. I take it and open my mouth to ask him what it is, but he presses a finger to his lips.

"*Aloe vera*," he mouths, glancing at the tent flap.

"For the burns?" I whisper. He presses his finger to his lips again and nods. "*Did you steal it?*" I mouth, silent.

The corner of Bowen's mouth lifts, and he says softly, "For militia use only. Not for Fecs. Took me an hour to find."

I open the bottle, squeeze green goo onto my palm, and slick it over my angry skin. Air hisses through my gritted teeth, but then I sigh. The fire in my arm seems to seep into the aloe. I slather the other arm and give the bottle back to Bowen. He tucks it into his jacket once more and pulls something else out. Ankle cuffs. I groan. Out loud. Feet scuffle outside the tent, rifles clatter to life, and then the tent flap is flung wide. The glossy black barrel of a gun jabs into the tent and hovers above my nose.

"You need me to shoot it, Bowen?" Tommy asks.

"Chill, Tommy. The kid's just moaning about his arms," Bowen says. Tommy drags the tip of his rifle over the burned flesh on my arm.

I whimper and jerk away. Liquid oozes from a popped blister and Tommy laughs. He swings the gun toward my other arm, but Bowen grabs it.

"Just leave the kid alone," Bowen snaps. He shoves Tommy's gun out of the tent.

"Whoa, man, you're the one who needs to chill. You're acting . . . sympathetic toward the Fec." Tommy drops the tent flap and grumbles something I can't quite make out.

Bowen shakes his head and crawls to my feet. Without a word, he pushes the hem of my jeans up around my knees and attaches the cuffs to my calves.

"Bowen, please don't—" Before I can beg him not to restrain me, electricity hums and my legs snap together, the cuffs clicking against each other as they lock into place.

"I'm not going to cuff your arms. You're welcome," he retorts.

With my fingers I comb my hair out of my eyes and glare at him. "Thanks," I whisper. He nods and tosses a wafer onto the floor beside me. And then he's gone.

Anger and frustration bring the sting of tears to my eyes. All I want is to be back in my house, the way it used to be, inside a thirteen-year-old body, with Jonah doing his homework in the music room while I practice the piano, and Dad in the kitchen cooking dinner, and Mom on her way home from work, and Lis coming home from college.

I glare at the wafer, feeling so sorry for myself I'm tempted to chuck it out of the tent and start the slow process of starving myself to death. But my stomach growls, feels concave, so I shove it into my mouth. It dissolves into the flavor of roast ribs and sweet potatoes and trickles down my throat. I close my suddenly heavy eyes and give in to the food-induced lethargy that steals the last bit of energy from my muscles and wipes the anger from me. My sated brain listens to the conversation going on outside the tent.

"Hey, guys. I'm going to try and get some sleep," Bowen says, his voice spinning with my groggy thoughts. "The kid's restrained again, and I gave him his ration."

"Maybe you should double his dose," Tommy says.

"Not funny, Tommy. The lab only pays for living beasts."

"It was a joke, Bowen. Don't worry. We'll keep the camp safe from the kid," Tommy says.

"Yeah. About that. Don't let *anyone* in the tent, all right? And do not leave your posts."

"You think he's on the verge of turning?" Tommy asks, suspicious.

"Something like that," Bowen says, his voice fading as sleep settles over me.

I am being touched, a warm hand caressing my cheek. The gentle touch reminds me of what I am missing—human contact—and leaves me wanting more, wanting my mother's arms around me, my father's hand patting my back, Jonah bumping his knuckles on mine, Lis painting my nails, Bowen . . .

I sigh and lean into the touch, letting it fill me with comfort, with longing, with sorrow. Tears sting my eyes. I am so starved for affection it hurts. But I'm so tired, I can't bring myself to open my eyes. The trembling fingers move from my cheek to my mouth, gently tracing my bottom lip. And then they clamp down, crushing my teeth into my lips.

Tiredness forgotten, my eyes shoot open. Dark surrounds me, as if I'm in the tunnels again. A firm weight settles on my hips, and breath pants against my face.

More hands touch me, sliding over my body, groping my chest. The bottom of my shirt is lifted, and cold metal touches my stomach. In one swift slice, the T-shirt is cut from my body. A flashlight flickers on, shining on my bound chest, and someone gasps.

"I told you it was female!" The voice belongs to the person straddling me. I struggle against the weight, but my head is still groggy from sleep, my muscles filled with exhaustion. Plus, both of my tender arms are locked beneath a pair of knees. And my legs are locked in cuffs.

The flashlight goes dark.

"She's been sedated, but hold her arms tight anyway!" the man atop me orders. Hands grip my arms, anchoring them to the tent floor. Again, I try to thrash, forcing a little more strength into my limbs, but I can't get free.

Warm breath wafts over my face. "If you move, I'll kill you," a man whispers into my ear. I open my mouth and scream, but his hand tightens and holds the noise in, grinding my cheeks against my molars.

A nose prods my neck, sniffing, nuzzling. "It smells like a woman, even after living in the tunnels. Hold her tight. We've only got a few minutes to get her out of the camp." The weight climbs off me and my mouth is released. I open it, ready to scream, but my head jerks to the side as something collides with my face, and pain explodes behind my eyes. My chin is pulled down, and fabric is shoved into my open mouth. I scream again, but it's muffled.

"You grab her legs, Mac. Jerrold, you grab one arm, and I'll grab the other."

"How much do you think we can sell her for?" another man asks.

"Enough for all three of us to pay our way inside the wall. Governor Soneschen is always willing to let people in for the right price. She'll bring in a bundle! On the count of three, we move her out. One . . . two . . ."

My blood surges, tightening my skin, making my breath come faster, devouring the exhaustion in my muscles and feeding them with strength. I growl and yank my arms from the men restraining them and sit up. My fingers curl into a fist and I throw all of my rage into swinging it toward the person closest to me. With an audible crunch, my fist contacts flesh, and the person plummets into the side of the tent.

The other two men curse and jump on me, slamming me back to the ground. "I knew this was a bad idea!" one man says.

I reach up and pull the wad of fabric from my mouth.

"Bowen!" My scream echoes through the quiet night before a hand is suffocating me. I wiggle against it, claw at the arm it belongs to, try to breathe.

Light flashes on the canvas roof and a pair of feet thumps outside.

"Dude! Let's get out of here. Help me with Len," one of the men says.

"Leave Len! This was his idea," the other says, his voice panicked.

The hands leave my mouth and arms, and the two men scurry out of the tent. I sit again and hug my knees to my chest, trying to catch my breath. A steady noise is growing in the camp—voices. And then Bowen is in the tent, flashlight in hand, hair messed from sleep. His eyes travel over my bare shoulders. When he sees Len, unconscious at my feet, Bowen's nostrils flare and he begins to tremble. Without a word he tugs his shirt off—a plain white T-shirt—and hands it to me. I pull the shirt over my head as Bowen crawls to Len.

"If you hurt her . . ." Bowen yanks Len by the front of his uniform, forcing him to sit. But Len's head bobs like it is attached to a loose spring. Bowen drops him and presses his fingers to Len's neck. He looks at me and says, "He's dead. Did you do this?"

"He's what?" I whisper, wondering if I could have possibly heard him right.

"Dead."

I open and close my fingers, staring at them, wondering if

my fist could have killed a man. It was just one hit. One punch. "I don't know. I didn't mean to kill him. I was just trying to stop him." The air starts rushing in and out of my lungs too fast. I press my eyes against my knees and try to calm down. I killed a man.

A hand rests on top of my head. "Fo, are you all right?" When I don't answer he says, "Fiona?"

My name, my whole name on his lips, is like the aloe on my arms. It leeches the pain and fear from me and gives me the courage to answer. "Yeah, I'm all right," I say without looking up.

"I'll be right back." The hand leaves my head and I don't move.

Within a minute Bowen's returned with others.

"I bloody *told* you not to leave your post!" he yells.

"Len said—"

"Len is not your superior officer! I am!" Bowen retorts.

"Bowen, man, chill. Len said you wanted us to take fifteen, to drink some caffeine." I recognize the voice—Tommy's. "There were three of them. I thought they could handle the situation. Why you freaking so bad? Did the Fec escape?"

"Len's. Dead. He—"

"Was killed by the Fec?" four voices ask at once, not letting Bowen finish. Guns click, feet scuffle, and the tent flap is thrown aside. The four guards peer in at me with scared eyes, their guns aimed at my heart.

"I don't know what happened. Len was in the tent," Bowen says, pushing between the guns and me. "But I've got to get the kid out of there. I'll put him in my tent. You guys take care of Len."

"Wait . . . you're taking him to *your* tent? He killed Len! He's on the verge! Have you lost your—" Tommy's mouth snaps shut as his dark eyes move between Bowen and me. "Dude, Bowen. Is the Fec wearing your *shirt*?" he asks.

Bowen clears his throat and glances at his bare chest. "Yeah. I guess so." He kneels beside me, releases my ankle cuffs, and helps me out of the tent.

"Whoa. You're *touching* a Level *Ten*, Bo. And he's not wearing wrist cuffs! It's no wonder he killed Len. For the sake of the camp, get him fully restrained!"

Bowen glares at Tommy. "I'm the one who is in charge of the Fec. I'll do what I deem necessary for the safety of the camp. Now, come on." The armed guard follows us as he leads me to his tent. He holds the flap up while I crawl inside, and then I am alone, segregated from the others by fabric walls. "Do not leave your post! No matter what," Bowen says to the men now standing outside his tent. "And if the kid does anything, *Tase* before you shoot. Tase to *stun*, not kill."

"Where are you going?" Tommy asks.

"I've got a few things to do," Bowen says, voice fading as he walks away.

I lie atop Bowen's sleeping bag with my head on his soft pillow. Wrapping my tender arms around my chest, I roll onto my side and stare at the darkness, wondering what's going to happen to me now. Now that I have killed one of the militia. Do they hang people for murder, even if it is self-defense? Are they going to stand me against the wall, line up, and shoot me?

My thoughts turn slowly from a tornado of fear and dread

for my future to a gently swirling oblivion, and my eyes refuse to stay open.

Quiet footsteps make my heart race and pull me from a sleep filled with nightmares. When the tent flap swings aside, I open my mouth to scream.

"It's me," Bowen says. His voice is salve to my fear. My mouth snaps shut as he crawls into the tent, barely illuminated by the first hint of a gray dawn.

"Where's your uniform?" I whisper. He's wearing faded blue jeans and a tattered Sprite T-shirt.

"I hid it." He stuffs some things into a backpack and slings it over his shoulder.

"Why would you do that?" I ask.

He looks at me, eyes troubled. "We're going rogue. Until Sunday."

"Rogue? You mean, we're leaving the camp?"

He nods.

"Why?"

"I can protect the camp from you, no problem. But . . ." He takes an empty backpack from the corner of the tent and crams the sleeping bag into it. ". . . I can't protect *you* from the *camp*. We're going out on our own until I can get you to the lab." He tosses the pack at me, and I catch it.

"What do you mean, protect me from the camp?" I ask, dread making me shiver.

"For starters, you killed Len with your bare hands. You're a girl. You shouldn't be strong enough to kill him. Extreme bursts of strength are one of the first signs of turning." His eyes meet mine. "Once the camp finds out, they'll think you're on the verge."

I swallow, wondering if I am on the verge. Am I about to morph into a bloodthirsty beast? I don't feel any different than I did yesterday. Not physically, at least.

"What do you think," I ask, searching Bowen's face.

Bowen catches his lip in his teeth and stares at me for a long time. "I would have done the same thing if our roles were reversed. But that's not the main problem."

"Then what is?"

"They know you're a girl."

I frown, confused.

"Most of them haven't set eyes on a woman in more than a year, Fo. Let alone a young, *pretty* woman."

"What about you?" I ask.

"That includes me. But I know me. And I trust me. I can't say the same for anyone else. We've got to get you out of here. Now. So put on the backpack."

CHAPTER 16

The camp sleeps, an exhaustion brought on by the fight the day before. Only a few armed militia patrol the border. They watch Bowen and me with heavy, curious eyes as we pass into the trash-strewn street, but do nothing to stop us.

Bowen walks with his hand on his rifle, and I walk beside him. His mouth is set in a thin, grim line, and his eyes never hold still, scanning empty alleys between abandoned buildings, peering through broken windows—glancing warily at me. Our feet on the cracked pavement make the only sounds in the still predawn.

The sun never rises, hidden by a gray dome of clouds. The world is shades of brown and gray, with only the color of Bowen's eyes and the word *Sprite* on his shirt to remind me that green plants once grew in this dead place.

We have been walking less than an hour when Bowen,

without a word, grabs the sleeve of my shirt and yanks me into a narrow alley between two brick buildings. He shoves me into the shadows and whispers, "Stay!" Balancing his rifle over his shoulder, he crouches at the alley's entrance and takes aim at something I cannot see.

Above the torrent of blood rushing through my body, I hear rain, the pitter-patter of hundreds of drops thudding on the ground. I hold my hand up to the gray sky, but it remains dry. I look up. There is no rain. But the pitter-patter is louder than a moment before, a downpour.

I press my hand to my mouth and stare at Bowen's back. The downpour is not rain. It's footsteps. Lots of them. Running.

Bowen sets his gun down and tears the backpack from his shoulders. With trembling hands, he unzips it and starts pulling things out—dehydrated food, water bottles, a grenade—and stops. He holds the grenade in one shaky hand and places the fingers of his other hand on the pin. The muscles in his jaw pulse. I creep to his side and squat so that our shoulders touch.

The rifle is cold and much heavier than it looks. I pick it up, check the safety, balance it on my shoulder, rest my finger on the trigger, and point it out the alley in the direction of the stomping feet. And, side by side, we wait.

The pounding grows steadily louder. My hands begin to sweat, making the gun slippery, making it hard to aim. My shoulder trembles against Bowen's, and I wonder if he can hear my heart trying to explode out of my chest. A lone bead of sweat trickles down my temple.

Bowen's shoulder sags against mine, and he takes his fingers off the grenade pin. I look at him, thinking he must be crazy. He presses a finger to his lips and then touches his ear. I tilt my head to the side and listen. The footsteps are still there, still loud, but fading. To a drizzle. A sprinkle. Silence.

Bowen lets out a sigh and sits on the ground, still balancing the grenade in his hand. I sit beside him and set the rifle down.

"What was that?" I whisper.

"An entire hive is on the move," he says.

"Hive?"

"The beasts. A lot of them. Heading in the direction of the camp." Bowen carefully returns the grenade to his backpack and hands me a water bottle. I drink and pass it back. "I haven't seen the beasts this stirred up in months. They attacked yesterday, and the day before. . . . Something's bothering them." He looks pointedly at me.

"You think it's me causing this unrest?" I ask, stunned.

"Maybe. You're sure creating a lot of unrest for me." He puts his backpack on and peers out of the alley. "Come on. We're almost there."

With the gun now affixed to his shoulder, his finger looped through the trigger, we continue on. I follow a step behind him, my heart jumping at the echo of our feet against the ground, the jingling of his backpack, the scuff of a shoe behind us.

I stop and turn around. A wisp of gray, hardly more substantial than smoke, darts into a building half a block behind us.

"Bowen!" I whisper. Before his name has settled into the air, he is in front of me, gun pointed in the direction I am looking.

"What is it?" he whispers.

"Someone is following us."

He sweeps the rifle left and right. "Are you sure?"

"Positive."

"How many did you see?"

"Just one. He darted into that building." I point.

Bowen slowly lowers his gun, staring at the building.

"Whoever it was is more scared of us than we are of him," he says. "Let's go." He takes my hand and pulls me down the street at a slow jog. I stare at our clasped hands, at the human contact, wondering why it almost makes me want to cry.

Without warning, Bowen yanks me between two buildings and, hand in hand, we start to sprint. Our backpacks thump against our backs, and our feet pound the ground. Within seconds, my legs feel too weak, and a clammy sweat breaks out on my brow. My stomach turns, and I feel as if I haven't eaten in a year.

We round a corner, and Bowen pulls me to a stop in front of a metal door. Light flashes overhead and thunder rumbles. I rest my hands on my knees, gasping trembling breaths of air into my lungs, and peer up at the gray sky. A drip of water splatters against my forehead. And I hear the downpour again—whether rain or feet, I can't say, because the sky is falling, a thick, cool downpour.

Bowen swears and rams his shoulder into the door. It doesn't budge. He does it again, throwing all of his weight into it.

"I think it's locked," I say. My voice trembles. He ignores me and rams his shoulder into the door a third time with no results. He groans and smacks the door with his fist.

"It's not locked. I glued it shut so that no one else would be able to get in. But the glue should give under pressure." Bowen tries again, but the door doesn't move. He rubs his shoulder and curses.

The downpour is getting louder, though it isn't raining any harder than it was a moment before. Which can mean only one thing. The beasts are closing in. My heart matches the growing throb of their footsteps, and I can see fear in Bowen's eyes.

"We have to run," he says. He reaches for his pack, and I grab his icy hand.

"On three, let's do it together," I say, turning my shoulder toward the door. He stares into my eyes for a moment and then nods.

"One, two, three," Bowen says. I throw myself into the door, expecting it to absorb my momentum. When my shoulder hits, the door swings inward, and Bowen and I fall into the factory, our arms and legs tangled. Bowen wiggles away from me and climbs to his feet, slamming the door and sliding a metal lock into place.

I blink at the darkness. We stand in a huge empty room with one small window in the wall across from the door. The air is stale with dry heat and utterly silent.

Bowen crosses the factory to a narrow staircase in the corner, and I follow. The second level of the factory has windows as tall as me, most of them broken. Rain is blowing through them, pelting my skin, cooling my burned arms. Bowen strides to an empty window and looks out. I follow, but when I get there, he grabs me and pulls me to the side, just behind the window frame, holding my back against his chest with an arm pulled tightly around my shoulders.

"Don't move," he whispers against my ear. "Look."

Thunder rumbles. The wind picks up and whips damp air into my face. The pounding deluge of summer rain swallows the sound of footsteps. Below, two blocks away, runs a large group of people. As one, they stop, fall onto hands and knees, and press their faces to the wet street.

"Are they praying?" I ask.

"Yeah, right. They can't even talk. They're tracking us by scent," Bowen answers. "If they see us . . ." I press against him, trying to move us out of the window completely. "Just don't move," he whispers, tightening his hold on my shoulders.

The beasts stand and take a few steps forward, then throw themselves down onto the soaked street again. They stand once more and start running. Away from our building. Bowen sags against me, pressing his forehead on my shoulder, and lets out a deep breath of air.

"They lost the scent," he says into my shirt. And then he laughs. He turns me to face him and grins. I can't help but smile back. "The rain washed away the scent!" He runs his hands through his damp hair and sighs again.

I follow him back downstairs, over to the wall with the lone window. He sets his pack down. I do the same and shrug my tight, weary shoulders.

"So, now what?" I ask.

"We hide here until Sunday."

"We're just going to sit in this building for four days?"

"Yep. Bathroom's over there behind that door." He points to a wooden door that's been taken off its hinges and propped at an angle against the wall. "It's nothing fancy—just a bucket and a roll of toilet paper." Bowen sits and faces the metal door we came in through, his back against the cement wall, and lays his gun in his lap. "Might as well make yourself comfortable."

I take the sleeping bag out of my backpack, spread it over the dusty floor, and sit.

"Bowen?" I say. He looks at me. The skin under his eyes is as gray as the world, as gray as the cement wall framing him. "I don't think you brought enough food and water for four days."

His eyebrows rise. "Don't worry about it, Fo. I've got everything under control." He leans his head against the wall again and closes his eyes.

"Bowen," I say again.

"What?" he replies, sounding annoyed.

"Why did you do it?"

He opens his eyes. "Do what?"

"Leave the camp. With me."

"To keep you safe."

"I know, but you risked a lot. I might turn. I might kill you," I say, yet even as I speak the words, I know I could never hurt him.

"You're right. You *might* turn. And you *might* have been safe at the camp. But what if you don't turn? What if you are the only person in the world who carries the mark who doesn't go insane? But because of your mark, someone sells you to the black market and you die?" He looks at me for a long time before adding, "I want you to live to have a chance to make it to the lab. I mean,

I *know* you—have known you my whole life, even if we were never really friends. I think you deserve a chance." He shifts against the wall, sinking into the cement as if it were a pillow. "I need to sleep," he says, shutting his eyes.

I lie down on my side, and the sleeping bag rustles. Bowen's bleary eyes pop open. They're filled with alarm. "I almost forgot," he says. He unzips his backpack and reaches in. I groan when his hand comes out.

I shake my head. "No. Please," I say.

Bowen's jaw hardens. "Fo, the only way I'm ever going to be able to relax with you around is if you're cuffed. I'll just do your ankles."

"I'm not a beast," I whisper.

"If I'm going to protect you sufficiently for four days, I need to sleep. If I don't have peace of mind, I won't be able to sleep. And then we'll both end up dead, because I won't be able to do my job. I promise to release your legs when I wake up."

"And if I refuse? Put up a fight?"

He looks at his gun and then back at me, and his eyes turn cold. "I could always kill you."

I glare at him, and then roll onto my back and glower at the ceiling. Bowen points the remote at me, electricity hums, and the cuffs clink together.

He leans against the wall again, one hand resting on the gun in his lap, the other holding the remote, and is asleep in seconds. I put my hands behind my head and stare at the cobweb-covered ducts attached to the ceiling. My eyelids grow heavy, and I let them fall.

Rain patters outside, and the occasional thunder rumbles, making a fog of sleep settle around my weary, aching body. And then I hear something different. My eyes fly open, and I roll onto my side, wondering if I was dreaming. Every fiber in my body is tensed, right down to my eardrums. Waiting. I hear it again—the sound of fingernails on a chalkboard—and I know it was no dream.

The door shakes. The lock rattles against the metal, and dust floats from it. I look at Bowen to see if he heard it, but he's snoring, head sunk to one side. I look back to the door and wait, but nothing happens.

Eventually, weariness overrides fear and I drift off to sleep.

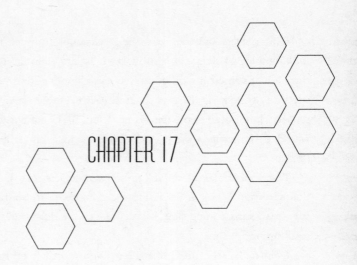

CHAPTER 17

The alarm is ringing. My clock radio must have fallen to the floor, because the ringing is muffled. I open my eyes and stare at a rectangle of sunlight on a cement floor. No alarm. No carpet. Just cement with a patch of sunlight. And I can't move my legs.

"What the . . . ," someone whispers. I roll onto my side. My shirt clings to my sweaty back. Bowen wipes sleep from his eyes and blinks. He clicks the remote at me and my legs are loose. "Come on." He grabs my hand and pulls me to my feet, hurrying upstairs.

Late-day sunlight glints off water pooled on the floor at the base of the broken windows. A repeating gong, like a church bell, echoes in the humid air. Bowen strides up to a west window and sunlight drenches him, casting a long shadow at his feet.

"You gotta be kidding me," he mutters.

"What is it?" I ask, standing behind him.

"They've opened the gate! For the first time in *ever*, they opened the gate on a Wednesday! And we're here and not there." He turns accusing eyes onto me. "I could have taken you to the lab right now and been done with you. Now I have to babysit you until Sunday." He shakes his head and pushes past me, grumbling under his breath.

"Gee, thanks. But you're the worst babysitter in the history of the world, Dreyden. Babysitters are supposed to be *fun*," I say to his back, and then I stick out my tongue. Very thirteen-year-old.

He turns and strides up to me, eyes full of fire, not stopping until our noses nearly touch. I gulp and force myself not to step back. "Nothing about life is fun anymore, Fo," he says. And then he leaves, feet thumping down the stairs.

I turn to the row of west windows and find the one with the least amount of broken glass below it and sit. The air is heavy with moisture and heat, clinging to my skin, gluing my hair to my scalp. My calves are worse, hot and itchy and sweaty beneath the cuffs. I sift through the glass shards littering the floor and pick up a long, triangular piece, wrapping it in the hem of my white T-shirt. And then I begin sawing just above my knee. The denim pops and tears against the glass. When I've made a sufficient hole, I tear the fabric, using the glass again to cut through the tough seams. And then the bottom half of my jeans separates from the top. I pull the cut denim over my shoe and stare at the glossy black metal encasing my calf.

"Stupid, stupid cuff," I say, and chuck the cut-off piece of denim out the window.

I start on the other leg, hacking at the fabric with the glass until I can tear it from the rest of the pants. I chuck it, too, and then jab at the metallic cuff encasing my calf. I take a second good, hard jab with the glass, gouging the metal, and gasp. Instinctively, I throw down the glass. The T-shirt protecting my hand has a small circle of red on it. The red spreads through the fabric, saturating the fibers, growing. I pull the fabric from my hand, and blood seeps out of a gash in my palm. The sight makes me want to gag.

I stand on weak legs and hurry down the stairs. Bowen, sitting with his back against the wall, gun propped on his bent knees, facing the door, doesn't look at me when I stop in front of him. His face is tight with anger, his brow furrowed.

"Bowen?" I say.

"What?" His eyes don't leave the door.

"Do you have a first-aid kit?" My voice shakes. He looks up, still glowering.

"Why do you need a first-aid kit?" he asks. Blood escapes my cupped hand and drips between his boots. His gun is on the ground and he is on his feet, pulling my hand to his eyes. "How did you manage to get hurt? Wait here." He lets go of my hand, and it falls limply to my side. Blood trickles down my fingers. "And keep your hand above your heart!"

I lift my hand to shoulder height, and blood trails down my arm and drips from my elbow. Bowen is gone for what feels like forever, a whole minute at least. When he comes back, he's holding a white box with a red cross painted on it.

"Upstairs. It's too dark down here," he says, gripping my elbow.

On the second floor, he pushes me to sitting and opens the box. "This will hurt," he warns, "but don't cry out!" He crouches beside me and pulls my fingers flat, making the gash in my palm gape. With his teeth he tears open a small white packet—it looks like a sugar packet from a restaurant—and holds it over my hand. Our eyes meet. And then his face is over my palm, and he pours little round white beads that look like fertilizer into the open gash. They hiss when they touch blood, and then absorb it until they turn red. The beads expand and the bleeding slows. Pressure fills the wound. I gasp and squeeze my eyes shut. Unable to stay upright, I totter and fall to the side.

Fire laces my blood, spreading from my palm to my fingers and wrist. Ice follows, traveling all the way to my elbow. And then the pain is gone. I wiggle my fingers. It feels like a rock is wedged inside the cut, and I can't make a fist. I take a deep breath and open my eyes. A knee supports my head, and fingers are brushing the hair from my sweaty forehead.

"I'm sorry," Bowen says.

I look up at him. "No. It's my fault for being stupid. I shouldn't have used the glass—"

"Fo," Bowen snaps, silencing me. "I'm not sorry the coagulant hurt your hand. You totally deserved it. But I'm sorry about what I said. About being stuck with you."

Sunshine spreads through my body. I sit up and beam at him. "Really?"

"Yeah. Really. Aside from you being my potential—and

most likely, terribly painful—death, you're not that bad." He smiles and I feel like I could float away. Without asking, he takes my injured hand and wraps it with stretchy tape.

"No showering for twenty-four hours," he warns.

My eyes grow round and I lean toward him. "Is there a shower here?"

He laughs and shakes his head. "It was a joke." A hot breeze stirs the air, and Bowen shuts his eyes. "Maybe we should sleep up here tonight. It's a lot cooler than downstairs. And with the cover of darkness . . . I'll grab our stuff."

He stands. I watch him go, then make my way to the west windows in time to see the sun disappear behind distant mountains. Shadows creep into the world, filling every corner and hollow. And one shadow on the street below moves. I crouch down for a better look.

The shadow crouches, too, and for a moment I wonder if it has seen me. But then it picks something up from the ground. Something pale and limp. The bottom half of my pants.

CHAPTER 18

I wake to the sound of a motor, and my eyes flutter open in confusion. The motor is right above me. Vibrations shatter the still morning. I lift my head in search of its source.

"No! Don't move!" Bowen whispers, pressing on my shoulder. "Look." He nods toward my cuffed and restrained ankles. Slowly I lift my head again and peer down the length of my body.

Above my stomach hovers a tiny bird, inspecting the crimson stain on my shirt. Its wings drone like a motor and I am filled with awe. This fragile hummingbird is the first living, wild animal I have seen since waking up in this dead world. Its bright-green chest and red-capped head are startlingly out of place.

"Where'd it come from?" I whisper, unable to take my eyes from it.

"The wall. There are hundreds of hummingbirds living inside

of it. Every once in a while one gets out. It thinks your blood is a flower. It's probably on the verge of starving to death."

The hummingbird, realizing my shirt isn't a flower, darts away, sweeping through an empty window and leaving the morning disturbingly silent.

Bowen points the remote at me, and my ankles release. I stretch my legs and think about going back to sleep.

After a moment, I hear another sound, reminiscent of the sound of a distant hoe scraping dirt. I open my eyes and look at Bowen—the source of the sound. A gleaming knife glides along his jaw line, scraping a thin lather of white foam and dark stubble from his skin. The scent of pine floats on the air. I stare, entranced, as he scrapes all the cream off, and when he is done, his smooth face looks thirteen again. Almost.

"Here." Bowen holds a water bottle out to me. I sit up, open it, and take a long drink. He smirks. "That's for you shirt, Fotard. You need to wash the blood out of it."

I open my mouth to ask him why, but before the words leave my tongue, he says, "Blood draws beasts—the smell."

"Oh." Horrified, I pull off my shirt. Bowen's smirk disappears, and his freshly shaved cheeks turn a shade pinker. He turns his back as if he's never seen me with just the binding that wraps my chest, as if the sight of me will make him go blind. "Bowen, I've still got the rags binding my . . . never mind." I turn the other way, hoping the back of my neck isn't as hot as it feels, and put my shirt on the ground. Pouring water on the blood, I start rubbing the fabric against itself. I pour more water and rub more, but the blood doesn't come out.

"I need soap or bleach," I say over my shoulder.

"I don't have any. Just give it a good rinse for now." Bowen's feet scrape on the ground, and he gasps. I turn and look up at him, every muscle in my body tensed for something bad. His eyes are fixed on my back, his mouth hanging open.

"What?" I ask.

"What happened to your back?"

I crane my neck to peer over my shoulder. "What are you talking about?"

He crouches behind me and trails his warm fingers over my skin, from the base of the fabric wrapping my breasts to just above the waist of my jeans. I shiver as warmth floods my body. His fingers move to the skin between my shoulder blades, just above the bindings, and trail up to my neck, leaving goose bumps in their wake.

"What is it?" I ask, my voice unsteady.

"You don't know?"

I shake my head.

"You have scars from here"—he touches my neck—"to here." His finger trails over the binding and down to the top of my hip.

"Scars?"

"Yeah. They look like they're from . . . fingernails." He presses three fingertips to my midback and drags them downward. His eyes meet mine. "What happened to Jonah?" he asks, eyes guarded.

"He's a beast," I say. The words scratch my throat.

"That's what I thought. He started the vaccine the same time you did, right?"

"Yes," I answer without thinking, a fact I didn't realize I knew until this very moment.

Bowen taps his chin with his finger and studies me. And then he's standing, tugging his Sprite shirt over his head. My body temperature surges, searing my neck and cheeks. He doesn't notice, is too intent on his chest. I follow his gaze.

His skin is suntanned and smooth over muscles earned by hard work. Right down the middle of his chest are five white lines, like five lightning bolts. I stand and get a better look. "Here, too." He points to his shoulder. I take a step closer and study the white marks, tracing the jagged crescent with my finger.

"That looks like . . ."

"Teeth?"

I nod.

"A beast bit me. And the marks on my chest are from fingernails." He pulls his shirt back on. "We need to go back downstairs. We're sitting targets up here. Are you hungry?"

"What?" I'm still staring at his chest, imagining the five scar-streaks beneath his shirt.

"Hungry. Do you want something to eat?"

My stomach growls. I haven't eaten in more than a day. He picks up my sopping shirt and hands it to me. I pull it on and follow him downstairs.

"When did you get those scars?" I ask.

"Three years ago. I was fourteen." The main level of the factory is dark and muggy compared to the second level. I can hardly see his face. "They had just completed the second level of the wall and were admitting more people inside, offering protection. If."

"If what?" I ask.

"If you qualified."

"And you didn't?"

"No, I did. But my mom? She didn't qualify. They turned her away."

An image wavers in my memory. A bathrobe and bunny slippers, and blood on snow.

Jonah and I were out front, taking turns pulling each other on a sled through the snow. It was my turn to be pulled, when a door slammed across the street.

She stood on the front porch, wearing a blue flannel robe. Twinkling Christmas lights clung to the roof of her house even though it was the end of February.

"Look, it's the crazy lady," Jonah whispered. "Dad says if you look at her wrong, she'll kill herself."

I tore my gaze from her and studied the purple plastic sled, wondering if Dreyden was embarrassed to have a mom like that—a mom who wore her bathrobe and slippers at four in the afternoon. A mom who left their Christmas lights on day and night.

The sound of Mrs. Bowen crunching through the snow of her unshoveled driveway echoed across the street to our house. A minute later a pair of pink bunny slippers matted with snowballs crunched into our yard and stopped beside the sled. Red dripped between those slippers, like the ticking of a clock . . . drip-drip-drip.

"I need help," she said. "I've accidentally cut my wrist." Drip–drip–drip.

I looked up, and Jonah rammed his boot into my thigh. "Don't look at her!" he warned.

I stood from the sled and stared at the blood melting a red hole in the snow between her slippers.

"I'll get Dad," I whispered.

"Why didn't your mom qualify?" I can still see the crimson snow when I look at him.

Bowen unzips his backpack and rummages around. "She didn't pass their health requirements. And if you aren't healthy, you aren't worth protecting." He takes out one of the meat-flavored disks, and my stomach rumbles. I don't know how I hadn't realized it before, but I'm ravenous. Eager, drooling, I hold my hand out for the disk, but he hesitates, his eyes full of guilt.

"What?" I ask, scared he might eat it himself. "We don't have enough food to last, after all?"

"No. These." He scowls at the disk. "They're for Fecs. And beasts. It is a flavored calorie tablet with an appetite suppressant, emotion inhibitor, and tranquilizer. And they're mildly addictive."

I stare at the disk, thinking of the pleasant, heavy exhaustion that filled me each time I ate one and made life seem more bearable. I should be angry, *furious*, that he was drugging me. Instead, I want to snatch up the disk and eat it before he has a chance to feel guilty for feeding them to me.

Bowen's fingers curl around it, and I reach my hand out with a small whimper. He looks at me and puts it back in the backpack. "Wait here." He crosses the empty floor and disappears behind the stairs.

I sit on the ground and stare at the backpack, tempted to find the wafer. I'm so hungry. Peering toward the stairs, I place my hand on the pack's zipper.

"Don't eat it," Bowen calls.

I jump and pull my hand away. Taking a resigned breath, I turn away from the backpack and, in the dim light, pull the medical tape from my hand and study my scabbed-over palm. Only, the scab isn't red. It's chalky white. After a minute Bowen returns with a can in each hand. He holds them out for me to see, and I forget about the disk and my palm.

"Spam and peaches in light syrup. Worth almost as much as honey," he says, sitting on the ground beside me. He pops open the lids on the cans, and my mouth fills with saliva. I swallow and take a deep breath, and smell the memory of flowers and breakfast and juice. He takes a knife from his pocket and slices a gelatinous chunk of pink Spam from the can and hands it to me.

I put the meat into my mouth and am transported to a world long gone. Tears of yearning for the past sting my eyes, so I close them and chew. My stomach heaves and jumps, trying to get the meat into it as quickly as possible. I can almost hear the clatter of silverware on plates, hear the quiet sound of classical music in the background, see my family gathered around the dining room table, sunlight streaming through the windows. When I open my eyes, Bowen is staring at me, a ghost of a smile on his mouth.

"Good?" he asks.

"So good," I say, wiping the tears from my lashes. He hands me the other can without a word. I take a sip of the syrup and slurp a slice of peach into my mouth. I want to melt into the floor. "Heaven," I say. "Where did you find them?"

"I've been storing food here for a while. Just in case . . ." He trails off.

"What?"

He shrugs and slices off another piece of Spam. "In case I ever decide to go rogue. Permanently. Colorado isn't the only state out there that cut itself off from the rest of the country and made its own government in an effort to survive. The rumor is, there's a place—a settlement—in Wyoming, where anyone's welcome. I figure one day I might want to see if the rumors are true. I don't have anyone holding me here—you know?" He puts the meat into his mouth and sighs. I pass him the peaches and take the knife from his hand, slicing more cold Spam.

"What happened to your mom?" I pop the meat into my mouth and force myself to chew when my stomach begs me to swallow it whole.

"She died. So I joined the militia," he says. The muscles in his jaw pulse, and he won't look at me.

"How did she die?" I ask, Spam momentarily forgotten.

His gaze doesn't leave the can of peaches in his hand. Juice sloshes out of the can, and he gently sets it down. His hand trembles, and he tucks it into his lap.

"What about your dad?" I ask, trying to change the subject. I hardly ever saw his dad. He drove a semi and was gone for months at a time.

"My dad's not worth talking about. He abandoned us," Bowen snaps.

"Where's your brother?"

Bowen's shoulders relax a bit. "He's inside the wall, making babies with a sweet sixteen-year-old wife."

"Sixteen?" I squeak.

Bowen laughs. "Yeah, sixteen. He loved her enough to wait a whole year for her. Fifteen is the new legal age. When you turn fifteen, you join the militia if you're a boy, and get married if you're a girl. The number-one priority right now is repopulation. Number two is to protect those repopulating the world, from the rest of the world."

I study his face—his green eyes, angled cheekbones, and soft mouth—and my skin suddenly feels too warm as my blood heats beneath the surface. "Why aren't you married, then?" I ask, finding an imaginary spot on the floor to scratch. "And making babies?"

He exhales, and I feel the air stir against my burning skin, feel his body shift in the space next to mine. "It feels wrong, looking at twelve-, thirteen-, and fourteen-year-olds as possible wives— not that I *get* to look, since they're all inside the wall and I'm stuck out here." Bowen picks up the can of peaches and hands it to me. When I take it, our fingertips touch and mine explode with fire. Bowen doesn't let go of the can. His eyes meet mine, and the factory air seems unbearably hot, too hot to breathe. After a heartbeat, he releases the can and turns away from me.

I peer into the can of peaches, wondering if the heat of my hand will make the sticky-sweet syrup boil.

"I need to get some sleep," Bowen says, his voice rough.

I set the peaches down and study his silhouette, bracing myself for the zing of my ankle cuffs. But the zing doesn't come. "You forgot my cuffs," I say. My sweaty skin itches beneath the metal. Bowen bites his bottom lip and stares at the cuffs for a minute. He lifts the remote and points it at my legs. I clench my teeth, waiting for the magnetic pull and discomfort of immobility. The remote clicks, metal clangs, and cool air swirls around my damp calves. I look at the cuffs, sitting useless on the cement floor beside me. I look at Bowen. He shrugs and lies on the cool cement ground, wadding the sleeping bag up for a pillow.

"You're not restraining me?" I whisper, afraid if I say it too loud, he'll remember I'm a Ten.

His eyes flicker to mine. "Do you feel like you're about to turn?"

I mentally tune in to every single part of my body. "No."

"I trust you, Fo," he says. He puts his gun over his chest and cuddles it, then shuts his eyes. The air temperature seems to drop ten degrees, going from unbearably hot to just uncomfortably warm, and I can breathe again.

Bowen has a talent for falling asleep the minute his eyes close. His face goes soft, his lips part, and quiet snores fill the warehouse.

I sit cross-legged in front of him and stare at his sleeping face while I eat the rest of the food, remembering how he looked when he was a kid. He always seemed two weeks overdue for a haircut, with scraggly bangs forever in his eyes. And his cheeks were rounder, though typically pale. As a kid he seemed thin to the point of malnourished, with knobby knees and gangly arms. Whenever my mom baked, if she saw him outside riding his bike, she'd call him over and give him a plate of warm cookies or a slice of pie.

Now he's filled out, grown into his body, the perfect image of golden-tan health and strength. He stirs and shuts his mouth, as if he can sense my eyes on him. Were I brave, I would reach out and touch him, brush his bangs away from his sweaty forehead or trace the line of his jaw. But the thought steals my breath, so I lean my back against the wall and spread my fingers, plucking a tune out of the air, hearing notes in my head. My fingers remember exactly where to touch, as if I'd played the tune yesterday.

Chopin's Nocturne no. 2 replaces thoughts of Bowen.

CHAPTER 19

By late afternoon, the air is so heavy that if I cry, I'm certain my tears will hang suspended before my face. I wipe the back of my hand over my forehead, pushing my bangs from my sweaty skin, and try to hold back the tears.

Bowen murmurs, thrashing about in his sleep. This has been going on for hours, since shortly after he fell asleep. And when his nightmares peak, he mumbles my name—*Fiona*, not Fo—and clutches the gun tighter to his chest, or spreads his palm over his chest, right above his heart. I can imagine his dreams—my claws in his skin, my teeth gnawing his shoulder, gnawing his chest to get to his heart. I am the source of his nightmares.

He gasps my name and whimpers. This time I can't stop them. Tears fill my eyes and my heart constricts. I rest my forehead on my knees, listening to the agonizing sound of my name on his restless lips. Lips I have been studying for hours.

Something thumps. I jump, my heart jumps, my stomach jumps, and I look at Bowen. Something thumps again on the other side of the factory. A soft fist on the metal door? I stand and tiptoe to the door, pressing my ear against the sun-heated steel.

Deep voices, barely more than whispers, carry through to my ear. And scratching, the sound of a match against stone. I sprint to Bowen and touch his shoulder. His entire body lurches as if electricity has tensed every muscle in one swift jolt. Eyes wide, teeth bared, he digs the end of his gun into my chest right above my stuttering heart. I flinch and get ready to die.

Recognition softens his wild eyes, and the gun falls to his side.

"What's wrong?" he whispers.

"The door. Someone's here," I answer, pressing a hand over my ballistic heart.

Bowen jumps to his feet and crams all our belongings into our backpacks—the empty cuffs, the sleeping bag, even the empty peach and Spam cans. He takes my hand in his, and we run to the stairs, but instead of going up, we go behind them. The wall below the stairs swings open, revealing a secret room.

Bowen throws the packs inside, then grabs my shoulder and turns me to face him, pushing me into the room until my back presses against something hard and uneven. He presses the length of his body against mine, his feet snug in between my feet, and pulls the secret door shut behind us.

"Sorry about the tight fit," he whispers, his mouth against my temple. "I never thought I'd be stuck in here with another person." Bowen shifts, his body moving against mine, and something clunks. "Ow!" he whispers.

"Are you okay?"

"Yeah. I hit my forehead on the stairs." His breath dances over my face and I breathe it in, inhaling deeply, my ribs expanding against his.

Outside our tiny room under the stairs, something explodes. The walls shudder, dust falls into my eyes, and I need to cough. I lean my face into Bowen's shoulder and force myself to take slow, even breaths. His arm moves around me, pulling me a millimeter closer, cradling my head.

"It's okay," he whispers. "We'll be okay." His chin bumps the crown of my head when he talks. "It's the militia. They won't find us in here. If it were a beast, or the . . ." His body shudders.

I turn my head to the side, pressing my ear against his chest, and listen to the sounds of his body. Breath moves quickly in and out of him, and his heart is like the hummingbird's wings—frantic.

Boots pound the ground outside our room, go up the stairs, and unsettle more dust. I turn my face back against his shoulder and hold my breath. Most of the boots echo overhead, but one pair comes back down the stairs. Another shower of dust rains down. I press my face harder against him and take deep, slow breaths. The smell of him makes me think of cool mountain lakes and pine trees and sweat. I take a deeper breath, letting my body melt into the firm angles of his body, the safety of his physical presence, and loop my arms behind him.

"Bowen?" someone yells.

I jump, gripping the back of his shirt with my sweaty hands. The voice thunders through the factory and finds its way into our tiny shelter.

"We need the Fec!" I recognize the voice. Mickelmoore, the gray-haired man. "Bowen, this Fec might be the most important person alive. It is mandatory that you turn her over to me."

Bowen's arm tightens around me, pulling me more firmly against him, against the rise and fall of his chest.

Feet thump down the stairs again, shaking our shelter.

"Sir, he's not here. Tommy might have given us false info. They were pretty tight," a different voice says. "Marshall thinks he saw something in the factory across the street."

"File out," Mickelmoore orders. "And have your guns ready."

Boots echo and fade as they leave. I lift my face from Bowen's damp shirt, relieved that they're gone, and dare a deep breath of the dusty air. "Why d—" His hand presses against my mouth.

"Someone's still here. They always leave one man behind, just in case," he whispers, his lips soft against my temple. My body goes rigid again. Our hearts beat against each other's, and his hand stays firm over my lips. The air in the shelter is suddenly so dense I can hardly breathe. Or maybe it's being pressed against Bowen that steals my breath. For a long time we stand motionless. And then the solitary sound of boots resonates through the factory, fades, and drifts into nothing.

Bowen's body grows slack, and he moves his hand from my

mouth to the back of my neck. His breath cools the sweat on my face, and I lift my face toward his. He sighs and rests his forehead against mine. Our noses bump, and something soft touches my lips—his—an accidental, feathery touch. But then his hand tightens on the back of my neck, and his lips move, tracing a line of fire from my mouth, along my jaw, to the soft skin below my ear. He takes a deep breath and moves his lips back to mine. They press against mine again, soft and firm. And very deliberate. His lips part, and I don't know what to do. I've never been kissed.

My stomach drops, and my knees forget how to stay straight. I grip Bowen's shirt and let my lips melt against his. But he pulls his face from mine.

The door opens. Cooler, dry air takes Bowen's place against my body, and he steps into the light. He runs his hands through his dark hair and curses.

"What?" I say, breathless. I lick my lips and taste salt.

He points to the door. Or what's left of it—a gaping hole in the side of the factory, surrounded by rubble. The mangled door lies beneath the solitary window on the opposite side of the factory.

He turns back to me, pulls me out into the open, and takes my place in the shelter. Kneeling, he begins filling the backpacks with food and water. The shelter is crammed with cans. From floor to ceiling. Except a small space big enough to fit one body. I look at Bowen's scowling profile and wonder, *Did I imagine his lips on mine?* I slide my tongue over my lips again and can still taste him.

"Take off your shirt," he says, peering up at me.

My heart jumps into my throat. "What?"

His jaw muscles pulse. "Don't ask questions. Just do it, Fo."

I pull the stained shirt over my head. Bowen stands and puts his hands on my bare shoulders and looks down into my eyes. My knees tremble and I lean toward him. He frowns and flips me around so my back is to him, and pulls the shirt from my hand. It falls to the floor by my feet.

"Arms out," he orders. I lift my arms. He slips something over my hand and up to my shoulder, the way my mother helped me put on my coat when I was four. The other arm is next and then he spins me back around to face him. He pulls a heavy black vest closed over my chest and zips it into place.

"Bulletproof?" I ask. His troubled eyes meet mine, and he nods. From the floor he takes my shirt and presses it into my hands. I pull it over my head, over the vest. The instant it's in place, he thrusts a heavy, bulging pack at me and slings the other over his shoulders. Then, without a word, without a backward glance, he turns and leaves.

"What about you?" I say, running after him, thinking of his scarred chest and shoulder—the only things hidden beneath his shirt. "Aren't you going to put on a vest?"

His stride doesn't slow. "There's only one."

"So, you're giving it to me? A Level Ten?" I ask, shocked, clumsily following him as I try to get my arms into the heavy backpack's straps.

He yanks the straps of his backpack tighter. "I suppose I am."

"Why?"

He slows and looks at me, and his eyes hold mine. I lick my lips again, wondering if I can still taste him. I can't. He lets out a deep breath, looks at his watch, and curses. "Come on. It's almost dusk. And shut up. We've got to be silent. And we've got to find somewhere to spend the night, fast."

CHAPTER 20

It is like playing capture the flag. Only if we're caught by the other team, we lose something much more important than a scrap of fabric and a game. Bowen leads and I follow, from doorway to doorway, alley to alley, our feet as silent as the rest of the shadowed world.

The sun sets and the sky darkens, and Bowen balances his gun over his shoulder, ready to shoot at any moment. I clutch the straps of my backpack with sweating hands. Every so often voices float over the still evening air. When this happens, we pause and Bowen tilts his head to the side, choosing a new direction. Always away from the voices.

Bowen's stance is as rigid as his gun. Tension oozes from his taut shoulders and finds its way inside me, making me jump at every sound, making my heart pound as we round corners and duck into buildings.

"If we're lucky, it's the militia," he whispers.

Who else could it be? "And if we're not lucky?" I whisper, wondering if I want to hear the answer. He glances at me over his shoulder, his face lost in shadows, but doesn't reply.

As we creep through the darkness between two tall buildings with gaping holes where windows used to be, the voices stir again, restless whispers bouncing between the walls. Bowen holds a hand out for me to stop, and when I do, my foot skids on the ground, a grating sound that destroys the silence, sends my heart into my throat, and makes a stream of sweat trickle between my shoulder blades. Bowen grips his gun, swinging it in a frantic circle, eye glued to the night-vision scope. I look around, but see nothing in the darkness.

A pebble falls, swishing the air in front of my face, plunking on my shoe like a fat drop of rain before settling between my feet. Together Bowen and I look up to the roof of the building on our right, Bowen through the gun's scope. Before I see anything, he yanks me forward, hard. My feet tangle in his, and we crash to the ground, his arm cradling my head. Something pops and echoes, and I expect a firework to bloom overhead, mingling with the first stars of the night. Bowen gasps and his body flinches, curling against mine. An instant later, he shoves me aside and leaps to his feet, pulling me to standing in the same swift movement. With our hands clasped we run, backpacks thumping against our backs, veering through starlit alleys, across deserted streets, and in and out of buildings.

Voices fill the dark, shouts that echo against buildings and disappear down alleys. Feet thud behind us, a staccato mess. I glance over my shoulder and see light dancing inside a building a block away. And then men wearing headlamps swarm out of it. Militia. Energy surges through me. I grip Bowen's hand and run faster, pulling ahead of him, around the corner of a building.

Gray against the gray dusk, like a plume of smoke, a shadow steps in front of me. My feet skid and grind on the pavement. Bowen slams into my back and throws an arm around my waist to keep me from spilling forward with his momentum.

"Why did you . . ." His words die and his arm tightens around me. The shadow, slight and wispy as the naked trees, takes my hand and pulls me and Bowen, his arm still around my waist, into the nearest building.

The building has windows, dark windows tinted to block out sunlight, whole windows in a world of broken glass. My eyes widen at the interior darkness, and my skin crawls. The building—there's something about it, something different from all the others we've been in, as if it is frozen in time.

Bowen's arm tightens and pulls me to a stop. Without releasing me, he maneuvers himself between the shadow and me and raises his gun.

"Who are you?" he whispers to the shadow.

A smell oozes around us, clings to my throat like grease. I breathe through my mouth and taste the oily tang of tunnels.

"Arrin?" I whisper, peering around Bowen.

"Shut up, Fo," she hisses. "Or we'll all die."

Arrin reaches around Bowen and takes my hand in hers

again. I tug one of Bowen's hands from his gun, and we wind our way, a human chain, through frozen darkness.

The voices get louder, the sound of feet pounds nearer to the entrance we just came through. Arrin pulls me faster, her grimy hand damp in mine. After a minute she stops and pushes me against a wall. Bowen stops beside me, his biceps against my shoulder, and, enveloped by the overwhelming scent of Arrin, we wait.

The sound of boots grows slowly louder. Flickers of light through the black-tinted windows shine into the building where we hide. Whispers tangle with the sound of blood pulsing in my ears, and then the square eye of a headlamp flashes in the doorway.

"Don't go in there!" someone whispers. The man in the door-way pauses, his headlamp swooping a wide arc against the floor, touching my toes, reaching deeper into the building.

"But what if they have?" the man with the light asks, his lamp still searching.

"Then, the beasts will kill them."

The man with the light freezes. Bowen's arm hardens against my shoulder.

"Beasts?" Headlamp Man asks. His light shines into the dark-est recesses of the building, and I forget to breathe.

Pale, dirty, muscular bodies litter the ground, their chests rising and falling. Stringy, long hair hangs in faces, drapes over closed eyes, falls into slightly open mouths. I hear the gentle sound of many bodies breathing, almost masked by my pound-ing heart, and turn away. If I see more, I will scream.

"That's a mapped hive. If you go in there, you're toast," the man whispers. "And if you're toast, no way you're going to live a long, happy life inside the wall if you even catch the Fec."

Headlamp Man turns, his feet silent, and creeps away from the building's entrance. The light outside the door dims and fades. Arrin sighs and I cover my nose and mouth against the reek carried on her breath, afraid that I might gag and wake the sleeping hive. Bowen grabs my hand and starts dragging me toward the doorway.

"What are you doing? Where are you going?" Arrin whispers. Bowen's hand tightens on mine and he doesn't slow. Arrin materializes beside us. "*Where* are you *going*?" she asks again, through gritted teeth.

He pulls me to a stop beside the door leading outside and moves between Arrin and me. "What were you *thinking*?" he hisses at her. "You took us into a mapped hive? They could have killed us. They still might!"

"They rarely stir after sunset. And besides—it's better than the *alternative*," Arrin whispers.

"What alternative," I ask.

Paper rattles, and the smell of Arrin makes me gag.

"What is that?" Bowen whispers. He drops my hand.

"The *alternative*," Arrin snaps, her heavy breath lingering in the air like a thick fog.

Light flickers, a finger-size flashlight, lens pressed against Bowen's palm. It gives off just enough light to illuminate a wrinkled piece of paper. Bowen hands me the light, pressing it

against my palm, and takes the paper from Arrin's hand. Over his shoulder, I read the words and gasp. Bowen curses.

"See," Arrin says. "I just saved Fo. Again."

WANTED:

Fiona Tarsis

Female

Age: 17

Height: 5'9"

Hair: blond

Eyes: brown

Level: Ten

Reward: Life inside the wall with no age-limit extermination.

Below the writing is a full-color picture of me. My hair is long and clean, spread over a crisp white pillow, and my eyes are closed. Sleeping Beauty. I blink and look closer. A finely wrought gold chain is around my neck, with a gold treble clef nestled in the dip between my collarbones.

"Where did you get this?" Bowen asks, eyes flickering over Arrin.

"They opened the wall this morning and posted them all over the place," Arrin says, dangling a pale-blue scrap of fabric in front of me. I take a closer look at the fabric and recognize the bottom half of my jeans. She grins. "I've been waiting for you to come out of that warehouse," she whispers.

Bowen folds the paper into a rectangle and stuffs it into his pocket. It is then I notice the jagged trail of black along his arm. I touch it and put my fingers into my mouth.

"Why are you bleeding?" I whisper, swallowing the coppery tang of Bowen. He glances at his shoulder. The sleeve of his shirt is torn and black with blood.

"The guy on the roof," he whispers, peering into the building, eyes cautious, as if making sure the smell of his blood hasn't disturbed the sleeping beasts. "Barely nicked me."

"Why are they trying to kill me?" I ask, horrified that Bowen took a bullet meant for me.

"They aren't. They hit their target," he says.

My mouth drops open, and hot panic surges inside me, mixed with confusion. "You? Why?"

"Because if I'm dead, you aren't protected. And if you aren't protected . . ." Bowen looks at Arrin. "What's your name, kid?"

She takes another step away and peers at Bowen through her bangs, a sly, devious smile on her face. A smile that makes my skin crawl.

"Arris," she whispers, the *s* a slow, drawn-out hiss. She perches on the balls of her feet at the exact moment Bowen points his gun at her. Arrin drops the piece of denim, leaps behind him, and grabs me, clinging to my back, her nails digging into my flesh. "If you don't let me leave, I'll kill Fo," she says, peeking her head around my shoulder. A blade jabs my spine, and I flinch. "And if you shoot me, you wake the hive."

Bowen lowers his gun but doesn't take his finger from the trigger.

"Bowen, this is the Fec who brought me to your camp," I whisper, trying to placate them both while easing away from Arrin's rusty knife.

"*Arris* brought you to the camp?" he says, eyes locked on Arrin, hands rigid on the rifle. "I thought you said you were brought by a girl."

"Arris, Arrin . . . she *is* a girl."

Bowen laughs a whispered laugh—a grating, miserable sound. "No. Arris is the most deadly, conniving, evil thing that lives in the tunnels. Arris is not a girl."

The knife leaves my back, and in a heartbeat, Arrin is gone. Only the smells of crusty feces and rotting teeth linger in the air. Bowen's gun is on his shoulder again, aiming into the shadows, but there's no trace of the Fec.

We ease toward the open door and step out into starlight and fresh air.

"Hold this," he whispers, thrusting the gun at me. "And don't hesitate to shoot anything that moves," he adds. I put the flashlight in my pocket, lift the gun to my shoulder, and let its weight settle, looping my finger through the trigger.

"You hold that like you know how to use it," Bowen whispers, crouched beside his open backpack.

"My dad taught me to shoot."

"Your dad?" The skepticism in his voice makes me stand a little taller.

"Just because he was partially paralyzed doesn't mean he couldn't shoot a gun," I snap.

He chuckles. "I'd say the wafers are losing their effect." He sets the first-aid kit on the ground and opens the lid. "Sorry. I didn't mean to disrespect your dad. He was a good man."

He takes out a packet and tears it open with his teeth, then peels back the sleeve of his shirt. In the starlight, a dark gash slices through the white bite-mark scar on his shoulder. Blood oozes from the gash and trickles down his arm in a dozen branches, like an upside-down tree. He pours a few pale beads into the open wound and sucks air through clenched teeth. His body stiffens and shudders, and then the air leaves his mouth in a swoosh. Sweat gleams on his shadowed forehead.

"You'd think that would get easier to bear with time," he whispers through clenched teeth. He takes a water bottle out of his pack and rinses the blood from his arm. "We need to get out of here. But we need to talk first." He takes my hand and leads us away from the building with tinted windows.

Pressing me against a white brick building, he puts his hands on my shoulders and looks right into my eyes. "Arris, the Fec, was wearing your old clothes?" he asks.

"You want to talk about clothes right now?" I ask.

"Was he or not?"

I frown. "If he was, they're a lot dirtier."

"He was wearing a pair of knee-length drawstring shorts and a V-neck shirt. Does that sound familiar?"

"Yeah." I nod. "Those were mine."

Bowen's lips thin and pull tight against his teeth. "We have to travel. Tonight. In the dark. We have to get away from

the militia. And that means we run the risk of intercepting raiders."

The intensity of his voice scares me. "What are raiders?" I ask, my eyes wide.

"They're ruthless slavers, rapists, and murderers. They keep beasts as *pets*, tied up, and beat them and then drink their blood. They take pleasure in other people's pain and hunt—for humans—at night." He hangs his head. "They're the reason my mom's dead."

I put my hand over his. "I'm so sorry," I whisper.

"The militia has orders to shoot them on sight. Because the militia patrols the wall twenty-four-seven, the raiders typically avoid the wall," he continues. "So if we stay near it, we probably won't run into them. But if we do . . ." He stares at me, the whites of his eyes visible above the shadowed planes of his cheeks.

"If we do?" I ask.

"If you get caught . . ." He takes a deep breath and shakes his head. "You *can't* get caught. If they find out you're a girl . . . a *woman* . . ." His hand leaves my shoulder and cups my cheek. "You can't get caught," he whispers, leaning his forehead on mine.

"Okay."

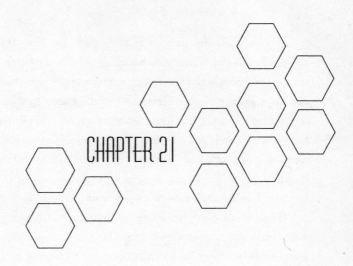

CHAPTER 21

We cling to the wall's dark shadow, leaving its protection only when we are forced to—the militia are stationed every quarter mile—not standard protocol according to Bowen. They've upped security, probably because of me.

Every few minutes, Bowen pauses and listens to the quiet of nothing, as if he's expecting . . . something.

We walk for what feels like hours, and I keep expecting the sky to brighten, the sun to rise. A slow, persistent ache grows in my lower back, and blisters form on both my heels. When I think time must have paused, trapping us in this forever night, the darkness takes on a different hue, like the fuzzy gray of pre-dawn.

Light flickers and glimmers between buildings, turning slowly from gray to red, and I realize my mistake. Not sunrise. Firelight.

Bowen pulls me to a stop and drags me into the closest building—an old apartment building with a walkway between numbered doors and a few tattered doormats littering the ground. He eases a door open, number 1C, and we step inside.

A hint of firelight shines in through a shattered window, between a broken pair of blinds, illuminating an overturned table and the frame of a sofa. He presses me against a wall, his damp hands tight on my shoulders. Firelight glows against the side of his face, leaving the other side black and featureless.

"There's someone out there," he whispers. "We've got to get away unseen." A wail, eerily human—yet not—echoes into the apartment building, and Bowen grapples with his gun, aiming it toward the window. "If they catch you," he whispers, eyes glued to the window, "you're a boy! But don't get caught! If I give you this signal," he pumps his fist three times, "that means run. Go to the north gate and turn yourself in. Don't get caught!" He lowers the gun and looks at me again. "You stay behind me. Do not make any noise! And stay in the shadows!"

His hand goes to his belt, and he removes something, a Taser, and presses it into my hand. He shows me how to use it and sets it to *kill*. And then, our feet silent, my heart thundering like a bass drum in a symphony, we step back into the night.

We haven't gone ten steps when the bass straining against my ribs is joined by more drums. Pounding. Throbbing. An entire bass-drum section being played at once. A sound that makes my throat constrict, makes me want to whimper.

Many footsteps, marching in synch.

Bowen whips around and grips my shirt, yanking me down

behind the nearest hiding place—a blue postbox cemented to the sidewalk in front of the apartment building. The two of us barely fit behind it, sandwiched shoulder to shoulder in a crouch, backpacks against the cold metal, waiting, hiding. Icy sweat drips down my back.

Shadows dance on the buildings around us, framed by the flickering, growing light of a moving fire. I peer to my left and see the light's source. Men, dressed in a mishmash of jeans, shorts, T-shirts, tank tops, or no shirts, all filthy and holding burning torches, are coming down the street. They look like the kind of grisly men I remember from road-warrior movies, who wore metal spikes around their necks, had tattoos and piercings, and rode motorcycles. Only, these guys don't have the spikes and tattoos and piercings. They don't need them to give off an air of ferocity. Instead, each man has four thick scars on his left forearm—a marking as deliberate as the tattoo on my hand. But there's a problem. The drumming feet? They don't match the uncoordinated steps these men take.

I look to the right, past Bowen, and understand. *They* look like militia, these men walking down the opposite side of the street in perfect unison, toward the scarred gang of warriors. Well, they *almost* look like militia. Only, instead of the stripes shaved onto the sides of their heads, the sides of their heads are bald, below slightly longer hair, like peach fuzz, on the tops of their heads. But the dark uniforms, guns, Tasers, rigid backs, set mouths, and lockstep walk make them look like militia.

"Bowen," a man's quiet voice calls from the street, from the clean-cut marching men. My mouth falls open and I look at

Bowen, wondering how a man who has just arrived knows we are here. Bowen gasps and presses harder against the postbox, eyes scrunched shut, like a kid playing hide-and-seek who thinks you can't see him if his eyes are covered.

"Company, halt!" a smooth, deep voice calls, and somehow it is familiar, like a song you never forget once you hear the tune, even after a long time has passed. "At attention. Tasers before guns," the voice orders in monotone.

Bowen opens his eyes, and his eyebrows pull together. Sweat gleams on his creased forehead. Slowly, millimeter by millimeter, he peers to the right, around the side of the postbox, and then eases back around, facing me.

"My brother's out there," he breathes. "That's the Inner Guard."

Feet shuffle to a messy halt on the left—the gang of men with torches—but even though they've stopped, something still shuffles in their midst. And growls. I try not to breathe, try not to blink, as I slowly peer around the side of the postbox. And then I try not to bolt. Or scream. Or pee my pants.

I gulp down the scream threatening to be my undoing, and an icy hand finds mine, squeezing an ounce of courage into me.

"What did you see?" Bowen whispers, eyes white-rimmed with fear.

"They have a beast!" I mouth, too terrified to whisper. *"Bound with chains,"* I add, and close my eyes, seeing it all over again. A sleek, glossy, masculine body, the kind that used to grace the cover of fitness magazines—ripped with fine muscle and zero body fat. Only the smooth, taut skin is speckled and slashed with dark flaws. I see the rusted chains, barely glinting in the

torchlight, wrapped around the beast's tethered arms, each ankle, and neck—the kind of chains you put on a dog. I see the four massive, muscle-heavy men giving the beast a wide berth while holding the chains. And burned into my memory are the eyes, looking straight into mine.

Chains rattle and a growl echoes off the building in front of me, and I force myself to take another look. The beast is yanking on its chains. Its muscles, marked with deep gashes that ooze blood, bulge in an effort to get at the postbox where Bowen and I huddle. I whip back around, too scared to take another look.

"It knows we're here," I whisper between gritted teeth. Bowen's hand leaves mine and rests on something on his belt.

"We will not commence this business until you get your pet under control," a calm, educated voice calls, a voice totally wrong for this dark, ruffian- and beast-filled alley. "Bowen, instruct your men to take aim at the beast. Guns, not Tasers."

"Company, aim to kill the beast," the familiar voice from earlier says. And all the pieces fall together, like suddenly hitting a perfect chord on the piano. Duncan Bowen, Dreyden Bowen's brother, is the man out there commanding the Inner Guard. It is his voice that I recognize, so like his younger brother's.

I stare straight ahead at the blank apartment-building front. It is like watching a movie, only, the actors are shadows. And none of it is make-believe. A shadow raises a torch and swings it downward into another shadow. Chains rattle. The second shadow falls to its knees and starts panting. The beast is down. Business can begin.

"That's better," the man says—the man who commands Duncan Bowen and the Inner Guard. A pair of clopping shoes, like dress shoes, echoes in the street, and a shadow moves forward, walks to the edge of the torch-bearing men, and stops.

Bowen—*my* Bowen—eases to the right, head barely around the post box, for a better look.

"Did you bring us the trade?" a man on my left, with a voice like cracked concrete, asks. I stare at the building in front of me, at the interplay of shadows. The shadow with the smooth voice is short and lean. The shadow with the gravel voice is beefy and towers over the other man.

The smaller shadow holds something up, but when the big shadow reaches for it, the first shadow yanks it away. Guns rattle and feet scuff.

"At ease, men," Duncan Bowen orders.

"I will not," the smooth voice purrs—the voice belonging to the smaller man, "part with this until you show me my payment."

The big shadow holds out his arm. Someone steps behind him and places an unidentifiable shadow-object into the man's hand.

The smaller shadow exhales a deep, satisfied breath of air and lunges toward the burly shadow, grabbing at whatever is in his hand. The objects are traded, and the smooth-voiced shadow cradles his object to his chest.

"Careful! It's glass," the big shadow warns. "You break it, I can't bleed my beast for you again. He's new. And he's a Ten. We all took a lot of blood from him, and it has made him weak. And

I still wanna know why you can't get yours from the lab anymore."

"That is none of your business," the smooth voice snaps.

The bigger shadow shrugs. "Suit yourself. Why don't you tell your boys to lower their guns before we turn our backs on you."

A throat is cleared. "There is one other thing," the smooth voice says. A paper rustles. Beside me, Bowen's body grows more taut and his breath hisses between his teeth. "This girl," the man says, and Bowen looks at me.

A rectangle of shadow is passed from the small man to the big man, and the paper rustles again. A grating, stone-crushing laugh vibrates from the bigger shadow. "I haven't seen one like this in years. Look at this girl, boys!" He holds the rectangle overhead.

It starts with whistling, then growling and howling. Soon, the street is filled with the sounds of wild animals snarling, teeth snapping, and panting. And I wonder, who are the *real* beasts in this land of desolation? Is there a difference between these scar-marked, grown men and the tattoo-marked beasts? The men can choose how they act—they still have a semblance of humanity to them. But the beasts have nothing human left in them. Do they have a choice in how they act?

"Her name," the smooth voice calls out over the din, and the noise dies down. "Her name is Fiona Tarsis! And I want you to catch her!"

My heart jolts in my chest, and fear condenses in a damp sheen over every inch of my body.

"Fiona is young, fresh, and not hardened by the streets like the other women you catch! She bears the mark, but that won't make her a hard target for men like you. And . . ." He stops talking, but no one makes a sound. *"She's on your side of the wall!"*

The raging starts again, shadows dancing, fighting with each other, men screaming, howling, tearing their clothes, pounding their chests.

And then the big shadow raises both his hands, dampening the noise from forte to mezzo forte. "What do we do with her when we find her?" he grates out over the sound of his men. "If you think we'll turn her over to you, you'd better have an outrageous reward waiting for us, and I can't guarantee she'll be impeccable on delivery." The roaring dies at the word *delivery,* as if cut off by the sharp blade of a knife.

"You misunderstand me. She *is* the reward. But if you find her—*when* you find her, because I know you will—do not let her get inside the wall!" the smooth voice replies, though the smooth tone is accompanied by a fevered need. "When you find her, kill her. I don't care how. But make all evidence that she existed disappear. Burn her remains."

The roaring starts again, throbbing painfully loud. Torchlights flicker. Men howl, their shadow faces aimed at the dark sky. I try to force myself to blend into blue metal. Become the box.

"Bowen!"

Bowen jumps beside me, his shoe scraping on the cement, a sound way too loud even with the men screaming around us. Someone has to have heard.

I stop breathing, stop moving—even my eyeballs—as I stare

straight ahead at the shadows on the building. One of them noticed the sound of Bowen's scraping shoe. I see the figure uncurl from the ground, see the shadow chains restraining it. Biting my tongue, I peer to my left, around the postbox, and look right into the beast's eyes—eyes that are twin to my own.

"Jonah," I whisper, as sorrow and fear thunder through me. His head tilts to the side and he lunges. Taken off guard, the men holding the chains fall forward with Jonah's momentum and he clangs free, dragging his chains behind him and running straight at me. My eyes grow round, and I shake my head a fervent no—I cannot imagine what will happen if I am caught, if he gives my presence away. And, as if he's the old, gentle Jonah, he pauses, the briefest release of his sculpted muscle. He blinks, looks away, and changes course, veering toward the opposite side of the street, sprinting away on one good ankle, and one ankle that is twisted painfully to the side.

The men erupt, feet pounding the ground. Gunfire echoes over the shocked, furious screams of men, and as if a vortex has sucked everyone away, the street becomes dark and empty in a matter of seconds. Only the smells of smoke and sweat remain, and trash gently flutters to a stop in the street.

Bowen sags against me, his breath ragged. Where our shoulders press together, my T-shirt is sopping with frigid sweat.

"What is going on?" he whispers, his breath like frost against my ice-sweaty skin.

"I don't know." My voice is almost a sob. "Who was that man with the Inner Guard?"

"The governor. From inside the wall. The ruler. My brother's employer," he whispers, still sagging into me as if his bones have been removed.

"Who was the other one? The big guy?" I can still hear his gravelly voice in my head.

Bowen lifts his head and looks at me, wiping damp bangs from his forehead. "Remember the gangs I told you about? The raiders? There are two of them—two main gangs. He's the leader of one of them. He's the man who stole my mom."

CHAPTER 22

My head throbs with tension that has me clenching every muscle in my body, and I don't know if I can go much farther. I push sweat-crunchy bangs from my forehead and force my legs to continue forward.

The glass skyscrapers of downtown Denver reflect the brightening sky, glowing with the promise of a very near sunrise. In between the slender skyscrapers, a few blocks away, the wall looms—a muddle of stacked, rusty train cars and cinderblocks.

Bowen pauses, and I almost walk into him before I realize he's stopped moving. I halt, wanting to fall to the dusty sidewalk and sit, but stay standing.

"Where are we?" I whisper, wobbling on unsteady legs. My voice is out of place in the quiet morning. Bowen tilts his face toward the sky. I follow his gaze and blink at a massive, ornate glass skyscraper that seems to touch the blazing blue sky.

"Marriott," Bowen states, sticking his head through the frame of a glassless revolving door in the building's exact center.

"The hotel?" I ask, wondering if my sluggish brain heard him right.

"Yeah. You need rest. And sometimes there's water in the toilet tanks, in case we run out. And if we are *really* lucky," he says, looking at me with a gleam in his weary eyes, "we might find a room with a bed that hasn't been destroyed. You can sleep in comfort."

In spite of the terror of the night, I smile at the thought of sleeping in a real bed. Bowen smiles back, an expression that reaches his eyes and warms my exhausted body. A moment later his smile fades and he presses a finger to his lips. I cringe and twirl around, expecting attack. A hand softly squeezes my shoulder, and Bowen turns me back to face him.

"It's okay. You're safe. When the militia passed the order to shoot raiders on sight, the raiders stopped coming out in daylight." He nods toward the remnants of the revolving door, presses his finger against his lips again, and tiptoes into the hotel.

Inside, sunlight glints off the glass-speckled marble floor—the glass from the revolving door—and I find myself in a ransacked lobby. Faded, once-red furniture has been pushed to the sides of the room. The stuffing is spilling out of most of the pieces, and I see a rat—a rat!—poke its head out of a hole in a sofa to watch us with beady eyes. Paintings hang crookedly on washed-out walls, and a layer of dust dulls everything.

In the lobby's center sits something out of my dreams. A dusty black grand piano.

A slew of music fills my head, resonates in the ugly minuscule sounds of this dead world. It turns into a haunting melody of snow and ice. Christmas music. At Christmastime I would dress in scarlet velvet trimmed with white lace and play the piano. *This* piano.

Child prodigy.

That's what my mother called me. That's what my teachers called me. That's the name my peers teased me with. That, and Fotard.

I can still hear my music theory teacher's voice: *With those fingers, she's destined to be one of two things in this life. A surgeon or a musician. But who would want to be a surgeon?*

My fingers could fly across the keys faster than human eyes could see, dancing to the music as they created it, brought it to life. If I wasn't doing homework, or spying on the boy across the street, or playing games with Jonah, I was sitting at the piano, filling myself with music—with joy. Or sorrow, depending on the piece. On that day, right before I turned thirteen, it was foreboding that overwhelmed me as I learned Beethoven's Seventh. I'd studied the piece the night before, memorized the translated words of a poem that had been sung to the tune, the words of "Figlio Perduto"—"Lost Son"—about a boy and his father going home, but the boy keeps hearing things and seeing things that his father cannot. And then the Erl King—a fairy king—comes to steal the boy away into another world. Only, the father couldn't see the king.

> "MY FATHER, MY FATHER, HE SEIZES ME FAST,
> FOR SORELY THE ERL KING HAS HURT ME AT LAST."
> THE FATHER NOW GALLOPS, WITH TERROR HALF WILD,
> HE HOLDS IN HIS ARMS THE SHUDDERING CHILD;
> HE REACHES HIS FARMSTEAD WITH TOIL AND DREAD,
> THE CHILD IN HIS ARMS LIES MOTIONLESS, DEAD.

My fingers pounded the keys, the song consuming me, haunting me, making me feel as if I were the one being stolen away by the Erl King's magic.

Dad's voice bellowed into the music room, military fierce. "Quiet!"

My hands jerked off the keys, my toe released the pedal, and I stood from the glossy black bench, shocked.

The television boomed from the other room, turned so loud the windows rattled. I closed the piano, pushed the bench in, and followed the noise.

Jonah and Lis sat on the sofa, leaning toward the television, their eyes wide. Dad sat in his wheelchair beside the sofa, square hands resting on the wheels, attention glued to the TV screen.

I glared at my family. No one had ever yelled at me to be quiet before. I was a prodigy, after all. "Why can't I play the—"

"Shhhh!" they hissed as one. Lis glanced at me, and without speaking a word, I knew something was wrong. She held up her hand and I clasped it and stared at the television, too. And the more I heard, the closer to the television I leaned.

"Because of the direness of the situation, we thought it best to speed matters along," said a man in a gray suit. He stood alone at a podium in front of a group of reporters. The reporters wore white masks over their mouths: the kind doctors and surgeons wore to avoid spreading disease. "If we didn't step in, bees would already be extinct and that would potentially lead to worldwide famine, possibly even the extinction of the human race."

"So, you're saying you fixed the bee problem? Honeybees are no longer on the endangered species list?" a woman from the crowd asked the man in the suit.

The man looked away from her, straightened his red tie, and looked right at the camera and stared, as if staring directly into our family room, staring into every room in America. "Yes. We found a solution," he said, his eyes fastened to mine through the plasma screen. "We have already genetically modified honeybees."

On the bottom of the screen, words zipped by. Flu death toll at a new high. Over fourteen thousand known deaths with thousands more expected. Hospitals too full to admit new cases. Entire East Coast advised to stay indoors. West Coast predicted to follow.

"So, you're saying, in the midst of this monumental flu epidemic, we finally have something to celebrate?" another masked reporter asked.

The man in the suit tugged at the collar of his white shirt, swallowed, and looked down. Slowly, he placed his hands, palms down, on the podium. "No," he said, unable to meet the camera with his eyes. "We modified the bees. But the GenMod bees . . . they killed the other bees. All of them."

Another reporter chimed in, "Well, that's okay, right? As long as they reprod—"

"They're the cause of the flu," the man blurted.

"What?" Lis said, dropping my hand. "How can bees be causing the flu?"

The reporters burst into a flood of questions, raising their hands, trying to be heard over each other.

The man in the gray suit coughed into his balled fist before saying, "We genetically modified the bees' sting to be more powerful, more deadly to its predators. Unfortunately, we discovered that when a human being is stung, the bee's venom causes flu-like symptoms, followed by aggressive behavior and then death. The bee flu is highly contagious, spreading through bodily fluids—something as simple as a cough makes the germs airborne."

Jonah's face drained of color. "The bees? That's why so many people have died? Because of your stupid bees?" he yelled at the television. Lis grabbed my hand once more, holding it tight.

The man, his face turning a sickly shade of green, tugged on the collar of his shirt again and pointed to a reporter who stood frantically waving his hand. The reporter tore the surgical mask from his mouth. "So kill them! Exterminate them!" he cried, his voice rising to near panic.

"We tried," the man muttered, eyes full of misery, shoulders slumped.

"And?"

He looked right into the camera again. Right into the eyes of America. "We modified them to withstand all known pesticides. We have come up with a new pesticide that kills them, but it is worse than the bee flu—a last resort. We're not sure if anything will survive its effects."

"They're going to kill the whole country," Dad whispered, knuckles white from his grip on his wheelchair wheels.

"Use the pesticide!" a reporter yelled. More join in, chanting, "Pest-i-cide! Pest-i-cide!"

"Wait!" The man at the podium raised his hands over his head. "There's hope. We've manufactured a vaccine, a sort of antivenin derived from the bees. There's only a limited supply, so . . ."

CHAPTER 23

"Fo?" Bowen is in front of me, his hand shaking my arm. "Are you all right?"

I blink away the memory and look at him. "The bees?" I whisper.

"Bees? What about them?"

"Are they dead?"

Bowen nods. "Yeah. They used some newly invented heavy-duty pesticide after they realized the vaccine was worse than the flu. Only problem was, it killed everything—bugs, birds, cattle, small animals, trees, grass, crops, even some people. That's why everything is dead."

My brain starts to freak out and I begin to tremble. My eyes search for a distraction, anything to take my mind off the bees, and lock on the piano. "I played the piano," I whisper, staring at the grand piano, swaying with the remembered pulse of music.

"I know," Bowen says, his voice drawing my gaze to his face. His eyes grow far away, clouded over with memory. "I could hear you from my bedroom if I opened the window. That's why I was always sick in the winter. My window was always open. And on summer nights when my dad was home yelling at my mom, I'd get my sleeping bag and pillow and put them on top of his semi, so I could fall asleep to your music. Remember in third grade? You hit me in the face with your backpack when we were walking home from school?"

A smile tugs at the corners of my mouth. "Yeah. I remember you called me Fotard and said playing the piano was stupid. So I stomped on your foot and then hit you."

He smiles. "Your mom made you write an apology letter to me, but you were too scared to deliver it, so you had Jonah bring it to my house. It said something like, 'I'm sorry I hit you, but if you don't stop teasing me about piano, I'll hit you again.' Did you know that when Jonah delivered the note he told me if I ever talked to you again, he and his friends would beat the crap out of me?"

My mouth falls open in surprise. "My brother stood up for me? Is that why you never talked to me again? Because of Jonah?"

He shrugs. "That and you were always walking around with your nose in the air, always acting better than everyone else."

"I was not!" I snap, indignant.

He takes a step closer to me, so that there are only a couple of inches of air separating us. "The only reason I teased you in the first place . . ." He pauses, brushes my bangs out of my eyes,

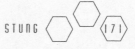

and I am painfully aware of the lack of space between us. "I teased you because I didn't know how else to talk to you."

"Oh," I whisper, at a loss for words.

He grins and puts a finger to his lips, nods toward a door at the far end of the lobby.

We pass the piano, and I reach toward the dusty keys.

Bowen's hand clamps around my wrist. "No. We don't know if this place is safe. Come on." He slides his fingers from my wrist to my hand and loops them in mine.

With my hand in his, held safe, it seems like everything will be okay. I tighten my fingers in his, and we cross the silent lobby to a stairwell filled with sunlit windows and littered with dead mice and bugs, which crunch beneath my shoes. We go up and up and up, my legs growing weaker and weaker with each step. When we get to level fifteen, Bowen pauses, letting go of my hand. There's a little window on the door leading to floor fifteen. Bowen peers through it and puts his hand on the doorknob.

"Don't make a sound," he whispers, and turns the knob, slipping through to the fifteenth floor. I follow and we creep down the dim hallway, past door after door—all closed—until we come to one that is barely cracked open, number 1513. Bowen presses his ear to the metal and closes his eyes. I count to thirty before his eyes open. He shakes his head and goes to the next door, 1515, also open a crack, and presses his ear to it. I wait again, adrenaline pumping, and after a solid sixty seconds, he pushes the door. It swings silently open with a breeze of warm air. Before the door comes to a stop the gun is on his shoulder, pointing into the bright room.

"Wait here," he whispers, and walks into the room. Balanced on the balls of his feet, he swings his gun from side to side, finger on the trigger. Poised for attack.

A sickening panic settles over me as I watch him disappear around a corner. He's not wearing a Kevlar vest, yet he's the one at risk. The seconds draw out as I wait for him to come back. Or get attacked. Or shot. As I wait to lose the only familiar thing in this world, I can't breathe.

He steps back into view and motions me in as he sets his gun on a mattress hanging halfway off a box spring. I step inside, but instead of shutting the door behind me, I stride over to Bowen and throw my arms around his neck, holding him close and pressing my face into his shoulder. He stiffens beneath my touch, and I remember.

I am his greatest fear.

But then his arm loops around me, backpack and all, and he turns his face into the side of my neck, his breath on my skin, his touch leeching the panic from my muscles.

After a long minute he pulls away and looks at me, his eyes devouring mine. Without taking my arms from his neck I stare up at him.

"What was that for?" he asks.

"Watching you walk into the room, I thought of how I would feel if anything happened to you." My voice trembles.

Bowen studies my face, his eyes moving from my eyes to my mouth and back again. "How *would* you feel?" he asks, his voice a whisper.

"I've already lost everything that I love. You're all I have left."

My face starts to burn as I realize what I've almost said. That I love him. I hide my face against his shoulder, too embarrassed to meet his eyes.

"You're just tired." He gently pries my arms from his neck. "You'll feel different after some sleep," he adds without meeting my eyes.

I know sleep won't make a difference, but I don't tell him. He steps from me and pushes the bare mattress back onto the box spring.

The room is covered in a layer of dust. The window is broken, and the curtains that once covered it are in a mouse-eaten pile on the floor. Bowen slips his arms out of his backpack and sets it beside the bed. I do the same, dropping my backpack to the floor with a clunk, and stretch my tight shoulders.

"Sleep," Bowen says, taking the sleeping bag from my backpack and unzipping it. "I'll keep watch." He spreads it over the mattress, and I lie down. Next, he riffles through his backpack and brings out a can of something and a water bottle, then steps in front of a mirror affixed to the wall above a dust-coated dresser. Opening the water bottle, he splashes the left side of his head, the side with four vertical lines shaved into it. Next he squirts mint-green gel out of the can and rubs it over the four lines until it turns white and foamy. From his belt he takes a knife and drags it through the foam. The knife leaves bald skin in its wake.

"What are you doing?" I ask, climbing from the bed to stand beside him, staring with fascination.

"Shaving," he answers, never taking his eyes from his reflection.

"I see that, but why?"

"I'm not part of the militia anymore. I'm on their most-wanted list, right up there with the raiders." He looks at me and touches his injured shoulder. "I'm on the shoot-to-kill list. I can't go back."

"Well, then, what are you going to do?" I ask, wondering if he can hear the hope in my voice. If he can't go back, maybe he'll run. I want to run with him. And never come back. And be with him forever.

He sighs and splashes water over the pale bald patch above his ear. "After I get you safely to the lab, I'll try to survive on my own. Try to make it to Wyoming."

Mention of the lab makes my hope turn hard and cold, makes the soft flesh in the creases of my elbows hurt. I fold my arms, pressing on the fading bruises. "I don't want to be the lab's guinea pig. Let me come with you. We'll survive together," I plead, my voice quiet with desperation. "I'm good with a gun. I'll learn to keep up. I'll help you survive, become your ally."

Bowen shakes his head. "Too dangerous," he says, wiping his knife on the edge of the dusty dresser, leaving a glob of shaving cream and hair.

I grit my teeth and glare at my tattoo, hating it more than I've hated anything in my life. It is a representation of everything Bowen hates and fears. Which means me.

"I don't think I'm going to turn into a beast, though," I say, still staring at my hand. "And if I start to feel signs of it, I'll leave. I swear. Please. Don't take me to the lab. Take me with you." I look up from my tattoo and stare at his reflection in the mirror as he slips the knife into a black sheath attached to his belt.

"It's not too dangerous for *me*. It's dangerous for *you*. What if I can't protect you?" He won't look at me. He turns and climbs onto the bed, knees bent, back pressed against the headboard. He picks up his gun and balances it on his knees. I climb onto the other side of the bed and curl up on my side, my arm beneath my head, my back to him, and stare out the broken window.

"I'm willing to take that risk," I murmur. "Because I don't want to leave you, Dreyden. I'd rather take my chances on the outside. With you."

He shifts, the mattress sagging beneath his weight, making me roll into him. When he speaks, his mouth is right above my ear. "I shot my mother in the head. It took me two tries to kill her," he whispers.

I turn and look up into his dead, cold eyes. His jaw muscles pulse.

"Why?" I ask, appalled.

"The raiders caught her. For two days I tried to get her free. For two nights, she screamed for someone to kill her. So on the third morning, when the sun rose, I finally got up the nerve." Darkness haunts his eyes. "It's not safe out there, Fo. I don't want to have to kill you, too. Life in the lab will be a lot more pleasant. Trust me. And you never know. Maybe one day they'll find a cure."

He climbs off the bed and I close my eyes, trying to forget the horror of his words, his hopeless eyes.

CHAPTER 24

I dream of grass and honey and flowers. Sunshine warms my skin and rose petals brush my lips, a feathery touch that makes me stir. I open my eyes, and Bowen's finger pauses against my lower lip. Slowly, he pulls his hand from my mouth. I stare into his grass-green eyes and wait for my heart to burst.

"You were talking in your sleep," he whispers. "Something about honey." He is curled on his side facing me, our knees touching, our faces mere inches apart. I look at his lips and remember how they felt against mine—smooth as honey and just as sweet. They curve into a warm, lazy smile. "Fo."

"What?" I look into his eyes again.

"You were staring at my mouth."

I squeeze my eyes shut and cover my face with my hands, and Bowen laughs.

"I have a surprise for you," he says, touching my cheek with cool fingers that smell like soap and bring heat to my skin. I open my eyes and stare at him. His hair is slightly damp, as if he's just had a shower and he smells like shampoo. "Come here."

I follow him into the bathroom and see nothing but a couple of dusty, sun-bleached suitcases that used to be some shade of purple and several empty water bottles. He points to the tub. Two inches of water shimmer in it—clean water, clear water. Bowen points to the sink next. A toothbrush and travel-size toothpaste are on the counter beside a full water bottle. And a comb.

"The water's not warm, or anything . . . ," he says, rubbing his hand over the bald patch above his ear

"Does this place *have* running water?" I ask, staring at the grimy sink.

He shakes his head and his tan cheeks flush, a hint of pink beneath the healthy gold glow. "While you were sleeping I gathered water from the toilet tanks in the hotel and carried it here in water bottles. It's not dirty or anything . . . I thought you'd like to get clean."

More than anything, I'd like to get clean. I stare at Bowen, and my heart grows too big for my chest. A sudden assault of tears blurs my eyes.

Bowen, seeing the tears, turns to leave but pauses in the doorway, not looking at my face. "There's stuff in those suitcases that should fit you, too." He shuts the door.

I peel off my grimy things, unwind the tattered binding from my breasts, and climb into the tepid water. When I sit, it only reaches halfway up my thighs. Even so, the water is heaven.

On the side of the tub are a little soap packet, a tiny bottle of shampoo, and a tiny bottle of conditioner. I lie back and scrub my scalp with the entire bottle of shampoo, then work the conditioner into my hair. By the time I've soaped every square inch of my body, the water is brown and I am too disgusted to sit in it any longer. I drain the tub and climb out.

Hot summer air whisks the moisture from my skin. Facing the mirror, I brush my teeth, then run the comb through my short, ugly hair, parting my long bangs to the side so my entire face shows.

The face in the mirror is odd, nearly a stranger's. Only my brown eyes are the same, set above unfamiliar, angled cheekbones and a mouth full of white teeth.

I rummage through the suitcases and find purple cotton underwear, a white camisole tank top, and a pink sundress. I pull the clothes over my clean body and twirl in front of the mirror. I feel like a girl again—almost like the old me. With a goofy smile plastered to my grown-up face, I leave the bathroom.

When I come out, Bowen stands looking out the window at the evening sky, his dark brows drawn together, completely lost in thought.

"All clean," I say, blushing.

He turns from the window, the beginning of a smile on his lips, and his face goes blank. And then he frowns. His eyes move all the way down to my bare feet and back up, lingering on my obviously female chest before returning to my eyes.

"No," he says. "You cannot wear that."

I look down at the sundress. "What's wrong with it?"

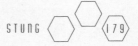

He drags a hand over his weary face. "You look like a . . . *woman*. It's not safe."

I think of the raiders and look back down at the dress. "When we leave, I'll change," I say. "But for now, it's comfortable. I feel like the old me."

Bowen presses his hands to his temples and looks back out the window. "Fo, you're not safe from me."

I stare at his back for a long moment, at the gun slung over his shoulder, the Taser on his belt. "You're going to shoot me for wearing a sundress?"

He turns his head and looks at me with danger-filled eyes. In three steps he's in front of me, his hands on my bare shoulders, fingers digging into my skin. "Fo, I'm a man, and you're a beautiful woman. But you're also a Level Ten, and when I look at you, especially when you're dressed like this, I can't think straight, because even though my brain tells me you're the most dangerous thing I've ever encountered, my heart . . . my *body*—" His mouth snaps shut and he stares deep into my eyes.

I get it, what his heart and body are doing, because mine are doing it, too. I ache for Dreyden Bowen, for everything about him. His smell, his touch, the sound of his voice, his presence. I tilt my head to the side and trail my fingers over his freshly shaved jaw line. He shuts his eyes and leans into my touch.

"I'm sorry, Dreyden. I'll change into something else," I whisper, letting my hand drop. His eyes open.

"*I'm* sorry. It's just, if I let my guard drop, even for a second . . ." His cheeks flush bright pink and he takes a deep breath. "I won't be able to keep my hands off of you."

I walk to the bathroom and find a pair of baggy jeans, an oversize T-shirt that hangs halfway down my thighs, and the strap of fabric that binds my breasts flat against my chest. When I come out Bowen is lying on the bed beside his gun, hands behind his head, ankles crossed, staring up at the ceiling.

"I need to sleep," he says. Without taking his eyes from the ceiling, he slides the gun across the mattress toward me. "Will you keep watch?"

I take the gun and nod, but he doesn't see. "Yes," I say.

"Don't use the flashlight. The raiders will see it through the window," he says, and his eyes slip shut. On bare feet, I walk to the short hallway beside the door and sit with my back to the wall, gun balanced between my bent knees.

Bowen sleeps, a restless sleep that makes him thrash and flinch. And when he thrashes about on the sleeping bag, it is my name he cries out. Sometimes he screams it and I cling to the gun, listening for the sound of anyone else in the hotel. Because if anyone's around, they know we're here now.

The sun sets and darkness creeps into the room. A crescent moon and stars illuminate the shadows, shining in through the window and casting a perfect ice-blue square over Bowen's sleeping body. With the darkness, Bowen's thrashing intensifies, my name spoken more often, accompanied by pleading whimpers or violent growls.

That he fears me so badly brings tears to my eyes. I hang my head, let my forehead rest on my knees, and try not to cry.

After he's been asleep for several hours and the moonglow has moved to the far side of the room, Bowen suddenly lurches, spine taut, and screams, "Fiona! No! Stop!" He keeps screaming and thrashing, mumbling words I can't understand.

Sick to my stomach, I set the gun on the floor and pad over to the bed. The sleeping bag is in a wadded ball beneath him, his shirt twisted around his torso.

"Bowen," I whisper. He whimpers and gasps my name, rolling onto his side, his body curled into a protective ball. "Bowen, wake up." I touch his damp forehead, and he flinches away from my fingers, curling even tighter into a fetal ball. I place both my hands on his cheeks. "Dreyden," I say. His eyes flutter open and focus on my face. He grabs me, pulling me against him hard, and I wonder if he's gong to thrust a knife into my ribs or strangle me with his bare hands.

"Fiona," he whispers, tightening his arms around my shoulders. I freeze, my head on his chest, my body beside his, his arms anchoring me there. After a minute his heart slows beneath my ear and begins to beat at a normal rate, and his arms loosen the slightest bit. Convinced I'm not about to die, I relax into him.

"Was it bad?" I whisper, imagining myself tearing him limb from limb in his nightmare.

"Yeah. Worst nightmare I've ever had. Even worse than after my mom died." His arms tighten. I spread my hand over his chest and, through his sweat-damp shirt, feel his pulse beneath my fingers.

"Did I tear your beating heart from your body?" I ask, struggling not to cry.

He lifts his head to look down at me. "What?"

"In your dream. Did I kill you and eat your heart?"

His head falls back onto the mattress and his ribs rise and fall with a deep sigh. "You tearing out my heart would have been a pleasant alternative to my nightmare."

I cringe and bury my face against his chest. His hand moves up to my hair and he trails his fingers through it. "Fiona. Look at me."

There's something in his voice—I know what he's about to say is monumental. I brace myself for bad news and look up.

"I'm not taking you to the lab." His arms fall away, and he rolls out from under me, climbing off the bed.

"You're not?" I ask, sitting, wondering if I heard him right.

"No. We're going to run, you and I together. But you have to promise me one thing."

My heart starts hammering in my chest. "What?"

"You *always* have my gun with you. And you *always* keep one bullet in the magazine. If you get caught, you use it. On yourself. Can you agree to that?"

I stare at his black silhouette. "Yes," I whisper.

"I'm going to get some supplies and another gun." He moves about the dark room gathering things, unzipping and zipping the backpacks. And then he is beside the bed. His hand finds mine, and something comes around my wrist. A tiny light glows, showing that it is 2:08 a.m. I am wearing his watch.

"Put your shoes on and leave them on, even if you sleep. If you have to run, you won't have time to waste putting them on. And make sure your backpack is always ready to go. If I'm not back by seven a.m. tomorrow—roughly twenty-nine hours from now—go to the north gate and turn yourself in. They'll get you to the lab."

His words jolt me. "Wait. If you're *not back*? You mean, if something happens to you and you die?"

"Yeah, something like that." He stands in the small patch of moonlight shining in through the window and pulls off his shirt. Taking the Kevlar vest from the floor, he zips it around his chest, and then puts his shirt back on. Next, he places something on the bed beside me. I reach out and feel dense, heavy metal. I sit up, afraid.

"You're not taking your rifle? But what if—"

His fingers cover my lips. "Fo. Keep yourself safe. I have my Taser. I'll be fine," he whispers.

I back away from his hand. "But what if you're not?" I cry.

He turns and walks away, and I can practically see the dark shadow of death marching on his heels. Before he can open the hotel room door, I scramble from the bed and run to him, throwing myself between him and the exit, wrapping my arms around his neck. Tears fill my eyes, so I press my face against his shoulder. His arms encircle me and squeeze.

"Fo, I'll come back," he says. I sniffle and press my face harder against him. He tries to pull away, but I won't let go. His hand finds my chin and forces it up, his thumb sweeping over my wet cheek. "Tears? For me?" he whispers.

I can't speak—just stare at his shadowed face.

"Fiona, I . . ." His fingers slide to the nape of my neck. Our noses bump and then his lips touch mine, finishing his sentence better than any words could have. His hands pull me closer and his lips press harder, start moving on top of mine. My mouth moves with his, my breath flows with his, my heart hammers against his. My salty tears make their way onto our tongues and are forgotten.

I push my hands under his backpack and run them over his back, over the unyielding Kevlar vest, up to his shoulders, and slip them beneath his sleeves against his warm skin. He groans, and his hands pull against the small of my back. Beneath his sleeves, I trace his muscles, find the teeth-mark scar and freshly scabbed bullet wound, and Bowen pulls his mouth from mine and gasps. He rests his forehead on mine and frames my face with his hands. They smell like metal and soap and shaving cream.

"Fiona, I . . ." The words disappear, their ending unspoken. I find his lips with mine, as if I've known how to kiss my entire life, and his hands tangle in my butchered hair. I taste Bowen and fresh tears, yet I'm no longer crying. I take my hands from his shoulders and press them to his face. Tears are streaming over his cheeks, down to our mouths.

I pull my mouth from his, and he buries his face against my neck, holding me tight. His body shudders against mine, and his tears come faster, soaking my skin. I cradle his head, my hand moving over his hair.

"It's okay, Dreyden," I whisper. "It's going to be okay." My words make his body shake.

He pulls away and peers down at me, his face nothing more than a silhouette in the darkness. "No, it's not okay," he says, voice ragged. "In my dream tonight, you were captured by raiders.

And no matter what I did, I couldn't save you. And I couldn't bring myself to kill you. They . . ." He takes a deep breath and pulls me against him. "You might as well have eaten my heart straight from my living body. I would rather die a thousand times at your hands than see you captured. Even if you eat my heart. Because you already own it."

He holds me for a long time, neither of us speaking. A long time later, he whispers, "Remember what I said about seven a.m." He touches my face with one hand and opens the door with the other. Darkness swallows him as he steps into the hall.

"Bowen, wait," I whisper. He stops and looks at me. "I love you." I'm glad for the dark that hides my flaming cheeks.

Bowen stands perfectly still for a drawn-out minute and then he steps up to me, cradles the back of my head in his hand, and presses his mouth to mine. Without a word, he releases me and strides into the hall's darkness.

CHAPTER 25

I sleep until the sun rises, heating the hotel room like an oven. With the gun in my lap, I sit on the bed, eager to run away with Bowen, watching the seconds tick away on his watch. I bring it to my nose and inhale. The band holds his scent.

When the watch shows twelve o'clock, I'm too restless to continue sitting. I go into the bathroom and sort through the old suitcases, putting things we might find useful—fingernail clippers, mouthwash, concealer, panties, and oversize T-shirts—into one pile, and the things we won't need—other makeup, lingerie, dresses, and high heels—in another. At the bottom of the suitcase I find a news magazine dated the year I turned thirteen—four years ago. I take it and the pile of useful supplies into the bedroom and drop them on the mattress, then lean against the headboard and open the magazine. The headlines make my head spin.

"New Bee-Antivenin Vaccine Discovered to Trigger Violent Behavior in Recipients."

"The Price of Life May Be Death."

"Cities Urged to Take Individual Government Control—White House Can No Longer Offer National Protection."

"Roving Gangs Taking to Streets, Preying on Women."

"Pediatrician-Induced Coma in Nine-Year-Old After Parental Consent. 'Anything to Stop Our Daughter from Attacking Us.'"

Reading the headlines, a fog seems to lift from my brain. I can remember hearing things like this, remember screaming at my mom that the vaccine wasn't making me violent. *I* wasn't going to start attacking people.

Lis sat behind me, humming, her back against my headboard, and ran the hairbrush through my long hair. Since I wasn't feeling well she'd skipped her nursing classes and had been sitting with me all afternoon while Mom took Jonah to the doctor's again.

"Do you want me to braid it?" Lis asked, gathering my hair at the nape of my neck. Before I could answer, Mom walked into my room, arms crossed over her chest, sting-proof netting still pinned in her hair like a bridal veil. At least she'd remembered to take it off her face when she came inside this time.

"How is Jonah?" Lis asked before Mom could say a word. "Where is Jonah?"

Mom's lips thinned and she studied the carpet. I leaned away from Lis and shivered—not because Jonah had gone to the doctor again; he'd been going on a weekly basis for the last two months—but because I was freezing on the outside while a fever burned hot inside of me, making my blood pulse through my body at an alarming rate.

"What did the doctor say?" Lis asked, dropping my hair around my shoulders before climbing from the bed to stand beside Mom. I buried my hands in the quilt's folds so Mom couldn't see the veins bulging beneath my skin.

"The doctor put Jonah in a straightjacket. That way he can't keep pulling out the morphine drip." Tears pooled in the corners of Mom's eyes and trickled out. Lis put her arms around Mom and spoke quietly in her ear.

Heat filled me. Sweat broke out on the bridge of my nose, and my blood vessels began aching with my pulse. I pushed my quilt off and swiped my hand over my forehead. "I don't see why you still give him morphine. It doesn't help anymore," I blurted, glaring at Mom.

Mom nodded and her bottom lip quivered. "I know. The doctor said there's another alternative." She sniffled and wiped her nose on the back of her hand, and for some reason that made me even hotter.

I clenched and released my jaw, poked my tongue in the hole where I'd lost my last baby molar. "What alternative?" I asked, fanning my face with the corner of the quilt.

"A medically induced coma. It might buy him some time while they try to find a cure." Mom looked up, right into my eyes, and I felt like I might throw up. Her tears were gone, replaced with bright, eager hope.

"No!" I shouted between clenched teeth. "You can't do that to him!" My body started to tremble, my heart beating too fast, pumping too much

boiling blood through me. Sweat trickled down my temple and dripped from my chin.

"He's scheduled for the procedure tomorrow morning, so we're taking you to the hospital tonight to say good-bye," she said.

Like I could say good-bye. Jonah had stopped talking a month ago. "Is Dad okay with all this? He's not going to allow it, you know. He loves us too much," I retorted. He always stood up to Mom when it came to really important things.

Lis gasped. Mom put a hand up to her mouth and tried to stifle a sob. "Honey. Fiona. Your father's dead, remember? Last month . . . Jonah . . ."

An image of my father flashed into my head, where he lay dead on the music room floor, his wheelchair overturned beside the piano. Jonah, my sweet, gentle brother, crouched at his side, weeping, muscles bulging. "I didn't mean to," he kept saying over and over. That was the last time he spoke.

Blood surged through my body, faster than before, making my ears ring. "There has to be another option," I whispered. "You can't do this to Jonah! Lis! Talk some sense into her!" My breathing sped up and I pressed on my temples.

"Fo, you're going in, too. To the hospital." I could barely hear her over the siren shrieking in my brain.

Slowly I climbed from the bed and took a step toward Mom and Lis. Pushing harder on my temples, I squeezed my eyes shut. "For a morphine pump?" I asked.

Mom didn't answer. I opened my eyes and took a step closer. Fresh tears shimmered in her eyes, and one eye was swollen and framed in black. I blinked and looked at my knuckles, black and blue and still swollen. I had put that bruise on her earlier that day, before Lis came over, before Mom went to the doctor's office. How had I forgotten?

"No," Mom said. "We're not trying morphine on you, honey. We are having the doctor induce comas in both of you."

At Mom's words, tears filled Lis's eyes and gushed out. Seeing my sister so sad made me want to scream. Made my skin feel too tight. Made me want to tear at my skin until it came off.

Instead, I jumped on Mom and tried to claw her eyes out.

I chuck the magazine across the room and curl up onto my side, letting tears splatter over my nose and onto the sleeping bag. My father is dead. He didn't die when the wall was built. He has been dead for four years. How could I forget that? Forget the fact that Jonah flew into a violent rage and killed him? I should have remembered. And my poor mother. I punched her in the face. Attacked her. And now she's most likely dead and I'll never get to apologize. I wrap my arms around my head and weep, soaking the sleeping bag with tears. Somehow I fall asleep.

Bowen lives in my dreams, in a world of green and gold, budding with new life. My mom is there, too, lazing beneath the shadow of a tree, netting covering her face, with Lis, my sister, at her side, mixing honey into porcelain teacups for the three of them. Lis sees me and smiles, swinging her long blond hair off her shoulder and motioning me to join them. Only, I can't move. My hand, my tattoo, is stuck to the side of a towering wall, and I can't pull it free.

Bowen waves me over, mouths the words, *Come on, it's time to go.* I pull harder but am stuck fast. His face falls, as if he thinks I don't want to come, don't want to run with him. He stands, shakes his head in disappointment, and walks off until he disappears against the horizon. Mom and Lis pack up the tea party and wave good-bye, blowing me kisses and leaving me in the looming shadow of the wall.

I wake sweating, still lying atop a sleeping bag in a deserted hotel, trapped in a blazing world. Sweat trickles down my neck and pools in my collarbone. And I am alone.

Night comes too slowly, a darkness that brings fear. It has been nineteen hours since Bowen left, and every hour that passes without his return, I imagine worse things happening to him. And worse things happening to me if he never comes back.

I hold the gun and stare at blackness, listening to the sound of air moving in and out of my lungs and the pulse beating faintly in my ears. My eyelids grow heavy, but my mind refuses to relax enough to sleep—anxiety claws at my nerves and eats at my belly.

The hours drag by. I find myself looking at Bowen's watch every half hour. And then every twenty minutes. And then every ten. By the time it is six in the morning, I look at his watch every five minutes, and every time I check, every five minutes that passes, it seems more impossible that he is coming back. I want to scream with frustration.

I lean against the headboard and force my breathing to slow. The anxiety has found its way into my muscles, my brain, even my lungs. But even slowed breathing does nothing to soften anxiety's fierce grip. I look away from the minuscule glow outlining the window. Dawn means Bowen isn't coming back. If I refuse to see the dawn, maybe it won't come.

I sit up tall and hold my breath. The air has shifted, a bare touch of breeze that cools my damp face. The hotel door eases open, slowly swinging wider. Hope and fear battle inside me, mingling with the ever-present panic. I lift the rifle to my shoulder and rest my finger on the trigger, hoping to hear Bowen's reassuring voice.

A shadow slips into the room, a gaunt wisp of a person, accompanied by the smell of the tunnels. All my hope fades with that smell.

"Arrin? Er—Arris," I whisper.

"Hurry! And it's Arrin. I only pretend to be a boy when it suits me," she whispers, and steps back out the open door.

"Wait! I can't go. If Bowen comes back and I'm not here . . ."

"He won't be coming. Come here and I'll show you why."

With rifle in hand, I climb from the bed and follow. The hall is black after the small amount of light from the hotel room. The smell of Arrin is what I follow. When she's halfway down the hall, she opens a door and the light of dawn stretches into the hallway. Heart pounding, I follow her into another hotel room.

She goes past the bed and straight to the broken window, pointing. I follow her and look. From up here I can see the whole city. It looks perfect, as if nothing has changed. Until I notice the complete lack of human life, complete lack of movement and sound.

A cool breeze flits through the broken window, carrying with it the scent of soil and grass. I fill my lungs with the mineral-rich fragrance and sigh the air back out. Surely I must be dreaming.

But then I gag on the smell of Arrin and wonder if I imagined the good smell.

The breeze stirs the air, and I smell green things once more.

"What is that smell?" I whisper, leaning toward the window. Arrin points again. We are close to the wall, maybe two blocks away. And from fifteen floors up, I can see what is on the other side of the wall. My eyes grow wide, and a yearning fills my chest, like my heart is trying to claw its way free.

Patchwork fields of green and gold fill the land inside the wall, where City Park Golf Course and the zoo used to be. Houses and buildings frame the green-and-gold fields. Men and women are walking toward the fields, hoes and shovels over their shoulders, baskets on their arms.

Something flickers inside my brain. A familiarity I can't explain, the feeling that I've been in there, seen the skyline framed by stars. A fleeting image of blue eyes and hushed words fills my mind.

"Now, look down there," Arrin whispers, shattering my thoughts. She puts a dirt-caked finger to her lips, warning me to be silent. I peer over the side of the window frame and stare down at the shadowed streets and rooftops below. For several minutes I stay there, waiting for something to happen. When nothing does, I look at Arrin with raised eyebrows.

"Look harder," she says softly, her eyes never leaving the street. I look again, following her gaze. And then I see it. Or them. And I forget to breathe.

They are hiding, squeezed into doorways, lurking in broken

windows, crouched on rooftops. And they are men, not beasts, with four thick scars in their forearms—the men Bowen and I saw two nights ago. Some of them hold guns. Knives and base-ball bats are in the hands of others. They are absolutely still, every single one of them looking in the same direction. I follow their gaze and stand tall.

Huddled in a shallow doorway is Bowen.

CHAPTER 26

Bowen has his back pressed against another man's—Tommy's. Bowen holds a grenade in one hand; the other hand pinches the pin. Tommy aims his rifle toward the street.

Arrin claws at my arm and forces me back down. "They'll see you," she warns, her eyes flashing.

"Then let them see me!" I say, my voice too loud. "Bowen is—" I am thrown backward, a hot, grimy hand clasped against my mouth, bony legs straddling my hips. Metal presses against my neck—Arrin's knife.

"Shut up or I will kill you. I didn't bring you here so you could get me caught!"

Anger warms my blood, makes my muscles taut. I yank Arrin's hand from my mouth and knock her other hand away from my throat, not caring if her knife cuts me. "Then leave," I say, glaring into her blue eyes. "I have to help Bowen or they'll kill him. And I don't *care* if I die trying." Because without Bowen, life will hold nothing for me.

"They *won't* kill you, Fo." Arrin's knife hand moves lightning fast, aiming for my neck again, but I grab it and hold it suspended in the air. Arrin raises one thick eyebrow. "They won't kill you," she says again, trembling with the effort to get her hand free from mine. "You'll only wish they did."

Something in her eyes speaks louder than words, making me more scared about my future than I have ever been before. A future as a slave, without Bowen.

"They never kill women. The women end up killing themselves, if they are lucky enough to find a weapon," Arrin says, a smug smile tugging at one side of her mouth, as if she knows she's won.

"All right. I'll be quiet," I whisper. "Just get off me."

She's off in a flash, shaking out her wrists as if I've hurt her. I swallow and hug the rifle to me, then stand. Without making a sound, I peer over the side of the window. I rest the rifle on my shoulder and take aim at the man closest to Bowen, tightening my finger on the trigger.

The rifle is jerked aside, and Arrin shoves her face in front of mine. "Are you bloody crazy? If you shoot one of them, they'll all come for us! I brought you up here so you'd know I'm not lying!"

"Lying about what?" I whisper.

"If you want to survive, you have to leave with me right now. I know a way inside the wall through the tunnels. *I'll* take you to the lab and collect the reward."

I cannot leave. Not when Bowen's down there facing almost-certain death.

"It's what Bowen would want, because there's no way they're going to let him walk away alive," she says, as if she can read my mind.

My hands start to tremble, so I hug the rifle to my chest. Can I leave him there and save myself? It *is* what he would want, and I know it. Just thinking it makes me feel as if I've been torn in two. "No. I have to help Bowen."

"You can't. He and Tommy have been sitting there all night, hoping the raiders would forget about them. We've got to run before it's too late. I'll show you where—"

"They've been there all night?" I gasp.

Arrin nods. "Why do you think it took me so long to get to you? I had to sneak like I've never snuck before."

Completely unconcerned for my own safety, I stand tall, shove Arrin aside, and put the rifle back on my shoulder, balancing my elbow on the windowsill for a steadier shot. Like a beacon of hope, the sun crests the horizon and shines on me, gleaming against the gun. Bowen's head comes up, his face turned toward mine, toward the flash of sunlight on metal. He waves at me to get down, but I've already decided what needs to be done.

I point the rifle at a rooftop half a block away, at the man closest to me. He's holding a gun, pointing it toward Bowen's hiding place. I take a deep breath and close my eyes, knowing this is the most important shot I will ever take in my life. And probably the last. My father's voice speaks in my head, teaching me how to aim a gun all over again. *It's just like learning to play the piano—all in the fingers*. As the air leaves my lungs, I open my eyes, brace for the recoil, and slowly squeeze the trigger. The sound of gunfire echoes off sunlit buildings.

I don't wait to see if I've hit him to find my next target. I aim and shoot again. And a third time.

"He pulled the pin!" Arrin whispers, her words barely making it past my ringing ears. I look at Bowen and Tommy. Bowen stands and chucks the grenade down the road, then he and Tommy run in the other direction. Gunfire fills the quiet morning. Bowen lurches and falls to the ground, and my heart misses a beat. Did he get shot? Is he dead? Tommy crouches down and pulls Bowen back to his feet. And then the grenade explodes, shaking the hotel, deafening my ringing ears, and creating a cloud of dust that hides Bowen and Tommy from view.

"We have to get out of here!" Arrin says, standing. Her voice sounds muted, like I'm hearing it through water. She darts toward the door. I take one final look below and swallow a surge of dread. While Bowen's hidden by dust, I've been seen. The men too far from the explosion to be hurt are pointing at me. Guns go off and bullets whiz by my head or send sprays of glass flying from the building. And men are running toward the hotel.

"Oh, crap." I sprint after Arrin.

CHAPTER 27

I sprint down the hall to the stairs, but before I make it to the thirteenth floor I hear the sound of feet thumping in the stairwell below, of someone coming up. Arrin stops and waits for me.

"They're about to catch us. No mercy," she says, her eyes hard. "Kill before asking questions." A knife appears in her hand, and she pivots on the balls of her feet, braced for a fight. I balance the gun on my shoulder and wait. The thumping of feet grows louder. And louder. When the sound of heavy breathing accompanies the feet, I know we are about to die.

Men come into view, and all I focus on is the place on a broad chest where I have to put the bullet. In spite of the gun pointed at them, they don't slow. I grit my teeth and find the trigger.

"No!"

I squeeze, and the gun discharges a split second before it is knocked out of my hands.

One of the men reels backward and topples head over feet down the stairs. Triumph swells inside of me. I've hit my target.

"What did you do that for!" someone booms.

"Fo," Bowen groans.

I lower the gun and stare in mute shock. Bowen lies in a crumpled heap of blood and clothes on the landing below. I run down the steps and grab his shoulders. He goes rigid at my touch. "Not so rough," he gasps.

I let go and stare at him. "Are you badly hurt?" I ask.

"You *shot* him, idiot," Arrin snaps, slamming the rifle against my chest. I clutch it and everything goes numb—my fingers, my ears, my brain. Unable to move, to speak, I stare at Bowen.

Tommy eases Bowen to sitting and slings Bowen's arm over his shoulders. Then he glares at me. "Never trust a woman with a gun. He comes here to save your life and you almost kill him," he says, staring at me like I'm trash. "Are you hurt bad, man?" he asks Bowen.

Bowen nods and cringes, peering down at his stomach. Blood is soaking his shirt, oozing onto his pants, and dripping onto the floor. "I need coagulant. Now. Where's your backpack, Fo?" Bowen asks. His voice is as unsteady as my hands.

"In the room," I say, unable to take my eyes from the blood. Every heartbeat that passes, his blood flows more quickly, dripping off the hem of his shirt and splattering into an ever-growing puddle on the dirty floor. I turn and start running up the stairs toward the fifteenth floor.

"Hurry!" Tommy calls. "We fused the stairwell door to buy some time, but we've only got a few minutes at most." I run faster, taking the stairs three at a time until I reach the fifteenth floor. I sprint down the hall to room 1515 and crash inside, jerking to a startled stop.

A small boy, maybe six years old, is sitting on the bed, an entire chunk of Spam straight out of the can in his hands—one of which is marked with the sign of the beast. He's gnawing on the meat so intently he doesn't notice me.

I take a step toward him and his eyes dart up to mine. The Spam falls from his hands to the mattress and he flinches. "Please don't hurt me," he whispers, wrapping his arms around his knees and pulling them against his chest.

"I won't," I say. "You can have the meat. There're peaches, too."

He lifts his head and stares at me with wide, shocked eyes.

"Where's your mom?"

"She's asleep in another room."

I jog to the backpack and pull out three cans of peaches, tossing them onto the bed. "Take these to her and tell her some bad men are coming and you guys need to hide." He puts the Spam and three cans of peaches into his tattered shirt and jumps off the bed. I sling the backpack over my shoulder and run back to the thirteenth floor.

Bowen is lying on the landing again, eyes shut. His face is so pale that a smattering of freckles stands out on his nose. Even his lips are gray. Arrin is kneeling beside him, staring at his face, and Tommy is gone. Arrin sees me and takes a knife from her pants. She lifts his shirt and puts the blade on Bowen's stomach.

"No!" I scream, leaping down half a flight of stairs and landing beside them, my feet slipping in blood. I yank the knife from her hand and stare at her, horrified.

"I was going to cut his shirt off, dimwit," she snaps, taking the knife back. "He's wearing a Kevlar vest and we've got to get it off him." She lifts his shirt and slices through the fabric. With unsteady hands I unzip his Kevlar vest.

"The vest didn't work," I whisper, staring at Bowen's bloody stomach.

"Hello! You shot him at close range! Vests don't work at point blank!" Arrin says, rolling her eyes.

I ease his arms out of the vest and cringe. His stomach is so bloody, I can't tell where the wound is. I take a packet of coagulant from the backpack and tear it open, then sprinkle it over his entire stomach.

He gasps and his eyes open, rolling back into his head. Arrin takes a scrap of his shirt and wipes the blood from his stomach. But when the shirt comes away, covered with blood and white beads, new blood oozes onto his skin so fast, I still can't tell where the wound is.

"You need more," she says. "Lots more."

I open another packet and hand it to Arrin. "You pour it," I say. I lift Bowen's head and cradle it in my lap. Leaning down, I kiss his pale lips. They are as cold and unresponsive as clay. Without warning, he jerks away from me as coagulant hisses

in his wound. He moans and curls up on his side facing me, clutching his stomach.

"What in the . . ." Arrin breaks off, face draining of color. She turns her head to the side and vomits on the stairs.

"What?" I ask.

She shakes her head, wiping her mouth on the back of her hand. "It went clean through him," she whispers.

"What did?"

She dry heaves and squeezes her eyes shut. "The bullet." Without opening her eyes, she points a bloodstained finger at Bowen's back. I lean over his body for a better look.

A chunk of flesh is missing just below Bowen's ribs, and blood is pulsing out of the wound. I gag once and then make myself take a deep breath. The air smells like blood and death, so I breathe through my mouth.

I grab my backpack and find three more packets of coagulant— all the coagulant I have left.

"Hold him down on his stomach," I say.

Arrin, eyes still closed, climbs atop Bowen's shoulders and pushes them to the ground so she is sitting on his back. I open all three packets of coagulant and at once pour the tiny white beads onto the gaping wound.

A scream tears out of Bowen's mouth, echoing in the narrow stairwell. He arches his back and thrashes, throwing Arrin from him, hands clawing at the ground. I jump on his legs but can't hold him still.

The coagulant fizzes and bubbles, mixing with blood and

expanding to fill the wound. And as it spreads, the bleeding slows. Bowen's body goes from tense to limp and then sags into the floor. I climb off his legs and put my hand on his cheek. His skin is ice cold and damp, his blue-tinged mouth hanging limply open.

"Bowen?" I whisper.

He doesn't move, doesn't even stir. I put my hand beneath his nose. There is no breath coming from him.

"You killed him," Arrin says matter-of-factly. "He couldn't stand the pain of the coagulant. Don't you know *anything*, Fo? If you use coagulant on major wounds, you have to sedate the person first."

"Bowen!" I pat his cheek, shake his shoulders, but he doesn't stir. The breath catches in my chest and comes out as a sob.

An icy hand finds mine and tries to squeeze. "I'm not dead." His eyes flicker open and meet mine. "Not yet. Help me up and bring me my pack."

I tug on his shoulders and help him sit, but he's too weak to stay that way unsupported. He wobbles and teeters to the side, and I grab him before he falls. I kneel behind him and support his weight, and Arrin hands him his pack. When she sees how badly his hands tremble, she unzips it for him.

"What do you need?" she asks.

"Water bottle, IV bag, and packet marked *blood loss*," he says. He leans against me and shuts his eyes, and his body goes utterly still. I can't even feel the rise and fall of his ribs.

Gunshots echo from below, three in a row, and Bowen stirs. "Hurry up, Fec. We've got three minutes at best," he says, words slurred as if he's almost asleep. Arrin holds out the water bottle,

IV bag with a long plastic tube and needle attached, and small vacuum-sealed packet. "Fiona, fill the bag to eight ounces with water and *don't* let your hands touch the water," Bowen instructs. Carefully, I fill the clear plastic bag. "Now pour in the *blood loss* packet." His voice is barely more than a whisper.

I open the packet and pour it into the water. It turns deep, dark green, so green I can't see through it.

"Good girl," Bowen says. "Now seal it and then hand me the needle." I seal the top of the bag, like a Ziploc bag, and then pick up the needle attached to the tube and hold it out. "Arris, get me a Mylar strap . . . a rubber-looking thing. Should be where you got the IV." Arrin rummages through the backpack and pulls out what looks like a really thick rubber band. "Fo, tie it above my elbow—tight." I take it and cinch it into place. Bowen takes the needle and jabs at an invisible vein in the crease of his elbow. The needle slides in. Bowen removes a little clamp on the IV bag.

"Arris, hold the bag above my head," he says. She lifts it, and green liquid fills the tube and goes into Bowen's arm through the needle. He shivers and droops more heavily against me.

Another gunshot rumbles the building.

"They've broken through the stairwell door. They're coming up," Bowen says. "Help me to my feet."

CHAPTER 28

I loop my hands under Bowen's armpits and heave, surprised that he isn't heavier. He stands and wobbles. His eyes roll back in his head and his knees buckle, his limp weight pulling me down as he crumples on top of me.

Footsteps echo in the stairwell, a frantic, staccato pounding that matches my heart. I struggle to get free, but with the floor slick with blood, and Bowen as limp as a corpse, I can't.

"I'm sorry. I'm too weak to move," Bowen whispers.

Arrin sets the IV bag on the ground and helps get Bowen off me.

"We have to go, Fo," she says. She grabs my wrist and pulls me to my feet. I look at Bowen, pallid and blood covered on the landing. "We have to leave him or we suffer a fate worse than a slow death!" She claws at me, digs her nails into my forearm, and pulls. I don't budge. "He's going to die, anyway! And he'd want you to save your own skin! Come on! I know a way into the tunnels if we can get to an elevator shaft."

"No. You go. Save yourself." I pick up the rifle and rest it on my shoulder, ready to fight.

"But he's going to die!"

"I am not leaving him," I say, looping my finger through the trigger. The footsteps are close. Bowen stirs, and his icy hand slides around my ankle.

"Arris is right. I'm going to die. Go. But Fo, I want you to know that I love you. I've always loved you." His hand falls away limp against the floor.

"I won't leave you," I mutter. The stomping feet are so near I can feel their vibrations in the stairs. I firm my shoulders and take aim.

"It's Tommy," Bowen whispers. "Don't shoot."

Tommy comes around the corner and jerks to a stop. "Don't shoot me!" he barks, his eyes wide, and I lower the gun. He runs to Bowen and drapes Bowen's arm over his shoulders. "Fo, get his pack and put it on—leave yours. Then get the IV bag and hold it as high as you can. If we get fluid into him, he might live to see tonight. If we survive that long. Now come on. We've got to find somewhere to make a stand." I nod and pick up the IV bag from the bottom step.

Tommy drags Bowen through the door to the thirteenth floor. I follow on their heels, IV bag held above my head, ultraheavy backpack pulling on my shoulders. Arrin is already gone. I never saw her leave.

As the door swings shut behind me, I hear the pounding of many feet coming up the stairs. Tommy pauses and presses something into the creases of the door. He spits on it, and it starts to fizz and smoke, tainting the air with an acidic, metallic smell and sealing the door shut.

"That'll buy us a few more minutes," Tommy says, turning down the hall.

We go into three different rooms before Tommy finds one he deems acceptable—one with a mattress for Bowen. He helps Bowen lie on the bed and hangs the nearly empty IV on the headboard above him. Next, Tommy opens his backpack and takes out grenades, ammunition, and two small guns.

"Where'd you learn to shoot?" he asks as he loads the guns.

"My father. He was in the air force when I was a kid—got disabled. He taught me how to shoot," I say, surprised that many words find their way out of my numb body.

Tommy looks at me. "You still are a kid." His words make me pause. For the first time since waking up in the wrong body, I feel older than I look. Ancient.

He hands me one of the small guns. "For when Bowen's rifle runs out of ammo," he explains.

I take the gun and tuck it into the waistband of my pants. "Why don't we go out the window? Down the fire escape?" I ask, peering at the shattered window.

Tommy laughs, a cynical sound. "No fire escape out that window."

"Then why don't we go to another room? With a fire escape?"

"Because," Bowen answers, voice strained, "there is no fire

escape. And if we go out a window, they'll get us. They're circling the building."

"Oh. How many are there?" I wonder aloud.

"At least fifty," Bowen says, watching me with half-closed eyes.

The thud of feet climbing stairs echoes in the hall outside our room, and my jaw drops. *"Fifty? And we're going to try to fight them?"* I turn to Tommy. "What if you and I die? What happens to Bowen?"

"He dies, too. Unless . . ." Tommy glances over his shoulder at Bowen and raises a thick black eyebrow.

"Dude! No," Bowen snaps, a sudden fire in his glazed eyes.

"Unless what?" I ask, a flicker of hope stirring in me.

"Unless I call in—"

"Tommy, no," Bowen says, his voice quivering, eyes frantic.

"Call in what?" I demand.

"Call in your location, Fiona Tarsis," Tommy says, studying me. "If I do that, the entire militia will be here in less than five minutes and the gang will run or die. Bowen will get help. And they'll take you to the lab."

The lab, where I will become a human guinea pig. I look at Bowen, at his ashen face and blue lips. "Call in our position. Now," I order Tommy. With those words, hope floods me, spills out through my eyes and trickles down my cheeks. I bite my bottom lip, savoring the feeling of hope when I thought all was lost.

"Fo." Bowen pushes himself to sitting and sways. "We have a chance against the raiders! We might make it out of here!"

"*Fifty* against *two*? I don't think so. If it means keeping you alive, I'll go to the lab. And if I survive the lab, I'll find you. I promise."

Bowen's mouth grows hard. "There is no *surviving* the lab. If you go in, you don't come out. Why do you think I decided to risk running with you?" he says, his voice as icy cold as his eyes.

"I'll come out. I promise!" I say, the hope of being rescued bleeding over into the hope that I will survive.

"No, you won't," Tommy says matter-of-factly, pointing his gun toward the door. "No one's ever come out of the lab unless they're in a body bag. You go to the lab, you forfeit your life."

Something pops and bangs outside our room.

"They got through the door," Tommy says, looking at me with raised eyebrows. "It's only a matter of time now."

Footsteps groan on the floor outside our door. And then the door crashes inward, and two guns jab inside. Tommy doesn't hesitate. He lifts his gun and fires. One man falls into the room. "I found them," the other yells from the hallway.

"Call. In. My. Location." I say it through gritted teeth. "Now!"

Tommy looks at me and nods, pulls a walkie-talkie from his belt. "This is Tommy. I've found the female Ten. Fiona Tarsis. We're—"

"Tommy, no!" Bowen wails.

"—on the thirteenth floor of the City Center Marriot. Surrounded by a gang of at least fifty." He puts the walkie-talkie back on his belt and looks at Bowen. "Sorry, man."

"Wait." Bowen plucks the IV needle out of his arm and climbs to his feet. A hint of color lights his cheeks. "Wait. We have one

other option." He turns to me. "Did I hear Arris say there's a way into the tunnels if we could get to the elevator shaft?"

I nod.

"There's a way into the tunnels from here and you waited until *now* to bring this up?" Tommy bellows.

Bowen glares at Tommy. "Sorry. I've been kinda distracted. But the Fec said there's a way into the tunnels through the elevator shaft. If we can pass the raiders and get there before the militia gets here . . ." Bowen wobbles over to my side and drapes his arm over my shoulder, leaning most of his weight onto me. "We might have a chance."

I wrap my arm around him and press my face into his shoulder. "Let's go," he says against my hair.

"Wait." Tommy holds up a hand and cocks his head. "Listen."

The deep, low throb of a helicopter pulses in the air. Bowen and Tommy look at each other and one of Tommy's eyebrows slowly lifts.

"They're sending a *copter* for her? That means someone's coming from *inside* the wall." Tommy turns his dark eyes onto me. "Why are you so important?" he asks.

I don't have an answer, but Bowen does. "She's *from* the lab," he says. His arm tightens on my shoulders, and he presses his chilled lips to my forehead. "Somehow she survived. And she's a Ten, but she has no signs of changing."

"I'm from the lab?" I say, staring at him.

"We don't have time for this!" Tommy snaps, shooting a spray of bullets out the doorway. I flinch and my ears ring. "You'd better get your mask. Can you share with her?"

Bowen nods and pulls me closer, putting his lips against my ear. "Tommy's going to drop a nerve-gas grenade. You can't breathe the air, or you'll have a mental breakdown," he explains. "You'll have to breathe through my mask. We'll take turns." He unzips the backpack, still on my back, and removes a palm-sized mask that only covers the mouth.

"When I say run, you two go to the elevator shaft and see if you can get it open. I'll cover you," Tommy says. He holds a pale-green grenade in his hand and then pulls the pin. He counts to five and tosses it out the door.

Bowen presses the mask to my mouth, and I take a breath that almost bursts my lungs. And then I hold it. The grenade pops and hisses, and slow tentacles of eerie greenish fog creep along the floor and into the hotel room. Outside the room, a man calls a warning, "Green Hell!" and then starts to scream.

"Run!" Tommy yells. I grab Bowen's arm and hold it tight around my shoulders, pulling him toward the door. He takes the mask from my face and inhales a deep breath through it, then presses it against my mouth again. I gulp a breath of air and keep going.

The hall is filled with green smoke, making it hard to see more than a few feet in any direction. As we stumble toward the elevator shaft, we pass a man who is panting and clawing bloody tracks down his own neck. We pass another who is weeping and clutching his stomach. He reaches out and grabs my ankle, and I fall to the floor. Bowen falls with me, landing hard, with a whimper of pain. The mask comes off my face, and I hold my breath, struggling to get out from under Bowen as he reaches for the dropped mask.

I manage to put my feet beneath me and help Bowen to his. He presses the mask to my face with a trembling hand. I gasp air into my straining lungs, hand the mask back to Bowen, and we continue forward. We pass eight more men writhing on the floor, some of them crying, others talking gibberish.

And then the elevator comes into view, a sleek metal door covered with grimy fingerprints, open just wide enough for a small person to squeeze through. I peer through the gap and my hope falters. A narrow ledge leads to a metal ladder. There's no way I can carry Bowen down that. I look at Bowen. His eyes meet mine, and he takes the mask from my mouth, pressing it to his and sucking in a breath of air. But the sorrow in his eyes tells me he knows what I'm thinking.

"Tommy will get you to the tunnels," he says through the mask.

He puts the mask back on me. "I'm not leaving you here," I say.

He shrugs and takes the mask from my mouth again, putting it back on his. "I'm not going to live much longer. You have to go without me." He takes one more deep breath, a final breath, and places the mask back on my mouth. Tears fill my eyes—tears of frustration. Hopelessness.

CHAPTER 29

A high-pitched wail fills the smoky air. "Militia's here," Bowen whispers, sagging against me as if he's already given up. A dark shadow looms up out of the green fog beside me, and I almost drop Bowen. Tommy steps past me and shoves the elevator door twelve inches wider. With a satisfied nod, he turns to me and my hope bursts back into existence. He holds a coiled rope. I look between the rope and Bowen and smile, my cheeks pressing against the mask.

"Take a breath, then come climb on my back, man," Tommy says through his mask, which is strapped around the back of his head. Bowen hesitates. "What? You thought I was going to leave you? You're my best friend. I'm tying you on, but hurry up before the militia get inside."

I take the mask from my mouth and press it to Bowen's. He takes a deep breath and then hands it to me. I strap it on behind my head.

"You take my mask off when you need air," Tommy says. "You think you can manage that?"

Bowen nods and steps behind Tommy. Tommy removes his backpack and drops it down the elevator shaft, and then hoists Bowen up, like a dad giving his kid a piggyback ride. He swings the rope behind Bowen, just under his armpits, and ties him into place. Next he loops the rope under Bowen's butt, then around his waist, careful not to put it directly over Bowen's wound.

"That gonna work?" he asks.

Bowen, face covered with a sheen of sweat, gives him a trembling thumbs-up and then takes the mask from Tommy's mouth for a breath of air.

Tommy steps up to the shaft and climbs over the side, working his way around the minuscule ledge to the ladder. Without hesitating, he starts down.

I follow, easing myself onto the inch-wide ledge, and cling to the wall, hoping that my heavy pack won't pull me backward. Millimeter by millimeter, I start my slow way toward the ladder, wondering how Tommy did it so fast. When I get to the ladder I grip it, panting into my oxygen mask. Slowly, I start working my way to the bottom.

Four rungs down, the sound of pounding feet and men's voices drift to me. I peer up through the gaping elevator door, into the smoky corridor, and see men in black uniforms, wearing oxygen masks, run past. The Inner Guard. I freeze and hold my breath, trying to blend in with the wall. When their voices fade to silence, I start climbing down once more.

Even though Tommy is burdened with Bowen, he's far enough below me that I can't see him or hear him. After a while, my sweaty palms begin to slip on the rungs and the muscles in my arms start to burn. Down and down I go into darkness, the ladder rubbing blisters on my palms, yet the shaft never ends. Twice I pass hotel floors with no elevator doors but never see another living person. Minutes drag by and my palms are rubbed raw, yet still I can't see the bottom in the fathomless shadows below.

By the time my legs are burning almost as much as my arms are, and my palms are wet with blood instead of sweat, the air changes. Dry heat is replaced with sweltering damp that clings to my skin and makes it hard to breathe. The lower I climb, the cooler the damp air becomes, taking on the smells of rock and dirt. And the tunnels.

I take another step down, and my foot doesn't land on a rung but on solid ground. Hands grab my shoulders and pull me backward, but it is too dark to see who it is. A callused hand tears the mask from my face and clamps down over my mouth. I sag with defeat, for I am certain I'm caught. Whether by the militia, the Inner Guard, or the raiders, I can't say.

I struggle against the hand, catch the calluses between my teeth and bite, but the hand doesn't release. "It's me, Tommy," the owner of the hand whispers into my ear. "We're not safe yet. So

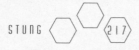

shut up, stop trying to bite me, and hurry." He releases my mouth and takes my hand in his, pulling me slowly through the dark.

"Where's Bowen," I whisper.

"He's gone. And shut up!" Tommy hisses.

Gone? As in dead? I can hardly walk. All I want to do is fall to the floor and weep. Bowen is gone, and now I have nothing to live for and nowhere to go. I hang my head and let Tommy lead me.

We don't walk far, but with every step the fetid smell of the tunnels grows stronger, the air thicker with moisture. Mist coats my tongue with each breath, and the hard ground gives way to water. Cool liquid oozes into my shoes and soaks my socks, filling the spaces between my toes.

Tommy slows his pace. "Stop splashing! You'll give us away," he warns. Do I care if I give us away? I care if I give Tommy away, but not myself. I silently ease my feet through the ankle-deep water. After we've taken too many steps to count, we stop.

"Duck," Tommy says, clasping the crown of my head and pushing down. I fall onto hands and knees, slopping slimy water onto my face. "Crawl." We slosh through the water. The hard floor grinds against my knees and stings my torn palms.

Tommy stops and then light fills the dark. A single match burns between his fingers. We crouch in a low-ceilinged cement tunnel filled with stagnant water and cobwebs. And huddled on the side of the tunnel are Arrin and Bowen.

Bowen's eyes meet mine and he smiles. I stand and throw myself at him, framing his face with my hands. He sags backward against the stone wall, totally limp, and I press my lips to his. His arm comes around my waist and lies lifelessly there, holding me gently to him. And then he returns the kiss like I'm the blood transfusion he needs to stay alive.

His lips are cool, yet spill warmth through my entire body. I hold his face firmly against mine and feel as if I'm going to burst with the knowledge that he lives.

Quiet laughter fills the tunnel. "Now I see why you're so attached to her, Bowen. You're gettin' sugar," Tommy says.

I pull away and look into Bowen's eyes. "I thought you were dead. Tommy said you were gone and I thought . . ."

The match flickers out, and I use the darkness as an excuse to kiss him again, deeper, slower. Another match scratches, and light flickers on the tunnel wall.

"Ew. You guys are gross," Arrin says. "Can we go already? Before she accidentally eats him?"

Bowen sighs into my mouth and I lean away, combing the hair off his forehead, studying his face for a brief moment. With a smile plastered to my face, I stand and help Bowen to his feet. He doesn't wobble, even a little, and my mouth falls open. He smiles again. "Guess the IV's working its magic," he says. "But I'm still weak. And still losing a bit of blood."

I peer at his bare, blood-covered stomach and wince. I am the one who did that to him.

The match flickers and goes out again. Tommy lights a third.

"Didn't you pack a flashlight?" I ask.

"You're so stupid!" Arrin grumbles.

"Of course I packed a flashlight," Tommy says. "But there's no way we're getting out of here that easy. Not with *you* along, Fiona Tarsis. The militia will scan the ground for any type of energy current, except fire. And I didn't pack a candle." Tommy turns to Arrin. "So, Fec, where are we going?"

Arrin shrugs, peering at him through stringy bangs. "You tell me. And I'm assuming I'll be paid? I'm not helping you for nothing."

"Will a can of peaches be payment enough?" Bowen asks.

"Double it and you've got a deal."

"Done," Bowen says.

"Well, then, where to?" Arrin asks.

I look at Bowen, hope burning in my chest. "Can we still run?" I whisper. "To Wyoming?"

He shakes his head. "Too weak. I'll never make it. And you'll never make it on your own."

Eyes pleading, I look at Tommy. He smirks and shakes his head. "I ain't running with you. And besides, even if you did run, even if Bowen was all right, there's no way you'd get far. Not with the manpower they've got on your tail."

"You can live in the tunnels," Arrin says, a sly gleam in her eyes.

"No!" Bowen and I say at the same time.

"Suit yourself. But where to? I can get you to the outskirts of the city or inside the wall, or if you want—"

"What?" Bowen says, interrupting her. "You can get us inside the wall?"

She spins around and grins at him, nodding. The match flickers out, and Tommy lights another.

"I don't believe it," Bowen says, his words a challenge.

Arrin shrugs. "Believe it or not. Doesn't change the fact that I know a way in. I know a lot more than just that. Like why the raiders always keep a beast in their camp. And why the lab wants *her* so bad." She nods her greasy head at me.

"Why?" Bowen asks, his eyes darting between Arrin and me.

"Because she's the first child to wake from a coma. And when she woke, she wasn't crazy anymore," Arrin whispers, as if it's the biggest secret in the world.

Chills dance down my spine.

"How do you know?" Tommy asks.

Arrin doesn't answer. Bowen does. "The Fec's clothes. They're standard lab uniforms. Patient uniforms. They used to be Fiona's. And I've never heard of a Ten who didn't turn. Except for Fiona. And the bruises in the creases of her elbows. They're from needles. She's from the lab."

Arrin nods. Tommy stares at me, eyes shining with amazement.

"Since you've got everything figured out, how did she get on the wrong side of the wall?" Arrin challenges.

"I haven't figured that out yet. Have you?"

Arrin shakes her head. "But I know why they want her so bad. They need her back so they can figure out how to cure the others. But . . ."

"What?" I take a step toward Arrin. "But what?"

"But . . ." She looks right into my eyes. "They're going to have to kill you to get the answers."

The match goes out and I'm blind. A cool, damp hand finds mine and folds around it. "I won't let the lab kill you." Bowen's breath is warm against my ear. His lips press against my temple. "Arris, take us inside the wall."

His words stun me. "Wait. Inside the wall? You *are* taking me to the lab?"

His fingers tighten on mine. "Never, Fiona. I'll *never* take you to the lab. But what if I'm right about your sister being alive and living inside the wall? Do you think she'd hide us?"

A wave of relief and hope shudder through me. My sister. Lis. "Yes."

"Then that's settled. Take us inside the wall, Arris," Bowen says, his voice sounding stronger every time he talks.

"Are you sure we can trust him?" Tommy asks.

"Do we have a choice?" Bowen answers.

Another hand finds my empty hand. A small, hot hand, with jagged nails and grit-covered skin. "Tommy," Arrin whispers. "Hold Bowen's hand so we're all connected."

Tommy splashes through the water. "Got it," he says, his deep voice echoing against cement. "You want me to light another match, Fec?"

"Nope. Darkness is my friend."

"Thank you, Arrin," I whisper, squeezing her scrawny hand.

"For what?" she says, her voice suspicious.

"Helping me."

She laughs, and another chill races down my spine.

CHAPTER 30

The water changes from stagnant to rancid and clings to my ankles like mud instead of splashing around them. Bowen's breathing has grown labored, and his palm has turned icy cold in mine. His hand begins to drag against mine, making me pull Arrin to a slower pace.

"Let's take a break," I say after an hour or so.

Arrin's hold tightens on my hand. "No. We're almost there."

I dig my feet into sludge and refuse to take another step. Bowen bumps into my back and drops my hand, clutching at my shoulder to keep from falling.

"Arrin, we need a break," I say, tearing my hand from her grasp.

"Whatever. But just shut up," she growls. "The tunnels are never safe."

Through the darkness and sludge, I guide Bowen to the damp tunnel wall. He leans against it, throwing one arm around me for support.

"Tommy, is there anything else we can give Bowen to help him?" I ask. I switch my pack around so it is in front of me but still looped to my shoulders and rummage around inside it for food and water. I open a water bottle and feel for Bowen's hand. He takes the bottle and drinks.

"We *could* do another IV," Tommy says, "but I worry about secondary infections. It's so dirty down here, he might die of blood poisoning if we puncture his skin. I have a vitamin tablet and an energy tablet. They might help."

"No!" Arrin blurts. "We're almost there!"

"How much longer," Bowen asks. His voice sounds as cold and weak as the sun in winter.

"Ten minutes tops," Arrin says, her voice nearly a purr. "I know you'll make it. Just . . . let's go."

I take the water bottle from Bowen and put it into the pack, then secure it on my back again. "I'm not leaving until Bowen eats a vitamin and an energy tablet," I say.

Arrin groans. Tommy sloshes to Bowen's side. "Open up, man. Now chew."

I hear the tablets crunch in Bowen's mouth. The sound eases a bit of the tension wound tight in my belly. "Now we can go," I say. But I don't want to go on. Something doesn't feel right.

We all grasp hands again and continue through the slop. Holding Bowen's hand is like holding an ice cube. Arrin's is like fire. And every step we take, dread coils more tightly in my belly.

We haven't been walking five minutes when the stuff squelching around my feet becomes thin liquid again, the stench less powerful.

"See? I told you we were almost there! Almost inside the wall," Arrin says, not keeping her giddy voice down.

"When you said you knew a way into the wall through the tunnels, you also meant you know a way up to the top, right?" Tommy asks, voice suspicious. Maybe he can feel the same thing I'm feeling—unease.

"Duh. Of course there's a way to the top. You just have to know where to go," Arrin answers.

We take three more steps through the pitch-blackness, when I jerk to a stop. Bowen walks into me again, and Arrin's hand slips out of mine. My heart is pounding, and despite the fact that the tunnels are already midnight black, I close my eyes, straining to hear.

"What now?" Tommy grumbles.

"I heard something ahead," I whisper. I reach forward for Arrin, but she's not within arm's reach. "Arrin?" She doesn't reply. We are stuck in darkness, trapped in silence. I hear a rustle from behind, and then a match flickers. Golden light hovers around Tommy's hand. And reflects against a dozen pairs of eyes.

One pair of eyes isn't as tall as the others. The short pair steps forward—Arrin, her mouth a hard line—and points at me. "That's Fiona Tarsis. The Ten."

"Oh no," Bowen whispers. His hand begins trembling in mine.

Tommy curses, and I know without looking that he's got his rifle on his shoulder, aiming at the eyes.

"Put your weapon down, militia man." The voice comes from the shadows. "We've got you surrounded. If you hand over the Ten, we'll let you go. If you try to fight, we'll kill you before we take her. So we win no matter what. You just have to decide how badly you want to lose."

I look around and gasp. There are people behind us, in front of us, on either side of us, even hanging in the pipes overhead. And most of them hold something that shines just like their eyes—weapons. Tommy grunts and tosses his gun to the side of the tunnel, out of the water.

"You too, Ten. Disarm. We are armed and we are many," the voice says.

I take the small gun from my waistband and slip the rifle off the backpack, and toss them to the side of the tunnel by Tommy's gun.

"You want to come with us now, Ten, or do you want your escort shot first?" The *click-clack* of a rifle being cocked echoes through the tunnel.

Without a second thought, I drop Bowen's hand and take a step forward.

"No! Fo, wait," Bowen pleads, taking a step toward me.

"Bowen, they'll kill you if I don't go with them."

"That's right. She's got to come now," the man in the shadows says.

"Who are you?" Bowen asks, his voice so strong he sounds healed.

"No one important. Just let the girl come to me," Shadow Man says.

"Can I have thirty seconds to say good-bye?" Bowen asks.

There's a long silence. "I'm feeling sympathetic today. Just don't do anything stupid."

Tommy's match goes out, but another light flares overhead. The man hanging in the pipes hands a lantern to us.

Bowen opens his arms and I step into them. He rests his forehead on mine and a new knot of worry tugs tight inside of me. He's no longer cold—his forehead is flaming hot against mine and parchment dry. "I'm pretty sure these guys are the men who run the black market, which means you're going to the pits," he whispers, eyes staring into mine. "I'll come for you as soon as I can. I promise. Just . . . don't give up hope. And fight to stay alive if you have to. Fight!"

A rough hand grabs my wrist and yanks me away. I reach for Bowen and catch his outstretched hand, our fingers clasping before I'm pulled away from him. Bowen's face tightens.

"Get the Ten out of here, boys, and escort Bowen and his buddy to make sure they don't follow us," Shadow Man orders. Bowen and Tommy start sloshing through the muck, a group of armed men at their backs. When I can no longer hear their retreat, Arrin reappears.

"Aren't you forgetting something?" she asks, gnawing on the side of her thumb. She bites a piece of skin off and nibbles it with her front teeth.

"Are you so hungry you're eating yourself, Fec?" answers Shadow Man.

Arrin spits and glares into the shadows. "Where's my *reward*?

You promised me sixteen ounces if I brought her in." Her stomach grumbles.

The man laughs, and Arrin pulls a knife from her shorts, growling, poised to kill. The man laughs harder.

"You'll get paid, don't worry. But do you really think you deserve honey? For selling Fecs on the black market?" He glances at the tattoo on her hand. "And what happened to that Three you promised earlier this week?"

"That was Fiona's fault. She got him killed in the camp," Arrin growls.

Dumbfounded, I stare at Arrin. "You were going to sell your own brother to these people?" I ask.

Arrin rolls her eyes. "I don't have a brother. And where's my honey? Pay me now so I can get out of here and trade the honey for some real food."

"The only payment you'll be getting is the same fate as the Ten," Shadow Man says. I swear I can hear a smile in his voice, though his face is still hidden by darkness.

Arrin gasps. "But who will get you Fecs for the pits? And what if the governor hears about this? He's trying to get her back inside the wall."

"Who do you think asked me to put the Ten in the pits in the first place?" Shadow Man says with a laugh. "He said use any means possible to find her. I wonder if he knew I'd use the Fec that supplies me—and him—with other Fecs. You're going to the pit."

Arrin's knife trembles and falls to the ground at her feet. "The p-p-pit?" she stutters. "But I get Fecs for the governor to bleed! If he finds out you put me in the pits, he'll kill you."

"That's where you're wrong," Shadow Man says with enthusiasm. The reason the governor hasn't yet shut us down is that he is too concerned with collecting the dead bodies we provide. He won't even know you're there until it's too late. Wonder what he'll think when he opens the body bag with you in it. Best bit of irony I've heard since the day I learned the elite children of the country were all going to turn to beasts." The man chuckles.

Arrin screams and tries to run, but the man in the pipes swings down like an ape and lands on her. Two more men step into the circle of light and take Tommy's and my rifles. Others move out of the dark. They are clean, neat men, with brushed hair, wearing clean, faded clothing. They look like the type of men who used to take their kids to the park on warm afternoons or wash their cars on Saturday mornings. Until you see the guns in their hands, and their shifting eyes.

Two men stop beside me. One pulls my arms forward and fits cuffs to them. "Are you familiar with electromagnetic cuffs?" he asks. He has brown hair, parted on the side and combed into place.

I nod.

"Good. I'd hate to kill you prematurely."

The cuffs hum and pull together. Arrin, pinned to the floor, is cuffed, too. As I'm shoved past her, she glares up at me, brown sludge caking her face.

"This is all your fault." She hisses. "If they put me in the pit with you, I'll tear your throat out with my bare hands."

I stare straight ahead and walk.

CHAPTER 31

Overhead, a circle of dim light appears, and I squeeze my eyes shut against the blinding shock.

"You want me to uncuff them, or are we going to hoist them up?" asks the man jabbing his gun against my spine, the man who has been guiding me through the tunnels, with his hair combed neatly to the side.

"A Level Ten? And *that* Fec? No way are we going to uncuff either of them. Hoist for sure. But bag their heads first," another man answers—Shadow Man. I've memorized his voice.

A thick, scratchy hood is pulled over my head, and the light is gone. Behind me, Arrin starts to scream and spit. Someone grunts and curses. The air crackles and the cuffs on my forearms grow warm. Arrin's scream turns to a whimper and then silence.

"You shocked the Fec?" someone asks.

"Yeah. Little bugger bit me," Shadow Man says. "I'm probably going to get some Fec disease."

Men chuckle like they're discussing a naughty dog. The sound makes me too hot, makes me want to jump on them and scratch their eyes out. Just like I tried with my mom. Maybe I am going to turn after all.

A rough cord is looped across my chest, under my arms, and behind my back. "Walk forward two steps, Tarsis." The voice is so close it makes me jump. I take two blind steps forward. "Now, don't flail. You'll fall and crack your head open if you do," the voice warns—the voice of my guide.

The cord bites into my armpits, chafing my skin through my shirt, and my feet leave the ground. I spin in a slow, lazy circle and try to catch my breath through the thick wool hood as I ascend toward the hidden circle of light. Hands are on me, pulling me to the side, and through the hood, pinpricks of light shine. My feet touch hard ground, and the cord grows slack beneath my armpits.

I'm herded over a floor that thumps hollowly beneath my feet. Small human sounds reach my ears—panting, whimpering, coughing, a snarl.

"Where am I?" I ask, my voice muffled by wool.

"You'll see soon enough," my guide says. His gun jabs my back, keeping me moving blindly forward.

The floor turns from smooth and hollow to grainy beneath my shoes—cement. A smell penetrates through my thick wool hood, and my mouth starts to water. Onions. And butter. I'm starving. A loud rumble comes from my stomach, and I wonder how I can even think of food at a time like this.

"Duck your head," the voice says.

I duck, and hands push me from behind, hard. I topple forward, my feet tangling together. The floor crashes into my face, and one of my cuffed hands pops under the impact of my body. Fire shoots up my wrist, and I writhe against unexpected pain.

"Careful with her! We don't want her bruised. She's going in the pit in the morning, and oh what a show it will be!" a deep voice says—Shadow Man.

"In the morning? Why so fast?" my guide replies.

"Governor's orders. He said if we acquired the Ten, put her in ASAP. Something about this kid scares him. And since we caught that other Ten yesterday—two Tens in one match. *Together*. Can you imagine the food that'll be trading hands? We'll be loosening our belts!"

"But the males aren't as aggressive toward the females," my guide says.

"This one will be, trust me," Shadow Man says with a chuckle. "He's injured and so psychotic, he killed three men on his way here. He attacks anything that moves, not to mention . . ." Feet shuffle away and their voices fade.

Something clicks, and then my cuffs lose their charge, and I am free to move my arms. I try to push myself up but gasp and fall back onto my face. I don't dare move. Not with pain burning from my pinky finger to my elbow and making me want to vomit.

Using my elbow, I manage to roll onto my side. Even that makes my hand hurt. With my uninjured hand, I pull the hood from my head. Metal bars surround me on three sides. On the fourth side is a smooth metal wall, and overhead looms a low metal ceiling.

Someone sucks in a deep breath. I look toward the sound and yelp. Forgetting the pain in my hand I scramble to my feet and crack my head on the low ceiling before falling back into a crouch. And then I see the bars separating us and sigh.

A girl, probably my age, squats in the cage beside mine. She looks human enough, except she has her narrow face pressed against the bars of my cage, her dilated eyes are devouring me, and drool drips from her chin.

She reaches one of her sinewy-strong arms through the slotted bars and swipes at me with jagged yellow nails of all different lengths. I freeze as air swishes against my face. When her reach falls short, she hisses and tries again, jamming her body against the bars to get her hand as close to me as possible. Her nail teases my hair and I whimper.

Never taking my eyes from her, I inch my way to the other side of the cage and press my shoulder blades against the bars. The female howls and slams herself against the bars separating us, making my cage rattle.

Behind me something stirs and groans. I look over my shoulder and stop breathing, stop moving.

In the cage on my other side is another beast, curled up in fetal position with his back to me. He is a broad-shouldered male,

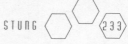

his skin covered with scabs and bruises and half-moon teeth marks. He whimpers and jolts, his hands and feet paddling the air like a dog dreaming about running. I scoot to the middle of my cage and sit with my back pressed against the metal wall. If I sit in the cage's exact center, neither beast will be able to reach me. Hopefully.

Stiff and rigid as granite, face forward, I breath shallow wisps of air that hardly make my rib cage move. The female beast lurches for me, her hand mere inches from my shoulder. After a few minutes she gives up.

Slowly, with the passage of time, I notice the throbbing pain in my hand again. Without moving my head, I look at it and whimper. At the sound of my voice, the female beast snarls and rams her body against the bars separating her cage from mine. She does it a second time, making the bars shudder. I scoot an inch toward the male beast on my left and close my eyes, cradling my swollen, deformed pinky to my chest, trying to ignore the panting coming from the female beast.

Minutes or hours pass. I don't know which. But my finger has doubled in size and turned purple, and the female beast has drooled a pool of saliva into my cage. And I smell food.

From the corner of my eye I see the beast to my left stir. He stretches his long, lean body and sits, staring out the front of his cage. Feet thump on the ground and something squeaks. For the first time I take a good look around, moving my eyes without turning my head. The room is long and narrow and lined with cages—like an animal shelter—and most cages are occupied.

But instead of holding stray dogs and cats, they hold beasts and Fecs. The cage across from me houses a slack, bony form with short, chopped hair, wearing my old shorts. Arrin.

A man pushing a cart with a squeaky wheel walks slowly in front of the cages, pausing before each to slide a plate under the two-inch gap beneath the door before dumping its contents onto the cage floor. When he gets to Arrin's cage, she doesn't move. Even when the man slides a pile of slop into her cage and dumps it onto the floor by her head.

One by one, he feeds all the caged things on the opposite side of the room and then starts on my side. He slowly makes his way toward me and pauses at the cage beside mine—the female beast's cage. Cautiously, he slides a plate under the cage, dumps the contents onto the floor, and then yanks the plate back lightning fast. The female beast sniffs but doesn't move from her position, staring at me like *I'm* dinner.

He comes to my cage and pauses, peering at me through the bars. Then he slides the plate under, dumping a heap of greasy meat and mostly onions on the grease-stained floor. He doesn't move on to the next cage but watches me like he did the female beast. And then he fills the plate again and adds a second helping to my first.

"You eat up," he whispers with a wink. My lower lip trembles, and my eyes fill with tears. This man is showing me compassion. I try to smile at him, but then he says, "I bet honey on you. Don't make me regret it!" My smile turns to a frown.

He stands and pushes the squeaky cart to the male beside me, and I look into the cage. The male beast isn't paying

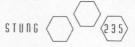
attention to his dinner. His face is pressed against the bars as if he's finally noticed someone is in the cage beside him. I meet his unblinking eyes—eyes I have known my entire life—and gasp.

The memory of pain burns down my back, fire beneath my skin, and Bowen's words come back to me.

"You have scars from here to here." He trailed his fingers down my entire back. "They look like they're from fingernails."

The walls were white tile, and light glared from them.

A man with thick white hair put his face in front of mine and looked right into my eyes. "You're only going to feel a little prick, and then everything will fade. You'll be at peace." He wore a white doctor's coat with a name tag clipped to it—Doctor Page.

I lay on my stomach. Thick leather straps held my naked body against a cold metal table. Straps that ground into my ankles, the backs of my knees, my bare hips, my lower back, my shoulders, even across my head. Jonah was in the room, too, right in my line of sight. Sedated, naked, and strapped to a stainless-steel table just like mine. Drool dripped from his slack mouth and pooled beneath his cheek.

"I don't want this!" I yelled. The metal clung to my sweaty cheek, making it hard to talk. The strap on my forehead made it impossible to see what was going on behind me, but I could hear people moving around— the doctor and someone else.

"You may not want this, but your mother does. She is your legal guardian. Her decision outweighs your wants. She's doing it in the hopes that you'll survive long enough for us to find a cure," Dr. Page said from behind me. "It's what's best, Fiona." He walked around to where I could

see him again, tilted his head to the side, and peered right into my face. A shadow of doubt flashed in his gray eyes, filling my entire body with panic. "You're much too sweet to give up on."

I snarled and lunged for him, making my table-bed lurch, yet I hardly moved beneath the leather straps. The doctor jumped away from me and frowned.

"Jonah," I cried. "Help me!" But he didn't stir. Didn't even close his mouth.

"Needle, nurse. The sooner we sedate her, the sooner we can induce the coma." The doctor held out his latex-gloved hand, and a hefty syringe was placed into it. "I'm going to inject this directly into your spinal tissue, and then you'll go to sleep. It will only hurt for a minute—a little pressure in your spine—and then everything will go numb," he said to me.

I looked at the needle, twice as long as my index finger, and screamed. The doctor stepped up to me and put his icy, latex-gloved hand on my naked back, pressing it against my spine. Something pricked my skin, like the sting of a bee, and then pressure built around my spine, hot and white, as if the needle were forcing its way between my vertebrae, wedging them apart. I screamed again and lurched, fighting against my restraints, making the needle dig against bone.

"No!" I shrieked. As if he could finally hear me, Jonah's eyes fluttered open and locked on mine, his massive pupils instantly shrinking. "Help me, please," I whimpered to him. My legs were going numb, a warm tingling sensation spreading from my thighs to my knees to my feet. I couldn't feel the table beneath them, couldn't feel the metal's coldness seeping into my skin.

"Jonah," I cried. "Get me out of here."

His eyes, so wild, so foreign, seemed to clear for a moment as they

focused on mine, as if there was a piece of him left inside. And then he grunted, long and low. A vein in his forehead popped to the surface. His face became red, his neck all sinew, and every single muscle in his body flexed. He trembled with effort, making the metal bed vibrate beneath him.

"Nurse, sedate him again," the doctor said. "Quickly!"

A hefty woman with graying hair and a syringe in her hand walked into my line of sight, intent on my brother. A pop echoed in the room, and the nurse stopped dead. The leather band around Jonah's shoulders fell to the floor, and the nurse took a step back. "Doctor, we have a problem," she said, backing away from Jonah until she crashed into my bed.

"Sedate him!" the doctor bellowed. "Now! I'm almost done with the girl!"

The leather holding Jonah's wrists popped, and then the straps tethering the small of his back and his ankles exploded simultaneously, until only the strap on his head remained whole. He tore it off, leaped from the table, and lunged for the doctor. They fell to the floor and Jonah lashed out at the doctor's face with his fingernails, smacking the doctor's head against the cold, hard floor.

I stared at Jonah's hands, gentle hands that built dinosaur models and did science experiments for fun; long, slender hands that played duets on the piano with me. Now, they were covered with blood.

The nurse screamed and huddled in a corner of the room.

Jonah leaped to his feet and tried to tear me off the metal table, his nails raking my back, my neck. I gasped at the pain, but then the tingly numb spread from my legs to my waist and oozed like warm honey along my spine, into my shoulders.

Red and blue lights started flashing overhead, and an alarm blared.

"Jonah. Run," I slurred. Even my mouth was turning numb, my tongue swelling with deadened warmth. My mouth sagged open, and drool trickled down my cheek. I forced my eyes to stay wide and watched Jonah ram the hospital door open with his shoulder.

And then he ran.

"You tried to save me," I whisper, staring into his feral eyes. At my words his eyes narrow and he grips the bars keeping us apart. The bars keeping me alive. His knuckles turn white, and the metal groans beneath his grasp, shifting a millimeter.

Oh crap.

I look away, straight forward again, and don't touch my dinner. I'm starving, yet the thought of food makes bile rise in my throat. In an effort to calm myself, I start to hum under my breath, random notes that have no tune.

Across the room, Arrin stirs. She lifts her head, and her sharp nose wrinkles. And then, cracking her eyes open, she shoves her face into the pile of onions and meat. When her food is mostly gone, she notices me watching. She sits and grins a grimy, grease-covered grin, and drags her finger across her neck.

"I'm going to kill you," she mouths.

Oh yeah? Wait in line, I think, listening to the sounds of the beasts breathing into my cage on either side of me. I press my back harder against the wall of my cage, cradle my throbbing hand, and for the first time ever, can't think of a song to distract me from reality.

CHAPTER 32

Somehow I sleep. I know because I lurch awake when my arms meld together and I topple sideways into a puddle of cold drool. Fingernails plunge into my cheek, and I'm yanked into the bars on the side of my cage.

The fingernails move, digging into my neck, cinching around my windpipe. My mouth opens, but no air enters my lungs. I stare across my cage at Jonah, my mouth gaping, struggling for air. He shrieks and throws his body into the bars separating us, straining to reach me.

I lurch against the claw-hold, but can't break free. Fire fills my air-starved lungs, and I wonder if this is how I'm going to die, before I ever see the pits.

"Taser! Cage eleven! Now! It's going to kill the Ten!" someone screams.

Electricity travels from the fingers gouging my flesh, into my blood, and heats the cuffs on my forearms. The fingers lose their power and fall away. The heat fizzles out of my body, but I'm too limp to move. I gasp and fill my burning lungs with air.

Somewhere, someone is screaming, "He's bending the bars! Taser thirteen!" Other voices call out orders and mingle with the scream. Cool hands find my neck and probe for a pulse.

"I'm not dead," I say, panting. My voice box hardly works.

Hands clasp my ankles and drag me out of the cage, through the pile of cold uneaten food. Outside the cage, I'm lifted into a chair. Metal cinches down on my wrists, ankles, and neck, pinning me immobile into the chair. My pinky throbs. My neck aches. My hair is plastered to the side of my face with saliva and cold onion slop.

I am wheeled past two clean-cut men talking to Arrin. One has a knife in his hand—a sparkling, new-looking blade. The man holding the knife looks at me as I pass and then hands the knife through the bars of the cage to Arrin. I crane my neck to see more, but someone smacks me on the back of the head.

"Face forward," the person pushing the chair orders. So I do.

We pass rows and rows of cages. Those that are occupied hold muscular beasts or filthy, boney Fecs. No one else like me—no one normal. We come to a door at the end of the cage hallway. A young man, probably about my age, types something into a keypad and the door opens. I am wheeled into a tan-and-green-tiled room occupied by four muscle-heavy guards.

I sit a little taller. Something about this place is familiar, with its rows of lockers and shower stalls, automatic hand dryers and sinks, and toilets in separate stalls. The air smells like . . . women—hairspray, lotion, perfume, powder—and bleach. Seeing the toilets reminds me how badly I need to go to the bathroom.

"Can I use the toilet?" My throat hurts too much to talk louder than a whisper.

There's a collective inhale of breath. "She talks," someone whispers.

"Are they sure she'll fight back?" another voice asks.

"Of course she will. Two Tens in one match? That's never happened before. If she doesn't fight she'll be killed," the young man, the one pushing my wheelchair, says.

My chair stops, and the metal bars release my neck and ankles. The young man walks to the front of my chair, followed by the four guards. From a hook on the wall, the young man takes a scrub brush affixed to the end of a ten-foot pole and examines me with nervous eyes.

"Do you want me to cuff her ankles, Lance?" one of the guards asks.

"I don't think she needs them," the young man—Lance— answers.

The guard ignores him and steps up to me, ankle cuffs in hand. "Better safe than dead," he says, kneeling in front of me. "Don't kick me or I'll zap you," he warns. He lifts my pants and slides the cuffs into place. They clink together and I'm immobile.

"Stand her up and hook her," Lance orders.

The metal slides off my neck and wrists, and retracts into the wheelchair. I am hoisted from the chair by two of the guards, their hands clamped on my elbows. They carry me, my feet dragging on the floor, to a shower stall, and hook my wrist cuffs onto a meat hook attached to a chain hanging down from the ceiling. The ankle cuffs are attached to another meat hook that's chained on the floor. I'm stretched tight between them, immobile. All I can do is turn my head from side to side and blink. My pinky finger pounds with building pressure, and my shoulders feel on the verge of dislocating.

Water turns on and falls onto me from above. Lance grips the ten-foot-long scrub brush, squirts something onto it, and swings it toward my head. He starts with my face, dragging the stiff bristles against my skin. Soap gets into my eyes, burning them, so I squeeze them shut. After a minute, Lance moves the scrubber to my hair and scrubs so hard I might go bald. When he's satisfied with the cleanliness of my hair, he moves the brush over every inch of my body—both clothing and skin—rubbing me raw with his fervor.

"What are you doing?" I splutter, and swallow a mouthful of soap.

The scrub brush pauses and Lance looks at me. "Getting you ready to fight. We've discovered that people feel more sympathy for the fighters if they're clean. And if they feel more sympathy, they make higher bets."

The water stops and I'm released from the chains and, sopping wet, sat back in the chair. The metal bars lock me in.

"Please don't put me in the pits," I say, my eyes darting between Lance and the four burly guards. The guards look at each other, then at Lance.

"Are you sure she's on the verge of turning?" one asks, his eyes worried.

"No, I'm not!" I blurt, staring at him with pleading eyes. "I'm norm—"

Lance's hand slaps fire to my face. My head jolts to the side, my skin stings, and tears fill my eyes. "Don't cry," he orders, glaring at me. "Of course she's on the verge. She's a Ten!"

"Why are you doing this?" I ask, blinking the tears down my cheeks.

The guard folds his arms over his wide chest and steps in front of Lance. "This is wrong," he says.

"Shut up," Lance replies, glancing nervously at me. "You're getting paid a double ration of food for your family to keep your mouth shut, remember? And she's a Ten!"

"This is wrong," he says again. "And I can't let you pass."

Lance looks over the guard's shoulder and nods. The barrel of another guard's gun is slammed into the back of the guard's head, and he flops into a pile at my feet.

With a renewed urgency, Lance locks me into the chair and wheels me to the other side of the locker room and through a door. The three remaining guards follow. And now I know why this place is so familiar. I'm in the old recreation center. The swimming pool is through a glass door on my right. But the pool looks different. Rows of stadium bleachers are set up around it. And people, mostly men, are filing in, fighting over the front-row seats.

"Wow. Big crowd," Lance says, pushing my chair away from the pool.

"Who are you betting on?" a guard asks.

"The female," Lance says, as if it should be obvious.

"Her? The Ten?"

"No way I'd bet on her. She's going down first. I'm betting on the female Five."

I am wheeled into an elevator that smells like diesel exhaust and urine. The door slides shut with a rusty groan, the elevator hums, and we go down. When we come out, everything is dark, and the smell of chlorine stings my nose. The chair's metal restraints open, and I'm prodded forward. I stand. The chair is whisked away, and behind me a door slams. My cuffs spring apart and I can move again.

I am in the dark.

And I am alone.

CHAPTER 33

The room is small and square, with a door at each end. A thin stream of light trickles around the frame of the door across from the one I came through, enough of a glow that I can barely see after my eyes have adjusted. The room holds nothing. It smells like urine and bleach and damp.

Overhead, the ceiling rumbles with the sound of pounding feet. Excited voices carry to my room, shouting and clapping and whistling. I plug my ears, lean against the wall, and start humming Maurice Ravel's "Pavane for a Dead Princess."

Time passes, but I have no way to measure it. Cold from the cement wall bites through my wet shirt and seeps into my skin, making me shiver. My hollow stomach rumbles, and I need to use the bathroom. Judging by the smell, I could pee anywhere in this room—the whole thing is like a bathroom. But I don't. Because I am not a beast.

Overhead, the frenzy of feet grows louder, shakes the room around me. I push harder against my ears, hum louder, but nothing will drown out the sound.

I hear a deep, rumbling echo—hear it way down in my chest—and take my hands from my ears. The pounding feet and voices have grown quiet. Only one voice buzzes in my head—the source of the rumbling.

". . . a real treat. A twofer! A double match for the price of a single, two for one!" the voice booms. Noise explodes, cheering, and I cover my ears. After a minute the deep buzz of the broadcast voice is back. I drop my hands and listen.

"That's right. A double match, ladies and gents! We are—" The voice stops and the crowd goes silent. I wait a long moment, the only sound my own heart, before the commentator comes back on.

"We have a special visitor, folks. It looks like Governor Soneschen is going to be joining us for today's match! This is another first—a day of firsts! Let's clear out the front row for him and his personal guard!" The crowd cheers again, but not with as much enthusiasm. "Now, like I was saying before our illustrious governor graced us with his presence, I'm going to start this twofer special with a matched fight—Level Four versus Level Four. So make your bets, get your popcorn, find your seats, and enjooooy the show!" The crowd grows eerily silent without so much as a pair of feet walking overhead. I strain to hear what's going on, waiting.

Something happens. Something changes. The air around me shifts, a faint stirring that carries with it the scents of fresh popcorn and body odor. Through the cracks in my door frame, I hear guttural breathing. I creep to the door and press my eye to the crack. My knees grow weak and I cling to the wall, but I don't take my eye from the crack.

Two boy beasts, the baby fat barely gone from their cheeks, stand in a brightly lit pale-blue room. They are facing each other, circling, their muscular bodies tense. One leaps for the other, and a clap of noise—cheering—vibrates my bones. The beasts throw their arms around each other, topple, and start rolling around on the floor. Scratching. Biting. Clawing. And people are *cheering*, like they're at a basketball game and their team just scored.

I shudder and move away from the door, swallowing down bile as I try to forget what I just saw. Yet, even over the thunderous cheering, sounds of the fight reach my ears—wet, smacking sounds and grunting. I press my hands against my ears and hum Beethoven's Fifth as loud as I can. And all I can think is, *Bowen, come and get me!*

After I've hummed the entire song, the deep buzz of the voice echoes into my room. I cautiously take my damp hands from my ears, braced for the disturbing sounds of fighting.

". . . in your seats! I know how eager you all are, but you need to wait to collect your winnings until after the second fight. Now, if you voted Beast One in this round, you . . . *lose, lose, LOSE!*" he yells. The crowd groans. "And now, we'll take a quick moment to clean up the pit before we get on to what you *really* came here for.

So, use the bathroom, place more bets, or just hunker down in your seats and give us a moment to prepare the pit."

I mentally brace myself for something horrible and peer through the crack in the door again. Both beasts are in the bright room, one lying motionless on the floor, the other hunched over it and panting. Both are covered with streaks of blood.

My cuffs zing with a surge of electricity, and the sitting beast's arm and ankle cuffs snap together. He snarls and writhes, tipping over onto the floor. Two men come into view and approach the beast with their hands up, palms forward. The beast lunges to his feet, and I gag. His face is nothing but scratches with eyes peering out.

My cuffs fill with electricity again, and the beast topples to the floor, his body convulsing, his stringy hair standing straight up with electricity. When the electricity stops, his eyes are shut and he doesn't move. His unconscious body is lifted from the floor, placed into a wheelchair, and locked into place with metal bars identical to those that were on my wheelchair. His head lolls to the side as they push the chair out of the room.

The other beast, the one lying on the floor, is zipped into a black bag.

I have seen enough. Too much. So I lean against the wall and close my eyes. I have just witnessed my first pit fight. And now I understand. Unless Bowen shows up with his promised rescue, I am going to fight next. And I am going to die.

The door with the light seeping through—*my* door—swings open. I flinch and cover my eyes. The door behind me, the door I came in through, moves toward me. It presses against my back and I dig my shoes into the ground. I do not want to go into the pit! But it sweeps me, forces me out of my tiny room and into blinding light. I fall to my knees and stare at the floor—pale-blue cement smeared with streaks of brick red and brown.

The air explodes with cheering, and the commentator's booming voice echoes over the sound. "Isn't she a doozy? Our first Level Ten of the day! Of the year! Our first Level Ten . . . *ever*!" The crowd goes wild. "Don't be fooled by her submissive appearance, folks. She might be on her knees right now, but it is all an act. She's been living outside the wall. She's tough. She's a survivor. And she's a Ten. She's got the mark on her hand to prove it!"

I glance at my hand, at the oval with ten legs, and shudder. The cheering grows louder and I look up. I am in the bottom of the indoor swimming pool—the deep end where the diving boards and platforms used to be. Above me is a thick sheet of Plexiglas, a seal locking me in. Around the glass seal are stadium seats crammed with people—sitting in laps, spilling over the edges, lining the walkways. And they are all staring at me and cheering.

In the front row sits a man dressed in a suit and tie, with a white-collared shirt. He is flanked on both sides by four short-haired men in black uniforms, with automatic weapons in their hands. I have seen this guarded man before. In a firelit alley. The man who told the raiders to catch me and keep me, and kill me. His eyes are locked on mine. I stare into his narrowed eyes and slowly climb to my feet. He is the governor.

"Now that you've clapped eyes on this beastly sweetie, you

might want to change your bets. Or increase them," the commentator says, the timbre of his voice niggling at my memory. I break eye contact with the governor and look around but can't see the commentator. The noise dies down as people scramble to give slips of paper to several men dressed in black, wearing black caps.

"And now. Brace yourselves! Men, cover your wives' eyes! The moment you've all been waiting for is here." Everyone leans forward in their seats. "It is time," the commentator continues in a quiet voice, "to introduce the *other three* before we open their doors. Door number one holds a Level Three male. Don't let his small size fool you, my friends. We've been trying to catch this wily Fec for *years*. He's the craftiest, fastest thing on two legs that has *ever* come from the tunnels. In fact, get this. He's the Fec that usually *sells* the other Fecs to the pits! What a cruel turn of fate for him." The commentator chuckles, and I recognize his voice. He is the man from the tunnels who always hid in the shadows. Shadow Man.

"Door number three," the commentator continues, "holds our second female. She's only a Five, but you know how female beasts are—they kill all other females so they can be queen bee. She's clawing at the door to get to our Ten as I speak!

"And from door number four, you'll see our second Ten. He's . . ." The crowd shrieks so loudly, the commentator's voice is completely swallowed. Even the black-dressed guards in the front row lean forward to peer down into the pool. Only the governor seems unaffected. When the frenzy dies down, the commentator continues, "This Ten is a male with a broken ankle and some superficial skin wounds. But don't let that stop you from betting on him. He's the strongest beast we have *ever* seen. He *bent the bars of his cage* trying to get at our little Level Ten female down there. Steel bars, mind you! No beast has *ever* done that."

I grit my teeth and force my legs not to buckle. *Why does it have to be him in here with me? What kind of sick and twisted reality have I been thrown into?* I wonder. *And where are you, Bowen?*

The ground beneath my feet rumbles as the crowd stomps their feet on the bleachers in unison. Stomp, stomp, stomp. Just like at a high school basketball game.

"And now. Silence, please. We will open the other three doors," the commentator says, his voice reverent. The noise disappears, as if it has been clapped beneath a hand. My ears ring with its aftermath.

Slowly, one of three doors built into the side of the pool slides open. A person is shoved into the light.

It's Arrin, cuffed hands shading her face. She uncovers her eyes and squints. Her face has been scrubbed clean, her hair isn't in her face, and her clothes are dripping. With her face clean, and her—my—clothes plastered to her body, she looks . . . male—square shoulders, hairy legs, and a beaky nose too big for her face. I can see it, now, what Bowen has said all along. I am looking at Arris—not Arrin. She *is* male. He grins at me and I shiver.

Arris's eyes flicker away from mine, up to the bleachers above, and lock onto the governor's face. He mouths the words, *Kill her and I'll get you out.* Arris nods and grins.

The other two doors open, and two freshly scrubbed beasts, wearing scraps of damp clothing and bound by ankle and wrist cuffs, are pushed out into the pool. One is the female beast that had been kept in the cage beside mine. I press my back to the wall and pray she doesn't see me. Or smell me. Or whatever they do.

When I look at the other beast, I can't breathe, wonder again what kind of sick and twisted reality I exist in, that I am facing my own twin brother in a death match. Jonah. He hovers on one foot, the other hanging at an odd angle just above the ground, his ankle swollen and purple beneath the cuff. His skin is slashed and scabbed over, and around his neck, ankles, and wrists are chafed bruises from the restraints that have been holding him. He glances at me—a flash of dark irises—so quickly I wonder if I've imagined it, and then his full attention is on the female beast.

So is mine.

She hisses. At me. And fights against the cuffs on her legs. She lunges for me and falls onto the pale-blue, bloodstained cement. Like a worm, she begins inching her way in my direction. I press my back harder against the wall.

Movement catches my eye, something bright, and I look away from the beast, squinting. Arris holds a knife in his clean hand, wiggling it so the bright new blade catches the light and reflects it into my eyes. He grins a brown-toothed grin and slashes at the air.

Memories flash in my head—my father, forever stuck in his wheelchair, teaching me how to defend myself. *Never get in a knife fight. You'll get cut.* Like that's going to help me now. *If your attacker grips your arm, twist toward his thumb. Don't punch—grab the soft flesh of the inner arm or thigh with your nails. Bite. Stomp on the instep or kick the Achilles tendon. Go for the eyes. Use your elbows in place of punching.*

His voice floods my brain, an onslaught of information in the blink of an eye that makes my heart ache for his presence. His protection. Gathering up all the bravery I possess, I take a step away from the wall, balance on the balls of my feet, and wait. The crowd applauds my bravery.

I will not die without fighting for a life I am not yet done living.

CHAPTER 34

The commentator's voice rumbles, but I don't take my eyes from the others in the arena. "At a down-count of ten, we will release the cuffs and the fight will begin!" he roars. The air trembles with an explosion of noise, and the count starts, shouted by the spectators as well as the commentator.

"Ten! Nine . . ." The numbers pulse against me, hammer my eardrums, and then fade to gibberish in my ringing ears. Until they get to . . .

"ONE!"

And then the arena explodes with action.

Cuffs release. Everyone leaps but me. Before I can move, before I can put my hands up to protect my face, I am buried beneath three bodies. My head smacks the pool floor, though I don't feel it, only hear the crunch of skull on cement, see stars in front of my open eyes. I cannot move.

Jonah throws Arris aside and then rips the female from me, rolling with her into the center of the pool, a thrashing ball of limbs and skin.

Arris scrambles to his feet and leaps onto me, his knees pinning my wrists to the ground, and stares into my eyes. He lifts his knife and grins, watching for my reaction instead of striking. I don't wait for his knife to find my flesh. With a grunt, I thrust my knee between his legs, hard. His eyes grow wide, the knife trembles in his hand, and he topples, rolling off of me to stare goggle-eyed at the glass seal overhead. And now there's no doubt. He's male.

I jump to my feet and watch him. The advantage is mine. I could take the knife from his hand and eliminate him from the fight, but I don't. The thought makes me sick. Instead, I creep past Jonah and the female Five to the other side of the pool and cower. Overhead, the crowd is staring, starved for action, insane with their desire for blood. The governor's eyes never leave me.

"What did I tell you, folks? Looks like our female Ten isn't as soft as she appears to be," the commentator cries.

Across the pool, Arris drags himself to his feet and glares. Hunched over, gripping his stomach, he skirts around the two flailing beasts and cautiously approaches me. In spite of his youth, his eyes are old and filled with a hatred so deep, I can feel it.

"Why are you trying to kill me?" I call out to him. "Why do you hate me so badly?"

The noise of the crowd dulls to nothing. Confused by the sudden silence, I look up. The people crammed onto the stadium benches are staring down at me, mouths hanging open, eyebrows knit in confusion, shocked. The governor stands and walks to the edge of the pool, stopping beside a short man dressed all in white, with a round belly straining his shirt. The governor says something to the man.

"Cut the pit sound," the man in white says, his booming voice annoyed. He is the commentator, the Shadow Man. And he's just been given an order he doesn't like. The governor nods and returns to his seat. "Folks, don't worry yourselves over the Ten. The governor just assured me that she *can't* talk. That was the Three speaking."

From the corner of my eye I see Arris leap. I lift my hands to defend myself and am slammed into the pool floor again, skidding across the rough cement. The breath whooshes out of me. Heat stabs my forearm as Arris's knife connects with it, slicing downward. His eyes, mere inches above mine, fill with glee.

I buck Arris off and roll onto him, grabbing his knife-hand wrist with both of my hands. But my injured hand won't grip. And Arris is strong—his thin, wiry, vein-covered arm no match for me. Recognition niggles at my brain. I have seen this before, in myself and in my brother, symptoms of violence that are accompanied by an inhuman increase in strength.

Arris is on the verge of turning.

He shoves me off him like I'm a thin, limp blanket, perches on my chest with his bare feet, and leaning over, brings the knife to

my throat. I clasp his wrist with both my hands and stop the knife a millimeter from my flesh.

"I hate you," he gasps, his body taut with the effort of getting his knife to my throat. "It's not fair that you're not a beast! And the militia helped you. Bowen helped you. No one ever helped me!" I struggle against him, trembling from the strain of keeping his knife off my skin, and he laughs. "All I have to do is kill you and the governor will let me live inside the wall," he says. "Finally, someone is helping me."

Heat fills my blood, fire tightens my muscles, and I move the knife an inch away from my neck. Confusion fills Arris's eyes. "You're strong. Stronger than you should be," he says. The confusion in his eyes turns to satisfaction. "But my knife is already at your throat."

The knife presses harder and Arris's eyes grow darker. I squeeze my eyes shut and focus every bit of strength I have into keeping his knife from my throat.

"Open your eyes and stare death in the face," Arris growls.

I open my eyes and stare into his. Little by little, the knife moves toward my neck until it brushes my skin.

I grit my teeth and close my eyes, and an unexpected heaviness flattens my body into the ground. I can't breathe, can't move, am completely trapped beneath Arris's slight body.

Did he just kill me? Is this how it feels to die?

I blink and stare into Arris's shocked, bulging eyes. Blue bleeds into his full red lips, and tan hands are cinched around his pale, sinewy neck. Arris's knife clatters to the pool floor beside my ear.

Jonah lifts Arris from me and drags him to the far side of the pool, and I think I just might live for three more seconds. Until a warm, hard weight crushes me.

The female beast stares down at me, knees straddling my hips. I grab Arris's knife from the floor and swing it at her chest, but she swats it out of my hand without taking her eyes from mine. Her hands grip my hands and slam them beside my ears, making my broken finger snap and flame with pain. She peels her lips from her teeth and stares at my neck.

"Look at this, folks! The female Five finally has her chance with the female Ten! She's going for the throat!" the commentator shrieks. "And by the way the Five is taking control, I'd say she's going to be victorious . . . but wait! Look at this, look at this!" He can barely contain his glee. "The male Ten! He's coming in for a piece of the fun, too! Both of them against the female Ten!"

Jonah jumps onto the female, crushing us both beneath his weight. He grabs her shoulders and yanks her up. She doesn't let go of me, grips my hands more tightly and pulls me to my feet. Jonah wraps his arms around her shoulders and flings her to the side. Her hands lose their grip on mine, claws raking my flesh. She flies through the air and strikes the side of the pool. And then I am living my worst nightmare—Jonah coming for me. He takes me by the waist and heaves me over his shoulder like a sack of potatoes.

"What? This is new!" the commentator blares. "Maybe he'll body slam her into the wall?" The crowd cheers. "Bash her brains out against the floor?" They cheer louder, and I cling to the threadbare shirt hanging on my brother's back.

Jonah hobbles to the side of the pit and stops, setting me gently on the floor with my back to the pool wall. He steps in front of me, faces the female, and crouches. I am stunned. Shocked. At this simple act of protection, tears sting my eyes, and my throat aches with the desire to sob.

The crowd starts booing. The female Five doesn't budge from her side of the pool—just stands panting and staring at Jonah.

"What in the world? This is a first! It looks as though the male Ten is actually *protecting* the female Ten! I don't believe it! Maybe he's saving her for last? For dessert?" the commentator barks.

The governor stands and walks over the top of the pool, his hard-soled shoes clicking on the glass seal, and stops beside the commentator. Unheard words pass between them, while Jonah remains crouched in front of me and the female beast stays on the far side of the pool. After a moment, the commentator grins and the governor sits back down.

"It's no wonder he got himself appointed governor! This guy is wily!" the commentator says with a chuckle. "He's suggested another first for the day! Listen to this, folks . . . shall we add a . . . *handicap* . . . to the male Ten?"

The crowd starts pounding their feet on the bleachers and chanting, "Yes! Yes! Yes!"

My cuffs fill with heat, but it is Jonah's wrist cuffs that meld together. The female, as if sensing her sudden advantage, hisses and takes a step closer. Jonah crouches lower and waits. The female begins pacing back and forth, her blood-streaked body tense, eyes never leaving Jonah. It is like watching two caged lions.

A drawn-out minute passes, and then two, and the crowd begins to lose some of its enthusiasm. I look up and meet the governor's nervous eyes. His mouth hardens, and he waves the commentator over. More words pass between them, and then the commentator moves to the very center of the pool, right above Jonah.

"Shall we add another handicap?" the commentator asks, lifting his hands into the air and spinning in a slow circle. The crowd cheers, chants again, *yes yes yes*. Jonah's legs snap together and he falls to his side. His elbow crunches when it impacts the cement and he screams, curling into a fetal ball. Bone, pink with blood, protrudes from his elbow.

The female doesn't wait. She's soaring through the air, teeth bared, eyes locked on me. I stand to run and trip over Jonah, toppling to the floor, palms skidding on cement.

Something cinches around my ankle just below the cuff, and I can't move. I'm dragged across the floor, back over Jonah's writhing body, and lifted up off the ground. The pool floor falls beneath me, wind whips my clean hair against my face, and with a hearty crunch, my shoulder and head smack into the cement wall. Stars flash before my open eyes, and a numb tingling works its way into my fingers and toes, legs and arms, saturating my whole body as darkness hovers around my open eyes.

"Ha! Did you see that? Slammed into the side of the pool!" Delight fills the commentator's voice. "And now, the male Ten has the Five's ankle and he's not letting go!"

Unable to move, I stare up at the glass seal, at the crowd of people staring down at me and cheering for my death. At the women—gasping, disgusted, but not looking away. At the men—drooling for violence and blood. And it hits me. They all want *me* to die. *Me!* Who cowers at the side of the pool instead of inflicting pain and death. Not the violent female beast who is obviously insane. Me. The piano prodigy, daughter of a retired war veteran, gentle me.

Because I have the oval with ten marks on my hand.

I ask myself, as I stare up into those faces, *Do I want to live? If I survive the pit, will I be forced to live in this world I see above me?* From where I lie, it appears to be a world worth dying to avoid. And so I don't care if I live or die.

Then a pair of brown boots steps onto the glass and stops directly above me. Someone dressed in militia brown falls to his knees, palms on the glass seal, looking down. His fist thumps the glass, and his mouth starts moving with a silent onslaught of angry words. And all of a sudden I remember something. I *do* want to live. Because if I am with the person kneeling on the glass above, I am home.

Bowen leans his forehead on the glass and looks right into my eyes. He opens his mouth and yells again. I cannot hear him, but I can see what he says, each movement of his lips forming meaning.

Fight! Don't give up! No matter what!

Hands grip his arms and jerk him to his feet. He starts fighting, kicking, flailing as two men dressed in black drag him off the glass and aim weapons at his chest.

"Uh, folks, it seems we have a problem," the commentator cries. He is standing at the side of the pool, hand rubbing his

round belly, eyeing Bowen nervously. "The militia just opened the south gate and are on their way here. They're insisting we stop the fight, so if you just remain in your seats . . ." The crowd groans.

The governor is on his feet and at the commentator's side in a flash, whispering into his ear.

"Wait, folks, wait! The governor has given his special approval to continue the fight!" the commentator says, voice uneasy. Bowen, despite the guns pointed at his chest, starts fighting again. It is time for me to do the same.

Taking a deep breath, I roll onto my side, ready to stand, ready to be done with the pits. The female, her ankle still held fast by Jonah, growls at me. On unsteady legs I walk up to her, bend my arm, and swing my elbow into her face. She falls to the side and in the same movement, rams her foot into Jonah's stomach, sending him flying to the other side of the pool. I jump onto her, ready to continue the fight, but she's fast—her hands whip up to my neck faster than my eyes can follow, and rough and hot, they clamp down. My body is flipped over and the beast is atop me, the pool grinding into my back.

Above me, Bowen becomes frantic, tearing away from the black-clad guards. He climbs onto the pool seal again, screaming words I don't hear. Pulling a handgun from his belt, he fires at the glass, but the seal holds fast.

I look away from him and stare at the female beast's face. Her chipped teeth are bared, a slight smile on her foam-flecked mouth. I claw at her hands, kick at her legs, but her hold tightens, as if my attempt to fight back lends her strength. My lungs start to burn, want to collapse, beg me to inhale. And I can't.

I look up at Bowen again, desperate, wondering if all the time we spent trying to stay alive, all the running and the hiding . . . was it all for nothing if it ends with my death? He quit the militia for nothing. He got shot for nothing. He fell in love with me for nothing.

His eyes meet mine and he takes something from his belt—a black grenade. He pulls the pin, sets it on top of the glass, and walks calmly to the side of the crowded arena.

"Folks! Folks! Look at this! Look at the male Ten!" the commentator shrieks, oblivious to the grenade. I turn my eyes to the side and meet Jonah's. His face is swollen and bleeding, his body smeared with blood, but he's standing on his cuffed feet. "By brute strength he's pulled his wrist cuffs apart, in spite of his shattered elbow! That's over five hundred pounds of force! Just think of the pain and agony he must be feeling—a pain he's willing to endure to satisfy his desire to kill!"

The commentator's right. Jonah's shoulder muscles bulge and tremble with strain, a glossy sheen of sweat coats his skin, mingling with blood, and his arms aren't melded together anymore. Six inches of space separate the cuffs.

Oh, my poor brother. There is nothing left of him.

My vision is turning black, everything fading from view, except Jonah, focused at the exact center of my sight. He takes a leap toward me and the female beast, and his forearms come down on either side of the female's neck. Jonah's cuffs, zinging with energy, wrench back together and snap around her neck just as my vision dims.

Her fingers go limp, falling from my neck and trailing over my shoulder. I gasp a breath of air, and the world reappears, accompanied by pain. Jonah, his cuffs still locked on the female's neck, drags her away from me. In one swift move he throws her aside, reducing her to a limp pile of death.

As if seeing everything in slow motion, I blink and look back up at the glass, at the commentator pointing at the grenade and running from the pool, the crowd pushing and shoving and trampling each other to get away, at the grenade that is about to explode. I curl onto my side and cover my head, waiting for impact. A weight settles on me—Jonah—covering my aching body with his, cradling my head in his hand, his panting breath hot on my skin.

The air seems to solidify and compress, molding my skin against my bones, forcing its way into my ears and pushing the breath from my lungs. My skull squeezes my brain, and my eyeballs want to pop with the pressure. Jonah's body mashes mine into the floor and then goes limp as the pressure in the air fades to nothing.

I open my eyes. It is raining diamonds.

CHAPTER 35

When I was twelve I went to an all-day pool party. I forgot sun-screen. My skin was so sunburned, I couldn't sleep that night. My skin feels just like that now. Burned to a crisp—all the way into my lungs. Every breath fills my chest with an inferno, feels like lifting the weight of the world, and I am too tired to lift any extra weight.

Cool hands touch my brow, fiddle with my wrist. A pair of green eyes peers into mine, eyes that remind me of summer. "You're alive!"

Stringy blond hair trails over my face as a weight is hefted from me. Now I can fill my lungs. But breathing air feels like breathing fire, and I cough and gasp.

"Fo? Fiona, can you hear me?" Bowen asks. His words are muted, as if my fingers were pressed into my ears. He frames my face with his hands and stares into my eyes. "Can you hear me?" he asks, eyes frantic.

"I hear you," I whisper, pushing my aching body to sitting, wondering how I'm still alive. Four blood-streaked bodies are in the red-splattered pool, yet I am the one who will walk away. If I can find somewhere to go. If I *can* walk.

Beside me lies a still form. His skin shimmers iridescent red, every blood-covered inch coated with diamonds—glass from the ceiling. Only Jonah's pale stringy hair gives away his identity. A tear streams down my cheek as I place a trembling hand on his bare chest. His heart beats against my palm, a weak, fast flutter.

"He's still alive," I say, looking at Bowen.

Bowen yanks the handgun from his belt and with trembling hands, points it at my brother's chest. Shocked, I lean over Jonah's body. "Don't shoot him! He saved my life!" I say, surprised at the energy in my voice.

Bowen doesn't waver. "Fo, he is a Level Ten. I watched him kill the other beast. There's nothing human left in him!"

I shake my head and cringe at the pain. "He saved my life," I whisper. "A part of my brother is still in there."

"Would you look at that," a voice says. *The* voice. The commentator. He's standing on the side of the pool, looking down in. "The female Ten is protecting the body of the male Ten! And I thought beasts didn't have feelings!"

Bowen glares and stands, his jaw muscles pulsing. He walks to the side of the pool and holds his hand up to the commentator. The commentator, round belly nearly popping the buttons off his white shirt, reaches down and clasps Bowen's hand, ready to hoist him up. But Bowen yanks. The man topples over the side of the pool and lands on his back at Bowen's feet. He blinks, stunned, and the crowd—those who have braved the grenade to see what is going to happen next—gasps.

Bowen balls his fist and hits the man in the face. The commentator's eyes roll back in his fleshy head, and his pudgy cheeks sag.

Placing his fingers on the commentator's ample cheeks, Bowen pries open the man's mouth and sticks his finger inside, removing a tooth-sized metal chip. He sticks it into his own mouth and glares up at the remaining people.

"Listen to me." Bowen's voice drones impossibly loud, vibrating my bones, just like the commentator's. "My name is Dreyden Bowen. This is Fiona Tarsis." He points at me without looking. "She's a Level Ten. And she's *not* a beast! She's been *cured*!" The crowd goes utterly still, staring down at Bowen with wide eyes. "Now take a good look at the boy beside her. That's Jonah Tarsis. Her *brother*! You all came here today to watch our only hope for survival, our first real hope for the future, be torn apart by her own brother! You disgust me!"

The crowd inches toward the pool, all eyes on Jonah and me. The low drone of whispers fills the room. Women blink back tears, hang their heads in shame, and leave. Some of the men shout apologies. Others shake their heads and follow the women out.

Bowen crouches beside me. "The militia should be here any minute, and doctors are on their way," he says. He frowns and breaks eye contact, studies his hands. "I'm so sorry, I didn't

know how else to save you." He looks as if he's about to be sick.

"What do you mean?" I whisper. The thought of medical help is a comfort to my throbbing body.

Without looking at me he says, "When they took you in the tunnels, I knew you were going to go to the pits. Tommy and I got back to south gate as fast as we could, but when we told them you were cured and needed to be rescued, they didn't believe us—locked Tommy and me up as traitors. But when Micklemoore came back to the camp—he had been out searching for you—and found out that I had info about your location, he set us free and had us contact the lab with your whereabouts. Then Micklemoore convinced the director of the lab to issue an order to open the gates for reinforcements, so the militia could help rescue you. So Tommy led the militia through the gate, and I came here through the tunnels." Finally, he meets my eyes. "Fo. The only way I could get them to agree to help was by telling the lab your location. I couldn't let you die in the pits. At least in the lab, you won't feel anything when you die. They're coming to take you." His cheeks are pale and sunken, and blue shadows darken the skin under his eyes. A definite improvement from the last time I saw him, but still far from the glowing picture of health he used to be.

I reach a trembling hand to his face and trail my fingers over his bristly cheek. "How are you?" I ask. Hope that he will live a long, prosperous life burns in my chest. I don't care if I have to go to the lab, as long as he survives.

He leans into my hand, and a hint of a smile touches his

blue-tinged lips. "I tell you you're going to the lab and you want to know how *I* am?" He tilts his head and kisses me so softly and so gently I could lean into his lips and fall asleep forever, but he pulls away and looks into my eyes. "I'm glad you're alive."

A door on the side of the pool opens. Bowen stands and grabs his gun, aiming it at a lone man wearing a long white jacket. The man puts up his hands and steps into the pool.

"Looks like the lab has arrived," Bowen mutters, lowering his gun. His lips harden into a thin, straight line.

I look at the man in the white coat and my eyes narrow. He steps over Arris's lifeless body and walks toward me. Dark brows frame pale blue eyes. My heart starts pounding and a memory floods my vision.

CHAPTER 36

Warm hands were on my icy skin, the first warmth I'd felt in a long time.

"I need you to wake up!" someone whispered. "We need to get you away from here before they find out you survived the recovery period."

I forced my eyelids open and stared into pale-blue eyes creased at the corners with worry and framed with black lashes. He looked away, and I followed his gaze to my arm. His warm, nimble fingers slid a needle out from the crease in my elbow. He moved to the other side of the bed and slid another needle out of the other arm. Tiny beads of blood pooled in the creases.

Next, he jabbed a needle into my bicep, emptied a syringe into me, and pulled it out. Fire seemed to spread up my shoulder and into my heart, making it pound, making it pump blood through my body so fast I started to tremble. "I just injected you with adrenaline," he said, wiping a drop of blood away. "It won't last long and we don't have much time." His warm hands clasped my shoulders and helped me sit. "Can you walk?"

"Of course I can walk," I said, and frowned. My voice felt broken, sounded as rough as a dog's bark. I put a weak hand to my throat and felt a fine chain beneath my fingers. "But, who are you?"

"I'll explain as we go." He gave me his hand, and I tried to clasp it but couldn't. My bones felt like liquid. He squeezed my hand and pulled, and helped me to my feet.

The moment I tried to stand, my knees knocked together and my arms flailed, like a newborn deer on brand-new legs. I threw my arms around the man's waist and sagged gracelessly against him.

Without a word, the blue-eyed man draped my arm over his shoulder, supporting almost all my weight. Together, we walked out of a dimly lit room that had a bed and nothing else.

The empty hallway was nearly pitch-black and lined with numbered doors. His shoes didn't make a sound on the floor. My white tennis shoes hardly touched it because my feet, like my legs and my voice, didn't remember how to work. We came to the end of the hall and stopped by a slick black wall.

"This is where it gets tricky," the man whispered. He took a small metal object from his pocket and put it to his mouth. "She's awake. Call Gary. We have to get her out of the lab tonight. I just took her off life-support, so it's only a matter of minutes before he realizes she's cured." He took my arm from his shoulders and stepped away from me. My legs trembled beneath my weight, but not as badly as a few minutes before. I braced my shoes against the floor and held on to the dark wall for balance as the man typed something into a keypad on the wall at my left.

Light flashed beneath my hand. I squinted at the wall and realized I stood beside a floor-to-ceiling window many stories above the ground. It was nighttime. In the near distance, I could make out a wide stretch of connected buildings against a star-filled sky.

The lights flashed brighter beneath my hand. Nearer. A helicopter.

The blue-eyed man looked out the window. "Oh no. We've got to go now!" he said, no longer whispering.

He grabbed me, lifted me off the floor, and cradled me in his arms like a baby. And then he ran.

My head bounced against his shoulder, lolling on a nearly useless neck, and I clung to his pristine white coat. At the end of the hall, we stepped into a pitch-black steam-filled room that reeked of bleach. He maneuvered through the darkness, stopped, and threw me down. I flailed before landing on my back in a mound of warm, dry cloth.

"Looks like we're going to use plan B," he whispered. A light flickered, a tiny flashlight, barely illuminating the man's face while he scanned my body with it. The small light stopped on my arm. The man jabbed a needle into my bicep again and injected something into my muscle.

He leaned toward me, and his troubled face swirled in and out of focus. Lifting my eyelids, he shone the tiny flashlight into each of my eyes and nodded. The light went out. A fresh mound of hot cloth dropped onto me, making it almost impossible to breathe, yet my hands felt as limp and weak as flower petals, too weak to move the mass from my face. I relaxed into the warmth, content to be enveloped. My eyes closed, my mouth eased open, and I sank deeper into the warm fabric.

"Where is she?" a woman's voice asked, barely making it to my cotton-filled brain. I tried to open my eyes, to see who'd spoken the words. Because I knew that voice.

"She's in the linens. But we have to get her out now! There's already a copter circling the building. He knows she's awake."

"Then Gary has to get her outside the wall tonight. He won't be missed. As long as he's back before sunrise, no one will suspect we had

anything to do with her disappearance, and as long as she's sedated, she won't wake until we're with her," the woman said.

"Outside the wall? But——"

"She'll be sedated. She'll be fine. And you know Soneschen's got too many eyes in the city. She'll be dead before dawn if we keep her nearby. The other side of the wall is the safest place," the woman insisted. Hands sifted through the warm linens covering me and circled around my neck. They fiddled with something and slid a chain away from my skin.

A lone pair of footsteps echoed on the floor. "Gary! Take her. Quickly," the woman said. "To my old home from before." The towels surrounding me started to move, being wheeled away.

Footsteps pounded on the ground. "Doctor Grayson! You're to be taken in for questioning in the disappearance of lab specimen fourteen," someone bellowed.

And then I floated.

"I know you," I say. The man smiles, a gesture that doesn't reach his eyes.

"You remember me, then?" He crouches in front of me and visually scans my body.

I nod and look at the name embroidered on his starched white coat—*Dr. Grayson.* "You moved me out of a bed and put me in some laundry."

"That's right." He glances over his shoulder, at the door he just came in through. "We need to get you out of here immediately," he says, looking at me again, pressing warm fingers against the pulse in my neck. "Can you stand?"

"Wait. My brother. He . . ."

"That's Jonah?" Doctor Grayson asks, looking at the blood-covered body beside me.

"Yes. He's still alive. Can you help him?"

The doctor crouches beside Jonah and presses fingers to his neck. His blue eyes meet mine and he pulls a tiny clip from the pocket of his white jacket, lifts it to his mouth. "We have an unconscious Level Ten in the pit. Get him medical help immediately. And take every precaution that he survives," he says into the clip.

"Thank you," I whisper.

The doctor's eyes move to Bowen. "Are you Dreyden Bowen?" he asks.

Bowen nods, eyes instantly wary. "How do you know me?"

"I'm the one who had you promoted to guardian."

"You? Why?" Bowen asks, his voice bitter. "Do you have a personal vendetta against me?"

Grayson smiles, and this time it touches his eyes. "No, no personal vendetta. I was . . . apprehended the night I had Fiona removed from the lab and wasn't able to get to her. Your gate was the closest to her childhood home, so I thought she might find her way there. And if she did, I needed someone in place who would protect her, someone who knew her and would recognize her. Based on your psych analysis, you have a soft spot for helping women. So, while I was being held for questioning, I secretly signed the papers for you to be promoted to guardian, and an accomplice smuggled them to the gate." He looks between Bowen and me, then holds out his hand to Bowen. Bowen, his face raw with surprise, puts his hand into the doctor's and shakes it.

"Nicely done. You've exceeded all my hopes." They drop hands. "Now, we've got to get Fiona out of here."

Bowen eases to his feet, slow and unsteady, and starts tipping sideways. His eyes glaze over and roll into his head, and his legs crumple. Doctor Grayson grabs at him, toppling onto the pool floor with Bowen cradled against his chest.

"Is he injured?" the doctor asks, looking at me.

I nod, suddenly clammy cold. "I accidentally shot him. I think it was yesterday morning. It went all the way through his back." The words make my head spin, make me want to vomit. The pool wavers and I turn my head to the side, dry heaving.

The doctor pulls up Bowen's shirt, exposing a semifilled hole in his back that is oozing pus and blood. He looks at me, and the color has drained from his face. "How has he survived?"

I have no words.

"Get me medical backup, now!" Grayson orders, the clip against his mouth once more. "I have two injured teenagers in the pit, one on the verge of death."

Verge of death. He means Bowen. I lie down on my side in spite of the bloody floor. I am too exhausted to keep sitting, too sore to move, and too scared to go on. My head pounds as if it's filled with too much blood, and I fight the urge to dry heave again.

The doctor studies me with calculating eyes. "You've been kissing him, haven't you. Kissing Dreyden?"

I stare at him, wondering why he's asking me something so irrelevant at a time like this.

"Fiona," Grayson says. "Kiss him."

I blink at the doctor's face, confused.

"*Kiss* him," he says again, frantic. "Just do it!"

I stare at him and wonder how hard I hit my head. I'm obviously losing it.

"You still carry trace amounts of the vaccine. It has certain advantages in very small doses, certain healing properties," Doctor Grayson calmly explains. "If you can pass more of them on to Dreyden, he might live."

I push up onto my hands and knees and crawl over to Dreyden, pressing my uninjured hand against his cold cheek. "Dreyden?" He doesn't move. I lean down and put my mouth against his slightly open mouth, but his lips are cool and hard. I kiss him anyway, and as my warm lips leave his, I'm certain it is the last time I will ever kiss him.

Feet scuffle and the doctor curses under his breath. I turn away from Bowen's cold, still face to see what's going on and gasp. I am seeing a ghost.

A man crosses the pool and falls to his knees beside Bowen. He presses his fingers against Bowen's neck. "What happened?" he demands, looking at Dr. Grayson with accusing gray eyes. "Why is my brother in the pits?"

"He came to save her," the doctor says, nodding toward me, eyes steel hard.

Duncan focuses on me, and I can hardly believe how much he looks like his younger brother. The only difference is his eyes—cold, flat gray instead of warm green. "You're not dead yet? But I was told the Fec . . ." His eyes move to the slash on my arm, the spot where Arris's knife wounded me. Ironically, the only spot on my body that doesn't hurt. At all.

I look at my arm and gently prod the oozing knife wound. My skin is completely numb. Thin veins spiderweb away from a sickly purple gash, spreading up my entire arm and disappearing beneath my shirtsleeve.

The doctor is at my side, eyes panicked, staring at my arm. "You've been poisoned!" he blurts. And then he does three things that make me wonder if I'm hallucinating. First, he tears the tie from his neck and cinches it around my bicep so hard that I yelp. Next, he takes the knife from Dreyden's belt and slashes it over Arris's knife wound—and I don't feel it, even a little bit. Last, he starts squeezing my arm like he's wringing out a washcloth, forcing blood from the numb wound.

"Stop," a calm, smooth voice commands. Hard-soled shoes click across the pool floor, and a man stops beside Doctor Grayson. Duncan Bowen jumps to his feet, spine ramrod straight, and salutes. The governor doesn't seem to notice Duncan, doesn't take his eyes from the doctor and me. "There's nothing you can do to save her now," he says, a satisfied gleam in his eyes.

"Get out of here or I will physically remove you, Jacoby." The doctor gently releases my arm and stands, looking down at the governor. He's a full head taller than the governor, has broad shoulders, and looks at least a decade younger.

The governor laughs and steps up to Grayson. "You think you can stop me?"

"I already have," Grayson says, his body trembling as if he's about to explode. "As soon as Mickelmoore heard that I found a cure and you've been covering it up, he has been rallying the militia to stand against your Inner Guard. They're taking over control as we speak. They outnumber you five to one."

"You have no proof that there is a cure," the governor says.

Grayson smiles and, without taking his eyes from the governor, nods at me.

The governor takes a deep breath. He slowly removes his suit jacket and tosses it to the side of the pool. Without warning, his hand darts out and he grabs the doctor's wrist, twisting. The doctor gasps and falls to his knees, his arm at an unnatural angle. "If I move your arm an inch, your shoulder will dislocate." The governor's muscles bulge beneath his spotless white shirt, the seams barely holding the cloth together.

"You're not going to be able to hide this forever," Grayson says through gritted teeth.

The governor laughs. "You have no idea who you're dealing with. I can hide anything. Without the girl, there's no proof. It will look like you fabricated this whole thing in an attempt to usurp me." He kicks the doctor in the stomach. "Bowen, get the bodies out of here, starting with the girl," the governor says, holding the panting doctor firmly in place.

"But the girl is still alive," Duncan says.

"Just do it," the governor orders. Veins are bulging beneath his skin, and a sheen of sweat has glossed his wrinkled forehead.

"Yes, sir." Duncan Bowen steps up to me. He bends down to grab me when something clicks. Duncan freezes and his startled eyes flicker past me. I follow his gaze to Dreyden, to the handgun in his quivering hand—aimed at his brother's chest.

"You touch her, Duncan, I shoot," Dreyden warns, his voice a hoarse whisper.

Duncan looks between me and his younger brother. "You've got to be kidding me! You'd shoot me? Over a beast?" he asks.

"You left Mom and me to fend for ourselves outside the wall. I should shoot you for that. But I won't," Dreyden says, voice weak. "But if you move a single inch closer to Fiona, I swear I'll kill you so fast you won't even feel it."

Slowly, eyes wide, Duncan stands and backs away from me. He hasn't taken two steps when Grayson crashes to the pool floor and the governor leaps toward me.

"Shoot him!" Grayson shrieks. Time seems to slow down. I watch the governor arcing through the air toward me, teeth bared, see Dreyden move his gun a fraction, hear him pull the trigger. The governor's eyes grow wide as he skids to a stop on the ground beside me. His brows knit, and he looks from me to the blood spreading over the chest of his white button-up shirt.

As if responding to the gunshot, men in brown storm into the arena and circle the pool, guns pointing in, aimed at Duncan Bowen and the governor. Mickelmoore strides to the side of the pool and looks in. "Tommy, Rory, restrain those two," he says.

Tommy jumps down into the pool with two pairs of electromagnetic cuffs in his hands and chuckles. "Hello, Governor Soneschen! Never thought I'd see the day I put a pair of these on you. If only my mother could see it. But you threw her out of the wall and got her killed on her fifty-fifth birthday."

He slaps the cuffs onto the governor, over his shirt. Rory jumps in next and cuffs Duncan.

Too woozy to keep watching, I roll onto my side and face Dreyden. He turns his head and we stare into each other's eyes. Inching his way to my side, he carefully lifts my head with cold, clammy hands, onto the crook of his shoulder. I tilt my chin up and press my warm lips to his cold mouth. I kiss him like I am the blood transfusion he needs to stay alive. Because, really, I sort of am.

My lips fall away and I nestle closer to him, my head cradled in the soft spot just below his shoulder where I can hear the gentle *thump-thump* of his heart.

"Sleep," Dreyden whispers. And I do.

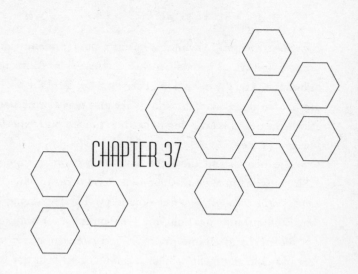

CHAPTER 37

I wake to pain. Everything hurts, even my eyebrows. My tongue is thick, my eyes grainy. I try to spread my arms, but only one arm works—the other is strapped to my chest.

I open my eyes, but heavy darkness fills my vision and I panic, thinking of tunnels where children eat worms and sleep on stale sewage. I wait for Arrin's knife—no, *Arris*'s knife—to find its way to my neck.

A light flashes on, illuminating a square of glass that frames a woman, like I am seeing her on television. My mind tries to understand her appearance, until I realize she is watching me from the other side of a window. She leaves the lit window. A moment later, a door opens, shining a rectangle of light across me, and she enters the room.

She's dressed in white, wearing a nurse's white cap, white shoes, and white nylons beneath a white skirt. With her back illuminated by the open door, I can't see her face. But I see what's in her hand and start thrashing. Because now I remember. I am at the lab. And I am going to be their guinea pig, experimented on until I die.

She pauses and the hand holding a giant syringe wavers. "Shh. I won't hurt you," she croons, and turns toward the door she's come through. She turns on an overhead light, and I flinch, my skull instantly too tight, my eyes so sensitive I want to vomit.

Warm hands frame my face, and something wet splatters on my chin. I thrash against the touch and lash out with my good hand.

"Fiona! Open your eyes!" the nurse says, grasping my flailing hand and holding it to my chest as if I were weak as a baby, which I am. Something about the voice calms me. I swallow and peer up at the nurse through my lashes, but the light is too bright. My gaze moves to her neck, to a golden treble clef hanging on a gold chain. I know this necklace. My father gave it to me on my thirteenth birthday. My good hand comes to my bare neck, and I remember how it felt against my skin. I look back at her face.

Tears are streaming down her cheeks, splattering onto my chin, my lips. She smiles and it warms her hazel eyes. I look from her face to her dress and the words embroidered over her heart—*L. Grayson, LPN*—and back to her face.

"Lis?" I ask, my voice a hopeful whisper. She nods, leans down, and kisses my forehead. I throw my good arm around her neck and press my cheek against hers. Joy warms me. My sister is alive. Another thought hits me and I turn cold. "Bowen? Is he alive?" I say, trying to claw my way to sitting. Lis puts her hands on my shoulders and eases me back down into bed.

"You mean Dreyden?" I nod. "He's doing better than you, actually. Lick your lips," she says with a laugh, wiping her damp cheeks. "You might taste him. The instant he learned that your saliva would help him heal, he's been taking full advantage. He left less than an hour ago and kissed you at least five times while he was here."

I feel my face heat and try not to giggle. I lick my lips. A smile finds my mouth, and my entire body melts into the mattress with relief. Bowen is alive. "What about Jonah?" I ask.

"He's alive," she says, looking away, "but barely. If he survives it will be a miracle." My heart hurts for my brother.

"Am I going to die?" I whisper.

Her brows pull together. "Of course not, silly. Do you really think I could kill my own sister?"

Good question. "Then what's in the syringe?" I ask.

"Painkillers and antivenin. You were poisoned, and until the poison is completely out of your system, you're gonna hurt. It'll help you sleep, too."

She inserts the needle into a tube leading from an IV bag to my good arm, but before she can inject, I blurt, "Wait! I don't want to sleep yet. Not until I see Bowen."

Lis removes the full syringe from the tube and pulls a small chip from her nurse-gown pocket. "Please inform Dreyden Bowen that he is needed in lab room fourteen," she says. "He'll be here any minute, I'm sure. I still can't believe Duncan Bowen's brother is the one who saved you." Her face twists with distaste and then darkens with anger.

"Why?" I ask.

She meets my eyes. "Duncan helps run the pits, collecting the bodies after the fights. He's the one who matched you and Jonah against each other, even though he knew you were brother and sister."

"No! Does Bowen know?"

Lis shrugs and her jaw tightens.

As if the mention of his name has called him, Bowen strides into the room, followed by Dr. Grayson. Bowen's face is golden tan again, his lips rosy red and smiling. He stops beside my bed and stares down at me like it's the first time he's ever seen me. I blink and catch my lip in my teeth, unsure of what to say, unsure if I can talk at all, with my entire body flooded with emotion.

"Fotard," he whispers. Without another word, he climbs onto my bed and gently lifts my head onto his chest, wrapping me in his warm, strong arms. "It took you long enough to wake up." He kisses my forehead.

"How long?" I ask, breathing him in. He smells like soap and clean clothes and shaving cream. I settle more deeply against his chest.

"Four days!" He says it like it's been a year. "And your brother-in-law won't let me sleep in here, so I can only be here during the day."

"My who?" I ask.

"Brother-in-law," Lis says, standing with her arms wrapped around Dr. Grayson's waist. "I got married, Fo." She grins.

I stare at him and remember being buried by laundry. "Why did you put me on the wrong side of the wall to fend for myself?" I say.

Dr. Grayson steps to the side of my bed and peers deep into my eyes. "Believe me when I say that what I did was safer than keeping you here."

"Why?" Bowen and I ask in unison.

"A year ago, I found a cure for the virus. But there was a problem. Every child I cured, who woke up from the coma, died within a day. I couldn't figure out what was going wrong. So I woke a child and stayed awake at his bedside for forty-eight hours. He survived. Until I left his bedside, at which point he went into cardiac arrest. Someone was murdering the healed children. Someone who didn't want them to be cured. It took me three months to discover who was behind the murders."

"Who?" I ask, though I have a suspicion.

"Jacoby Soneschen."

"The governor? Why wouldn't he want them cured?" Bowen asks. "Think of all of the lives it would save! It would mean putting an end to the wall, an end to the rules. An end to . . ." He sits up and his face slowly hardens, taut with anger. "If a cure was discovered, and it was publicized, the wall would come down. And that would mean an end to Soneschen's power."

Dr. Grayson nods. "That, and something else. He's been bleeding beasts. Somehow he figured out about the healing properties they carry. Their blood is sort of like a fountain of youth, increasing health and strength. He's been drinking it to make himself stronger and healthier, and feeding it to the Inner Guard to make them—and ultimately himself—more powerful. The irony is, he didn't know that the beasts still carry the health benefits after they've been cured."

"So," I say, "the night you put me in the laundry is the night you hid me on the other side of the wall."

"Where else was I going to hide you?" He reaches out and ruffles my hair. "The governor has eyes and ears everywhere, even outside the wall. If I kept you on this side of the wall, you wouldn't have lived to see a sunrise, so Lis and I got you out. We were going to try to get you to Wyoming, beyond the governor's reach, and then start a movement to distribute the cure to the rest of the country, but Lis and I were imprisoned minutes after we got someone to smuggle you to the other side of the wall. We couldn't come for you."

I look at Lis. "You were in prison?" I ask.

She nods. "But only for a few days. When the governor couldn't find you, he let us out and had us watched day and night. He probably figured we'd lead him to you." Lis clears her throat and gives the doctor a look.

"That's enough talking," he says. "You need to rest, Fiona. You have a concussion, broken pinky, broken hand, seventy-eight stitches, and severe bruising. In addition to blood poisoning. Beast blood or not, you've got a lot of healing to do."

I try to wiggle my bandaged hand, and pain zings in my bones, all the way to my elbow. "Will I ever play the piano again?" I whisper.

Lis frowns and sighs. "Oh, Fiona, honey. I don't know. We'll do our best to get your fingers back to normal."

"Can I have a sec with Fiona?" Bowen asks. Lis nods and watches us with a small, satisfied smile. "Alone?" he clarifies.

Lis looks at Dr. Grayson before tugging him toward the door.

"Three minutes," the doctor says over his shoulder, sounding just like a . . . doctor. "We don't want to tax her strength." He glares at Bowen as Lis pulls him out the door. The door shuts with a quiet click.

Bowen presses his lips against my temple and I think he's kissing it, until his lips start moving against my skin.

"I want to apologize for my brother," he says, his breath warm on my face. "And wanted to let you know he's sitting in prison with Soneschen."

"I'm sorry," I whisper, heartbroken that Bowen's only surviving family member is locked up, leaving him completely alone.

"You're sorry? He would have killed you. He's where he deserves to be."

"But he's your only family," I say.

He's quiet for a minute before answering. "No. You're my family now, Fiona."

Tears flood my eyes and spill down my cheeks.

"Tears? For me?" he asks, his voice a hungry whisper. I turn and look into his eyes. They're ravenous, almost like a beast's, and they devour mine. He puts his warm hand against my face. "I love you," he whispers. "I didn't know if I'd ever get to tell you that again."

"I love you, too," I say, clinging to him like he might disappear.

And then his lips are on mine and my body seems to meld precisely into his. Cautiously, so I don't bump any of my injuries,

I slip my good hand behind his neck. Inside his mouth, pressed to his palate, I taste something slick and smooth. I'm curious what it is, but not curious enough to stop kissing him in order to ask. I tighten my hand in his hair and kiss him deeper.

It feels like mere seconds have passed when a door opens, feet walk quietly into the room, and someone clears her throat.

"Time to go," Lis says.

Bowen pulls his mouth from mine and scowls at her. "She's helping me heal, though," he says.

Lis grins at Bowen. "Nice try, buddy. It's been *ten* minutes! I talked the doctor into giving you extra time already! I don't think he'll approve if you kill her because you can't control your hormones."

He sighs and looks into my eyes.

"What's in your mouth?" I ask.

He opens his mouth wide, tilting his head up so I have a good view. Pressed to its roof is a small silver chip that catches the light.

"What is that?"

"A little something I stole from the pit commentator," he says with a gleam of mischief in his green eyes. "I have a present for you. And you," he adds, looking at Lis again. "Don't medicate Fo yet. Turn the television on in fifteen minutes." He kisses me once more, fast and gentle, and then he climbs from the bed and strides out of the room.

Lis raises one eyebrow and gives me a look that makes me duck my head under the covers and giggle. Very thirteen-year-old. But I don't care.

CHAPTER 38

Fifteen minutes later, Lis brings a small flat screen into my room and sets it in my lap. She hovers behind the head of my bed, watching with me. The words *Being Broadcast Live* scroll endlessly across the bottom of the screen.

The television shows the walled city just before sunset, from the high view of a helicopter—green fields, houses, buildings, people. In the distance, a man is standing on the wall, arms raised, voice booming above the throb of the helicopter. It circles closer to the man, and the camera focuses on his face.

My heart starts pounding as I stare at the screen, mesmerized.

". . . a cure!" Bowen shouts. The setting sun glows orange on his skin, frames him with light and hope and salvation. "I repeat! We have found a cure for the beasts, and for the Fecs," he yells, voice as loud and strong as thunder, thanks to the chip he stole from the commentator.

The helicopter crosses the boundary of the wall. In the distance loom Mile High Stadium and the Pepsi Center. The camera dips and bobs and focuses on the dead, dusty world just outside the wall—buildings with broken windows, trash-strewn streets, cracked pavement. And, surprisingly, people. They are creeping out of buildings, climbing up from sewer grates, skulking on rooftops, leaning out of windows, and they all have their faces turned up toward Bowen.

"I repeat," Bowen calls, "we have found a cure! There is hope. There is an end! A new beginning!"

The camera zooms in on the people outside the wall, on their gaunt, dirty, haggard faces. Scared faces. Weeping faces, with tear-streaked cheeks. Laughing faces, eyes full of hope. Shocked faces, mouths hanging open. People start jumping up and down. Clapping. Dancing. Embracing. They start calling out the news, passing the words to others farther down the street, who pass it on to more people farther down the street. And then they dance, until as far as the camera can see, people are dancing in the streets.

I can literally see the news spreading through them, wiping away despair like a physical wave, and I understand what is happening.

For the first time in four years, they have been given hope.

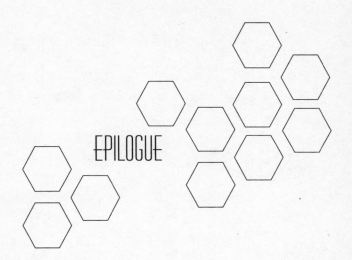

EPILOGUE

WARNING: FUGITIVE
FORMER GOVERNOR JACOBY SONESCHEN
HAS ESCAPED FROM PRISON
Age: 48
Height: 5'9"
Weight: 150
Hair: Brown with gray temples
Other: Recent bullet wound to chest
Possibly running for Wyoming
Reward: 8 oz honey for any information
leading to his recapture

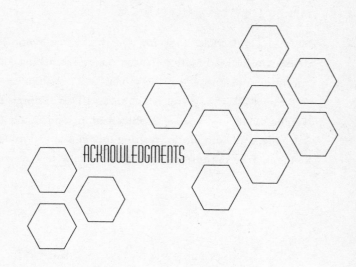

ACKNOWLEDGMENTS

I must first thank my husband, Jaime, because without my picking his brain about possible plot scenarios, this book never would have made it past page one hundred. Also, he turned this book's dedication into something beautiful.

As for the sleep-destroying nightmare that became chapter 1—thank you!

Marlene Stringer, my dear agent, you rock. Enough said.

Emily Easton, Nicole Gastonguay, Laura Whitaker, Melissa Kavonic, Regina Roff, Donna Mark, Patricia McHugh, and everyone else at Walker Books who has put time, thought, effort, and sweat into this book, thank you! It amazes me what a group effort book publishing is, and I am eternally grateful for your professional expertise.

Bonny Anderson and Kristin Wester, you are the best critique buddies a girl could hope for. On that note—Elana Johnson, thank you for reading the first ten pages and asking a hundred questions. You opened my eyes to endless possibilities.

Last of all, thank you to Mom and Dad, Tiffiny, Brittany, Natalie, Matt and Ashlee, Ashlee's mom and sister, Jennifer, Michelle, and Eamonn for reading this in manuscript form and loving it. Your enthusiasm is what makes me love to write.